"Does that turn you on Miss Sloane? Watching Julie make love to two men at once?"

She jerked around to find Jake standing not more than two feet away. Barefoot and shirtless, he stood wearing only a pair of jeans. The starlight gave his body a luminous glow, defining his ripped pecs and abs.

"Oh God," she whispered, staring up at him in shock, unable to move.

"Does it turn you on?" He repeated, obviously aware of her arousal.

A loud moan from the bedroom caused Amanda to blink. He glanced past her shoulder and smiled. "It's amazing how much pleasure two men can give a woman." He reached out and put one hand on the back of her neck, pulling her close.

She raised her hands, pressing her palms against the smooth muscles of his chest, trying to push away. Slowly, deliberately, he leaned down and kissed her, his hand behind her neck keeping her lips turned up toward his. With his free hand, he held the small of her back, pulling her closer. Then his hand slid up to caress her breasts, his fingers pinching and twisting her nipples, sending currents of electricity straight to her pussy.

For a long moment, he continued the kiss, his tongue probing deep, searching. His kiss ignited a desperate need and she kissed him back, her limp arms finding life, lifting to encircle his shoulders and grasping urgently at his neck.

One Hard Ride

by

M.M. Bordeaux

\#

One Hard Ride

Contact Information: info@thewildrosepress.com

Cover Art by *Angela Anderson*

The Wild Rose Press, Inc.
PO Box 708
Adams Basin, NY 14410-0708

Visit us at www.thewilderroses.com

Publishing History
First Scarlet Rose Edition, June 2012
Print ISBN 978-1-61217-398-6
Digital ISBN 978-1-61217-397-9

Published in the United States of America

Trademarks Acknowledgement

The author of this work of fiction acknowledges
the following trademarks:

Jeep: Chrysler Group LLC

Dedication

To K, my soulmate.
Thank you for your encouragement and advice
and especially for your love.

#

Chapter One

Amanda groped for her ringing cell phone, knocking the alarm clock and her vibrator off the nightstand before she had the damn thing in her hand. She fully intended to hang up but made the mistake of checking the caller ID.

"'Lo Sarah," she said sleepily. "What's up?"

"Time to rise and shine sweet cheeks. It's eight fifteen on a beautiful sunny day in Manhattan, and you owe me breakfast. Get your pretty ass out of bed and get dressed. I'll see you at Beans in twenty minutes. I've got a big surprise for you."

The cheery voice was like a suddenly raised window shade, flooding the room with bright light. "Jeez." She held the phone away from her ear. "How do you know I'm not already dressed? Maybe I've just come in from a two mile run."

"Yeah, right. And I'm the Queen of Sheba. It's just past eight on a Sunday, so I know you're still in bed. The question is, where and with whom? You still seeing that blonde Viking? Are you at his place or yours? I would really love to see the mast on that man's longboat." Sarah giggled.

"Well, you would be very disappointed, just like I was," Amanda groused. "And I'm afraid that relationship is over."

"You're kidding! After just a month? You two seemed like the perfect couple."

"I guess things aren't always what they seem, are they?" Amanda's question dripped with sarcasm, but failed to breach Sarah's optimism.

"I want to hear all about it over breakfast. See

1

you in twenty." The phone finally fell silent.

"Make it thirty!" she yelled, but Sarah was gone.

Leaning over the side of the bed, Amanda picked up the alarm clock and her vibrator, sighing as she sat the vibrator on the nightstand. It was frustrating to think that a battery powered piece of plastic could offer more satisfaction than a flesh-and-blood man. Why couldn't she find a man who could unlock her libido and awaken the sensual being she'd always been afraid to reveal?

Wondering about Sarah's big surprise, she took the vibrator into the bathroom for a wash-up and then took a quick shower. Scrambling through a drawer of lingerie, she selected a tiny thong in fine mesh trimmed in lavender lace.

She was very conservative in the way she dressed, except for her lingerie. Her one fashion indulgence was very erotic lingerie from high-end shops. The sexy panties and bras she wore, like her vibrator and shaved pussy lips, were her secrets, something only a few men ever got to see.

She slipped into the lace thong and looked in the mirror. She liked the feel of the thong on her ass and she didn't have to worry about panty lines. She also enjoyed feeling the material of her skirts and pants on her bare skin.

She kept the small dark triangle of pubic hair just above her clit neatly trimmed and, as she adjusted the panties, she made a mental note to make a wax appointment.

The matching lavender bra clearly showed her nipples through the transparent cups. Her nipples were large, sometimes embarrassingly so. When she was aroused or cold, the tips grew even larger, tightening almost to the point of pain.

She slipped into a pair of indigo skinny jeans and a black T-shirt. A pair of sandals completed the outfit. With a quick dab of makeup, she was off to meet Sarah at Has Beans, their favorite coffee shop/breakfast bar, where the walls were decorated with photos of celebs the paparazzi had lost interest in.

Amanda made it to Beans by nine and immediately spotted Sarah at their favorite corner table. It wasn't difficult. The neon pink mohair sweater she was wearing, which matched the inch wide strip of pink in her raven black hair, stood out like a beacon in a room crowded with New Yorkers dressed in de-rigueur black.

Sarah was an administrative assistant to Richard Patterson, Amanda's boss at Peabody, Patterson & Cope. She was also Amanda's closest friend.

In addition to Sarah's day job, she was a modestly successful artist, specializing in male nudes. The paintings were very popular among gay collectors, including their boss.

In appearance and personality, Amanda and Sarah seemed like polar opposites. Sarah, with her full red lips, eyebrow stud, and streak of pink in her coal black page boy reminded Amanda of a new age pin-up. She even wore bomber bras, garters, and stockings under her outrageous fashions, unless she was painting. Then her retro underwear was all she wore.

Amanda envied Sarah's wild non-conformist streak, which was coupled with a wickedly uninhibited libido. She was sure Sarah never let a man walk away without giving her an orgasm. Even if it meant she had to bring out the whips and handcuffs. Sarah's uninhibited sexual lifestyle made Amanda's lackluster sex life seem even more depressing by comparison. But she did enjoy hearing about some of the outrageous situations Sarah found herself in.

"Hey girl." Amanda slid into a chair across the

table from Sarah. "Love the outfit." Beneath the mohair sweater, Sarah had on a cone shaped bra that lifted and pointed her breasts like a fifties-era starlet.

Sarah smiled. "So tell me all, sweetie. You and Sven are no longer an item?"

"His name is Arne. And yes, we are no longer dating. What's in the box?" She nodded at a large box on the chair next to Sarah.

"You'll see. I want to hear all about your breakup with Arne."

When their waitress appeared, Amanda ordered a biscotti and cappuccino and they both ordered eggs Benedict. As the waitress walked away, Sarah asked, "Was the sex that bad?"

Amanda looked at Sarah in surprise then quickly leaned across the table. "Shhh! Keep your voice down." She looked around to make sure Sarah's comment hadn't caught some patron's attention. "What makes you think the sex was bad? There might be a dozen reasons we decided not to see each other."

"Name two."

Amanda tried to think of something. "Well...it might be..."

Sarah grinned. "Look. The man is successful, handsome, and has a killer bod. I only met him once, but he seemed nice enough. Maybe even charming. And he certainly wouldn't dump you. So it must be him and it must be the sex. Right?"

Amanda blushed and glanced around again. "You're right. The man has no idea how to please a woman. I haven't had that many lovers, but I deserve more than a five minute grope and poke, even if it is followed by a sincere 'thank you'."

Sarah made a face. "That bad, huh?"

"Worse. The man doesn't have a clue."

"Any chance you could train him? He is damn

good looking."

"I don't know." Amanda dipped her biscotti in her coffee. "We tried three times and it was bad every time. For me at least."

"Honey, three times in one night isn't bad."

"I meant three times in a month."

"Oh. That's bad. Did you tell him what you wanted? I mean, what you wanted him to do to you?"

Amanda blushed again, the glow rising from her neck and shoulders to her cheeks. "Well, I didn't say exactly what I wanted. But I hinted around and even suggested that we try oral sex sometime."

"And?"

"And nothing. I think it's too messy for him. Doing me, I mean. The man is a total priss when it comes to keeping things neat. The second time, we were at his place and he put towels down so we wouldn't get wet spots on the sheets."

"What about you doing him?"

"He never even asked. He just wanted to bang, bang, bang, get it done. Come and go, so to speak."

Sarah grinned and leaned back in her chair. "So this whole past month, you haven't had an orgasm?" This was said just as the waitress delivered their breakfast. Amanda glanced up to see the young girl smiling. When the girl left, Amanda leaned across the table and whispered. "Will you keep your voice down? Everybody in New York doesn't need to know about the sad state of my sex life. Or lack thereof. Besides, I've had orgasms lately. Just not with a man." She paused and frowned. "In fact, I'm not sure I've ever had an orgasm with a man. At least not in the classic big O sense."

Sarah leaned forward and lowered her voice. "Honey, you just need a good fuck with a man who will unleash your inner wildcat. Maybe I should set you up with one of my models. Seriously. Just for a nice fuck. No strings attached. With a guy who will do whatever you want."

Amanda smiled. "That sounds like an offer I'd be foolish to refuse. But for right now, I think I will. Thanks anyway."

"Okay," Sarah sighed. "You've got my number if you change your mind." She grinned. "Or if you run out of batteries."

There was a moment of silence as the two friends finished breakfast and sipped their coffee. Maybe I should take her up on a nice fuck from a handsome model, Amanda thought. What could it hurt? Even if it would only be a mercy fuck.

Glancing up, she saw Sarah looking at her with a Cheshire cat grin. "What canary did you swallow? And what's in the box?"

Sarah waited for the server to clear the table, then handed Amanda the carton. The box was big, half the size of the table, but not very heavy. Amanda looked at her friend with a lifted eyebrow, and then slid the lid off the box. Inside, to her total surprise, sat a brand new felt cowboy hat. The hat was pearl grey with a black braded leather band around the crown. The crown was creased and the brim pre-rolled into wearing shape.

Sarah was grinning and squirming happily on her chair, unable to sit still. "Put it on," she said excitedly. "See if it fits."

Amanda looked at the hat, then at Sarah. She glanced at nearby tables and saw several people looking at her and the hat. "I'm *not* putting this on. And why on earth are you giving it to me?"

Sarah's grin grew brighter as she answered Amanda in a slow drawl. "Cause yer gonna need it shugga. Down thar in Texas."

Amanda stared at Sarah as if she were daft. "Texas? What the hell are you talking about?" Just then her phone rang.

"That will be Richard," Sarah said. "Don't tell

him I told you about Texas. Or that I gave you the hat."

"You haven't told me anything about Texas," Amanda lifted the phone to her ear. "Hi Richard. What's up?"

"Mandy, darling." Richard sounded somewhat breathless. "Have you read your e-mail?"

"I only look at blogs and tweets on Sunday. And my laptop is at home. I'm having breakfast with Sarah."

"I know, sweetie. Has she told you anything? I told her I wanted to tell you."

"She gave me a cowboy hat. Said I would need it in Texas."

"You will, sugar. Maybe some boots, too. Do you have any cowboy boots? Never mind. You can buy some."

"Richard, would you tell me what in the world you're talking about?"

"You're going to Texas, sweetie. Tomorrow. Sarah's made all the arrangements. Tickets, hotel, reservations for a car. You leave tomorrow morning."

"It's too early in the day to be joking, Richard. And I didn't get much sleep."

"Darling, you need your beauty rest! And I'm serious. You are going to Texas. Tomorrow."

Amanda paused, trying to wrap her head around what she had just been told. "You're really serious?"

"As a heart attack, sweetie. I need you in Texas tomorrow." Her boss practically purred.

"But Richard, I don't do Texas. I do Western art but not on location. I barely know where Texas is. I may have flown over it once or twice." She glanced at Sarah, who was grinning from ear to ear.

"You don't have to know Texas sweetheart. Just art. Western art. This is right up your alley."

"Who's the client Richard? What is this all about?"

7

"A pair of brothers—Jake and Justin Morgan. They've got an honest-to-God cattle ranch out in West Texas about three hours northwest of Austin. Jake Morgan called me and said he wants to sell a painting. From his tone, I suspect he needs to raise some cash. Maybe cattle ranching hasn't been a growth industry for the past few years."

"What kind of painting Richard? Who's the artist?"

Patterson couldn't seem to conceal the excitement in his voice when he replied. "You won't believe this sugar, but the man sent me a jpeg of a signed Charles Randell painting titled 'Cowboy on a Horse.' Typical Randell scene."

"That could bring in a nice commission," Amanda said.

"Oh, that's not all. I've studied everything I could find on Randell. As far as I can tell, this painting has never been cataloged."

"Do you think it's real?"

"It could be. Morgan said the artist gave it to his great granddaddy back in the late 1800s. It's been hanging on a ranch house wall for a hundred years. If it is an unknown Randell, it will be worth a small fortune."

Amanda felt a slight constriction in her chest and realized she had been holding her breath. "No. It could be worth a big fortune if it's the real deal." She was trying to remember all she knew about one of America's most famous Western artists. He had given away lots of paintings and drawings when he was first starting out. "Jesus, Richard. This sounds exciting!"

"Go home and open your email. But do it in the bathroom because you're liable to pee your panties."

Amanda's mind raced. Charles Randell had done four thousand paintings, drawings, illustrations, and sculptures. Who could say he hadn't done four thousand and one, or four thousand and two? It seemed every twenty years or so a new Randell painting or drawing surfaced somewhere.

"This could be a major find Richard, if it's real. Do you know what the last unknown Randell brought at auction?"

"I do know, sugar. It made a very cool twelve million. That's why you need to get your cute butt down to Texas. We need to make sure it's authentic, at least as much as we can. And we need to get the Morgan brothers to sign with Peabody, Patterson & Cope as their exclusive brokerage firm.

"This could be huge for us Mandy. We'll have to put it through the ringer to verify authenticity, but just in case it might be the real deal, we need you in Texas, shaking hands with the Morgan boys."

"I'll pack tonight," Amanda said, already wondering what she should wear. "Do you really think I need cowboy boots?"

"Wouldn't hurt," Richard replied. "And wear the cowboy hat. Put on some tight jeans, too. We need to take advantage of your natural ass-ets!"

"You know I could sue *your ass* for sexual harassment, Richard. I only let you get by with all that 'sugar' crap because you're as gay as a maypole."

"I know, darling, I know." Richard giggled. "Have fun in Texas. I can't wait to hear what the Morgans have hanging on their wall. You should plan on spending the night at their ranch. They have a guest room and there are no hotels or motels within a hundred miles. Call me as soon as you know something. Anytime, day or night."

Amanda clicked off and looked at Sarah, who hadn't been able to wipe the grin from her face.

"Texas!" Amanda said.

"That's right partner. Where they drive around with cow horns on the front of their land yachts. I've made your reservations. You change planes in Dallas. There will be a car waiting for you in Austin."

Amanda smiled then slowly lifted the cowboy hat and sat it on her head, not caring that several people nearby were staring at her. "Texas," she said again.

"And cowboys," Sarah added. "Rugged, handsome cowboys."

"Yeah, right. Those ranchers are probably fat and fifty. I'm interested in seeing the artwork." She paused a moment. "I'm thinking about buying some cowboy boots. Want to go shopping with me?"

Sarah grinned then stuck her leg out to one side of the table. "No need to," she said, pointing down at her foot. "You can borrow mine."

Amanda looked down, then shook her head and grinned. Sarah was wearing a pair of pink ostrich skin boots. A wild collage of colorful jewels formed a peacock pattern on each side. "Thanks, but no. I don't think a rhinestone cowgirl is who they will expect from a prestigious New York art brokerage firm."

Amanda thanked Sarah for the cowboy hat, gave her an air kiss, and hurried home to look at the photo of the painting Richard had sent her. She spent the rest of the morning at the computer researching Charles Marion Randell. She couldn't find any Randell works that matched the Morgan painting. And from what she could tell from the jpeg, the Morgan work had the same brushwork, color palette, and style as a genuine Randell.

The more she researched, the more excited she became. At five thirty she decided to take a break and, on a whim, searched the net for Manhattan stores that sold cowboy boots. She found a shop called Wayne's Wild Wild West just blocks from her apartment. The shop closed at six on Sundays so she took a taxi, stopping to pick up batteries for her vibrator on the way. Half an hour later, she was back with a beautiful pair of hand-stitched boots in chocolate brown leather. Unlike Sarah's bejeweled and dazzling pink pair, her new boots had a simple design of an eagle done in gold stitching on each side.

By nine, she was packed for an overnight trip. By ten she was in bed, hoping to get a few hours sleep before getting up at five to catch her flight. Sleep, however, fell victim to the excitement of possibly finding an uncataloged painting by one of America's best known Western artists, and to the trip to Texas itself. She'd never thought about going to Texas. There were lots of places higher on her must-visit list. But now that she was going, even if just for overnight, she was looking forward to some scenery much different than Manhattan's concrete canyons.

Chapter Two

Texas. Texas!

Her only connection to the state was a girl from Dallas that she had roomed with during her senior year of art school in Pennsylvania. The girl, another art history major, was an attractive, big-breasted coed named Nichole. Nikki—or Nookie to a large number of male students—was the epitome of what Amanda's mother called a slut. She was also one of the brightest people she had ever met.

For the first few weeks of the semester, they were roommates. She didn't care that Nikki spent more time smooching and groping boys than she spent studying. Amanda's time was spent with her nose in art history books, not in Nikki's business. But by the fourth week, the smooching and groping had turned into fucking, and Amanda spent almost every night lying awake in the dark, listening to Nikki getting it on with one stud or another and sometimes two at the same time. To Amanda's amazement, Nikki somehow managed to screw her brains out and still maintain a 4.0 grade point.

Even though the two women had very different personalities, especially when it came to sex, for a short time they became very good friends. As with her friendship with Sarah, Amanda seemed to be drawn to women who actually did the sexual things she only fantasized about.

There was no question in her mind that Nikki enjoyed a highly active libido. But did that make her a slut? And if it did was that such a bad thing after all? Would it be terribly wrong to enjoy making love to two men at once?

Forget about it, she thought. She hadn't had a whole lot of success with just one lover. Thinking about fucking two at a time might be overreaching a bit.

****

With the exception of a squalling two-year-old and lightening-laced thunderstorms that kept the plane in a holding pattern for an extra hour, the flight from New York to Austin via Dallas was uneventful. Amanda spent the time on her computer, studying everything she had downloaded about Charles Marion Randell and several other Western artists working in the late 1800s and early 1900s. When the plane finally landed, she had a good overview of the artist and his contemporaries.

By the time she picked up the rental car, it was almost noon, and it looked like she would have to spend at least one night at the Morgan ranch. She'd wanted to avoid staying at the ranch, if possible, since God only knew how rustic a cattle ranch in Nowhere, Texas, might be. Economy and ecologically minded Sarah had rented her a new little hybrid for her drive to the ranch. Amanda didn't own a car of her own and didn't need one in New York, but she knew how to drive and the rental didn't appear to present too much of a challenge. Before she left the airport, she used her computer to access the university faculty roster for Nichole Nelson, hoping her former roommate hadn't married or at least was still using her maiden name.

She was in luck. Nichole Nelson was listed as professor of art history in the College of Fine Art. She dialed the office number listed and Nikki answered on the second ring. "Nichole Nelson."

"Hi Nikki. It's Amanda Sloane."

"Oh my God! Mandy Sloane. I haven't heard from you in years. What are you up to? Did you get that job in New York you wanted?"

"I did, with Peabody, Patterson & Cope. I'm in Austin, on my way to a ranch to look at a painting that might be an uncataloged Charles Randell."

"How exciting. Will you be here a while? We need to try to get together."

"That would be fun. But it will have to be on my way back. I'll be at the ranch a couple of days."

"Doesn't matter. I'm here all week teaching classes. Call me when you get back in town. We can at least have lunch or dinner."

"I'll try to. It would be good to see you. We can talk over old times."

"You mean *wild* times."

"I think they might have been I little wilder for you than me."

"Guilty as charged. You said Amanda Sloane, so I assume you aren't married."

"Nope. And no immediate prospects. You?"

"The same. There are too many good looking men out there to be tied to only one. And right now, I'm swamped. They've appointed me acting dean of the College of Fine Arts for the next two years."

"Nikki that's great! Congratulations!"

"Thanks. Listen, I've got a meeting in ten minutes. Call me when you get back to Austin. Early or late. It doesn't matter. And take down my cell number."

She jotted down the cell number. "It was nice to talk to you Nikki. I'll call you in a couple days."

"Please do. I'd love to see you."

Chapter Three

Amanda left the airport and half an hour later she was enjoying the rolling terrain of the West Texas Hill Country. It was late May and the hillsides, splattered with colorful Black-eyed Susans, Blue Bonnets, and bright red and yellow Indian Paintbrush, looked like an Impressionist painting. Even more amazing than the rolling hills of wildflowers was the vastness of the Texas sky. From horizon to horizon, the vault of the sky stretched in an azure arch, totally cloudless except for remnants of the thunderstorms that had delayed their arrival now skidding off to the east.

Rolling all the windows down in the little car, Amanda let it fill with fresh Texas air. Even though she'd spent endless hours studying the art of Western painters like Charles Randell, she had only been west a couple of times; once to Santa Fe and Taos and once to Denver. This trip, she decided, was more like a short vacation than a business trip. And if the Randell turned out to be genuine, that would just be icing on the cake.

She checked the map she'd printed out before she left, making sure she was on the right road. She had phoned the ranch from her cell to explain that her flight had been delayed due to weather, but had gotten only their voice mail. She left a message that she would be arriving sometime between three and four, wondering as she did just what the Morgan brothers were like. Whoever had spoken on the answering machine had a resonant baritone voice, deep but mellow. Not that it mattered. Her objective

15

on this trip was evaluating art and hopefully finding a hundred-year-old multi-million dollar painting.

A swirling cloud of dust suddenly blew across the road in front of her and she felt the car pull to the right. Adjusting, she looked toward the west and saw puffy white clouds billowing high into the sky. Another gust of wind pushed her toward the edge of the road and she twisted the steering wheel, almost over-correcting. She'd left the main highway an hour earlier and was now on a state road, paved, but just two lanes. According to the map, she would be turning onto a county road next.

To the west, the puffy cottonball clouds billowed higher and higher, maybe thousands of feet, but they still looked miles and miles away. She could see curtains of rain stretching to the ground in three or four places. Hopefully, she would make it to the ranch before she got caught in a rainstorm. As if to punctuate her thought, lightening forked from the clouds to the ground in the distance. Several seconds later, Amanda heard a sharp crack, followed by the faint rumble of thunder.

Turning off the two-lane county highway, she found herself on a gravel road. A couple of miles later, the gravel turned to dirt and strong gusts threw up clouds of dust around her car.

Damn, this can't be right, she thought. The gravel road is supposed to lead to the ranch house. She glanced at her watch. She should easily be at the ranch by now. She stopped the car, wondering if she should turn around. Suddenly, a huge glistening brown eye in a white face was staring at her, just inches from her open window. She screamed and jerked back from the window, scrambling to find the button to roll it up. Another face appeared on the passenger side and then a dozen more brown bodies and white faces surrounded her, bleating and slobbering from their mouths and noses.

It was the first time Amanda had seen a cow up close and her immediate reaction was to scream and honk the horn. At the first beep, the cow on her side of the car leaped away, crashing into another cow. Two more cows leaped out of the road in panic, trying to get away from the blaring horn. One of the frightened animals defecated, splattering cow shit all over the front fender of the car.

With her car surrounded by bawling, mooing cattle, she couldn't move forward or backward. Suddenly, in place of the cow at her window, there was a boot in a stirrup with a silver spur on the heel leading up to a well-worn pair of leather chaps. A gloved hand reached down and knocked hard against the car window. She looked up into the face of a very angry cowboy, leaning down from the saddle of his horse. The man twirled his hand indicating that she roll down her window. Amanda rolled the window down an inch. At the expression on the irate man's face, she rolled the window down a few inches more. Although the man was obviously very angry, she couldn't help but note he was also ruggedly handsome.

The cowboy tipped his hat back so he could lean in closer as he yelled. "Lady, stop honking your Goddamn horn. You're gonna have steers climbing all over your fucking car." Amanda jerked her hand from the steering wheel, unaware that she had been honking the whole time.

"Sorry," she apologized, but the cowboy had risen up and was shouting at another man up ahead.

"Jody! Go get that bunch headed to the creek!"

The other cowboy cut away from the herd, riding quickly after a small group of reddish brown, white-faced cattle that were running down the hill. A black and white border collie ran ahead of the cowboy's horse, nipping at the heels of the wayward cows.

The cowboy at her window had finally cooled off

17

a bit and she was getting over her initial fright. "I'm sorry. I didn't mean to scare your cows. They just—"

"What the hell are you doing out here anyway?" The cowboy was close, hanging on to the roof of the car as he leaned down into the window. She noticed his boots were round toed and scuffed and worn, nothing at all like the shiny new pointy-toed boots she was wearing.

"I'm trying to find the Morgan ranch," She said, regaining some of her composure. "Isn't it dangerous for you to drive cattle down a public road?"

The cowboy studied her for a moment. "The road to the ranch is a mile back. Then you go a mile and a half north. If you're the art appraiser, they're waiting for you. And this isn't a public road. You left that two miles ago."

Amanda looked out the front window at the half dozen men who were rounding up the frightened cattle. When she looked back at the cowboy, he was staring at her chest. Her nipples quickly hardened under his admiring gaze.

That morning, she'd left New York wearing jeans, her new boots, and a long-sleeved flannel shirt over a gossamer bra and a thin white tank top. The shirt, in a dark blue plaid, was unbuttoned and open, clearly showing the fullness of her breasts and the hardness of her nipples against the material of her bra and tank top. She pulled the lapels of the shirt together, covering her nipples.

The cowboy looked up. Although he had been caught blatantly staring at her breasts, he showed no sign of embarrassment. Instead, his slight smile sent a flush up her neck to her cheeks. When he saw her blush, his eyes, a luminous emerald green, twinkled mischievously.

Amanda suddenly realized she was looking at an amazingly attractive man. Christ, she thought, unable to stop staring at his face. Men are not supposed to have eyes that pretty. Certainly not in a face that handsome.

"Sit tight for a minute," the cowboy said. "We'll get the herd around you. Then you can turn around." He reached into a pocket of his leather vest and took out a cell phone. "If I can get a signal, I'll tell them you are coming." The cowboy looked over his shoulder at the lowering sky. "This weather coming in fast, I'd try not to take any more side trips."

Side trips! I wasn't on a side trip, you arrogant ass. I was trying to follow your lousy directions. She frowned at the man but he wasn't paying attention. Still fuming, she watched in her rear view mirror as the cowboys drove the remaining thirty or forty cows around her car and on down the road. When the last animal passed, the green-eyed cowboy followed, tipping his hat slightly as he rode by. She could see he was dressed in full working cowboy regalia—hat, boots, spurs, chaps, and a red flannel shirt under a leather vest. His horse was a beautiful reddish brown with white stocking forelegs and a white blaze on its head. *Holy cow,* she thought, watching his posture in the saddle. *I just met my first honest-to-God cowboy. Too bad I pissed him off.*

A crack of lightening and a rolling peal of thunder made her look out to the west. The billowing storm clouds that had seemed so far away were much closer now, so close she could smell the rain in the air. She worked at turning the car around in the narrow dirt road, then drove back the way she had come.

At exactly a mile on her odometer, another gravel road angled north. This road, barely wide enough for two cars to pass, had barbed wire fences on each side, set back behind bar ditches that were three to four feet deep. On her right, to the east, the road was lined with occasional groves of cotton-woods. Beyond the tall trees, she could see pastureland sloping up to gently undulating hills. To the west, the land was treeless and flat, stretching in an empty plain toward the distant horizon.

Except now the horizon seemed much closer and was filled with dark curtains of rain sweeping rapidly toward her. A bright flash lit the sky and she jumped, startled by the boom of thunder that seemed to explode right above her. As the thunder rumbled away in the distance, the first big drops of rain hit the car, splattering loudly on the metal and glass. In seconds, the rain came down in torrents.

The car's lights had come on in the weather's gloom, but she could still barely see the road ahead. The wind-whipped rain came at her sideways in sheets, rattling against the shaking car like gunfire. She stopped in the middle of the road, unable to see more than a few feet in front of the car. She turned the caution blinker on, unsure whether to pull to the side of the road in case another car came along or stay in the middle away from the steeply sloping ditches on each side.

The rain pounding against the car grew in intensity, becoming louder and sharper. Thunder and lightning were almost constant now, one flash and boom and rumble following on the heels of another. Outside the car, she could see small white pellets hitting the ground, striking the hood, and piling up along the front edge of the windshield.

Fuck! It's hailing. As she watched, the pellets grew from dime to nickel size, then as big as quarters. She had seen hail in New York, but nothing like this. As the hailstones thumped against the hood of the car, she knew they must be making hellacious dents on the roof and hood.

Between the howling gusts of wind that drove the rain and hail against the car in blinding torrents, Amanda could see the dark shape of trees arching over the road in the near distance. Hoping the overhanging branches might offer some protection, she eased the car forward, her windshield wipers whacking uselessly at the pounding rain and hail.

Just as she reached the shelter of the overhanging trees, she saw an opening in the fence to her right. Through the opening, a narrow rutted drive wound toward a grey, weather-beaten barn a hundred yards up a slight hill. The rutted road, now thick with mud from the rain, led directly to large double doors in one end of the long low-roofed structure. One of the double doors had been rolled aside a couple of feet.

At the far end of the barn, she could see a wooden railed corral that stood empty. Along the side of the barn a flat-roofed canopy jutted out, held up by wooden posts. A farm tractor sat under the protection of the canopy roof, out of the hail. There was an empty space next to the tractor, and she decided she would try to get the car up to the barn and out of the hail.

Gunning the car, she slipped and slid her way up the muddy ruts, finally pulling off to one side under the shelter of the canopy.

The absence of the sound of hailstones hitting the roof and hood of the car was a relief. The rain was still coming down in buckets, but the space under the canopy was relatively dry. She opened her door and got out of the car, standing for a moment to watch the rain and hail. The ground was not completely covered by hailstones, but in places the pellets had drifted up enough to look like patches of melting snow.

The wind was dying down somewhat and the hail had tapered off. The pellets were smaller, once more dime sized or less. Amanda felt that in a few minutes she might be able to get back down to the gravel road and make her way to the ranch. Slipping her cell phone out of her jeans pocket, she scrolled to the preprogrammed number and pushed the call button. NO SIGNAL. She sighed and slipped the phone back into her pocket. Just then a loud whinny came from inside the barn.

She turned. On the other side of the tractor was a small opening in the side of the barn, about two feet square. The opening had been framed like a window but without the glass. Stepping around the tractor, trying to avoid the wet grass and mud beyond the canopy, she made her way to the opening. She had expected the barn to be empty. But looking in, she saw that wasn't the case at all.

Two bare light bulbs suspended from the ceiling cut through the gloom enough for her to see the barn's interior. The barn, long and narrow, had been divided into six or seven stalls on each side, with a dirt floor between them running the full length of the building. Two of the stalls held bales of hay, stacked almost to the low ceiling. Another stall was filled with saddles, bridles, and other tack. At the end of the barn to the right, where one of the double doors had been partially rolled aside, stood a large black extended cab pick-up truck.

Another sharp whinny split the air and she looked quickly toward the other end of the barn. Two cowboys, one tall and one short, were working with a pair of horses. The horses, both dark brown with black manes and tails, were not saddled but had halters and lead ropes.

One of the horses stood facing into a stall, its head tied close to a rail next to the barn wall. The short cowboy had hold of the second horse's lead rope, pulling it toward the rear end of the hitched up horse. The two cowboy's backs were turned toward her, and they had no idea she was there.

"Yup! Yup! Come on Rocket! Get up!" The taller cowboy was behind the horse outside the stall, urging him into the stall with the other horse. Then she realized he wasn't urging the horse into the stall, but on top of the first horse.

Oh my God, she thought, now seeing the stallion's huge cock that was swinging menacingly under the big horse's belly.

"Sheeup! Sheeup Rocket!" The short cowboy was standing on a rail outside the stall holding the mare, pulling hard on the lead rope of the stallion, trying to lift its head and pull it forward. The cowboy's voice sounded shrill, mixing with the snorting and huffing of the stallion and the high whinnies of the mare.

Amanda was transfixed by the stallion's huge cock, which had to be two feet long and as thick as the business end of a baseball bat. She could see that the massive instrument, a mottled pink and black, was already dripping fluid. Both horses pranced anxiously, their back hooves digging up chunks of dirt from the floor. The mare, her wild eyes trying to see the stallion behind her, had her tail up, waving it like a flag as she danced from side to side.

The stallion suddenly reared up, snorting as his forelegs landed on each side of the mare's rump. Amanda watched in amazement as the stallion's massive cock suddenly lifted and speared forward, sliding halfway into the mare. Working his back legs for traction, the stallion lunged forward again, burying his cock deeper.

Jesus, she thought. *How could any animal accommodate a cock that big?*

Hunching his hips, the stallion worked his forelegs up the mare's back, finally burying his cock completely in the mare.

The stallion fucked the mare rapidly for a few minutes and then it was over. The stallion stepped backward, his penis sliding out of the mare. As he backed up, the mare whinnied and bucked.

23

"Goddamn it Dolly, stop that! You've had your fuck." The tall cowboy slapped the mare's rump with the quirt, then grabbed the stallion's lead rope and led him away. At the end of the barn beyond the stall sat a set of double doors identical to the doors to Amanda's right. The cowboy rolled one of the doors aside and stood watching the last of the rain. After a moment, he unhooked the lead rope and let the stallion loose in the wood-railed paddock. The stallion bucked a couple of times as he left the barn, then disappeared from sight.

Stepping back inside, the cowboy turned toward his partner, who had walked up behind him. Suddenly, he leaned down and kissed the short cowboy, who immediately wrapped his arms around the taller man's neck.

Holy shit! Amanda stared, stunned. Just then, the shorter man's hat fell backward onto the floor of the barn, uncovering a thick mane of blond curls. After the unexpected shock of seeing what she thought were two men kissing, she was relieved to find that the short cowboy was actually a cowgirl.

The couple moved out from under the hanging bulb that lit the stall until they were primarily in silhouette. But it was obvious the man was squeezing the woman's breast as they kissed, and one of her hands had drifted down from the man's neck to his rear.

As the couple continued kissing, Amanda felt her nipples harden again. Her pussy was also tingling and she realized, to her embarrassment, that watching the stallion and mare had turned her on much more than she would ever admit. Now, watching the couple groping each other in the barn, her arousal was rapidly growing in intensity.

Amanda knew she should turn away, go back to the car, and give the lovers in the barn their privacy. But the voyeuristic arousal she felt kept her transfixed. She put her hand on the crotch of her jeans, pressing hard, trying unsuccessfully to quiet the tingling hum of blood rushing to her swelling pussy lips. She closed her eyes for a moment, wondering if this could actually be happening. When she opened them, she saw that the woman was now squatting on the dirt floor, balancing as her fingers worked quickly at the man's belt. A moment later, she pulled his unbuckled jeans aside and hauled out an impressively large cock. Even in the shadowy dimness, Amanda could see the cowboy's dick was at least nine or ten inches long, longer than any she'd seen outside of the few porn movies she'd watched. With the girl's hand wrapped around the base, another five or six inches extended out from her fist.

The cowgirl angled the cowboy's cock upward slightly and took the head in her mouth. The sight quickly dialed up the silent buzzing under Amanda's cotton thong. As the woman slowly sucked the man's cock, Amanda slid one hand down inside her jeans and the other up under her tank top to squeeze her breast.

Suddenly remembering where she was, she looked quickly over one shoulder then the other. The hail had stopped completely and the rain had dwindled to a light sprinkle. The landscape, still gray from the cloud cover, was wet and glistening but completely empty. She saw no signs of life, not even a cow. She leaned forward an inch or two and peeked back inside the barn.

The cowgirl had abandoned the blowjob and turned her back on the cowboy. She was now bending over at the waist, holding on to a rail of one of the horse stalls, while the cowboy struggled to pull her tight jeans down her legs to her boots. Once he had her jeans down to her boot tops, he took a condom from his pocket, opened it, and rolled it down his amazing length.

Amanda still had one hand inside her own jeans, but realized the fit was too tight to allow the finger movement she craved. She quickly unsnapped and unzipped her jeans, pushing them down just enough to access to the damp, swollen flesh between her legs. Slipping one hand down inside her thong, she slid her index finger into the wet slit below her clitoris just as the cowboy slid his cock into the cowgirl. As he fucked the cowgirl, Amanda finger-fucked herself, stimulated by the scene in the barn and the memory of the stallion thrusting his giant cock into the mare. To her surprise, and increased arousal, the face of the cowboy with the pussy-melting emerald green eyes also flitted among the images that were overwhelming her.

In the inhibited part of her consciousness that normally ruled her sexual urges, Amanda could not believe she was actually standing outside a barn in the middle of Texas, finger-fucking herself as she watched two people doing the nasty inside the barn. But the physical sensation spreading up into her belly and down the insides of her thighs was proof enough of just how much she was enjoying it.

The cowgirl had been moaning softly but now her cries of pleasure were growing in intensity. The level of Amanda's arousal was keeping pace, her fingers working her wet slit faster and faster, sliding deep between her swollen lips, then back up to circle eagerly around her clit.

The cowgirl bucked her bare bottom against the cowboy's thrusts, suddenly climaxing and crying, "Yes! Yesss! Fuck me, Luke! Fuck me hard!"

Amanda's fingers flew rapidly over her pussy, pushing her to the edge of orgasm. As one hand worked inside her jeans, she squeezed her breasts with the other, pinching her erect nipples to the point of pain. She desperately needed to come. She was close. So close that her knees felt weak. She backed up, supporting herself against the huge tire of the tractor. Her eyes were closed tight, her breath coming in short gasps. Any minute she would find her pleasure.

****

Jake Morgan nudged Ginger up the rutted road toward the barn where the art appraiser's car was parked under the overhang. As he approached, he saw the woman standing next to an opening in the barn. She was peering intently into the shadowy interior of the barn, her back to the road. The hail had stopped, but there was still a steady drizzle of rain. He started to call out to the woman, but stopped when he saw what she was doing.

"Son of a bitch," he murmured, reining Ginger to a halt. The woman had one hand inside her jeans, obviously rubbing herself. With her other hand, she was squeezing her breasts. She apparently was so enraptured by whatever she saw inside the barn that she was paying no attention to anything else.

What the hell was she watching that had her frigging herself out in the open? He smiled. Luke and Julie were supposed to be breeding Rocket and Dolly in the barn. Maybe she was watching that. Or maybe Luke was breeding Julie. It certainly wouldn't be the first time. Whatever it was, it was damn sure turning her on. From the action of her hand inside her pants, she was definitely aroused and needed to come.

He had been royally pissed when she drove her car into his herd and scattered them with her goddamn horn. It had taken the cowhands an hour to round them back up and moved to pasture. Still, he had to admit that she was damned good looking. When he had arranged for an art appraiser to come look at Great Granddad's painting, he had half expected a matronly woman in her sixties with her gray hair up in a bun. He certainly hadn't expected this sexy lady. She was pretty. And she had an amazing pair of tits.

She'd blushed beet red when she caught him looking at her nipples. What the hell will she do when she realizes he's caught her with her hand down her pants?

He nudged Ginger again and the horse snorted as she moved forward. He was less than forty feet from the woman when she finally opened her eyes and saw him. Her face went instantly ashen and then turned sunset red. He couldn't keep from smiling when she whipped her hand out of her jeans and tried to zip them up without him seeing what she was doing. Damn she was pretty when her cheeks turned rosy. It wouldn't be bad at all to have her around the ranch for a few days. If she was horny enough to frig herself in broad daylight, what would she be like in the dark? The shy ones often turned into wildcats once their campfire was lit.

He watched her in silence, but couldn't keep a glimmer of amusement out of his expression. He touched the brim of his cowboy hat and calmly said, "Howdy ma'am."

"I—I—I was just getting out of the—the—hail," she stammered.

"Good idea. Hail storm's no fun to be out in." He nudged Ginger toward her and stopped ten feet away. The lady finally stepped away from the tractor and faced him. She was still beet red from embarrassment, but took a deep breath to introduce herself.

"I'm Amanda Sloane. From Peabody, Patterson & Cope. I'm here to examine some artwork."

"Figured as much." He swung down off Ginger and stepped forward. He slipped the leather glove off his right hand and extended his arm. "I'm Jake Morgan. My brother Justin and I own this spread." He took her offered hand, holding it as he looked into her eyes. After a long moment, she averted her eyes and pulled her hand away.

She looked at his horse just a few feet away. "Your horse is pretty. What kind is it?"

"This is Ginger," he said. "She's a sorrel Quarter Horse. Most of our horses are Quarter Horses. Do you ride?"

Amanda stepped forward and laid her palm on Ginger's nose. "No, not at all," she said. "The closest I've come is a horse-drawn carriage in Central Park."

"We'll have to fix that," he said. "But right now, Justin is probably waiting for us. We'd best get on up to the ranch house. Our granddaddy built it originally as a hunting lodge." He swung back up on his horse. "We were worried you might be having some trouble in the storm, so I thought it best if I come fetch you. I'm glad you found some shelter from the hail."

There was the sound of dual mufflers rumbling and a moment later a big black pickup pulled around the corner of the barn. As the truck pulled up alongside Jake and Amanda, the window rolled down. "Hey Jake. What's up?" The cowboy addressed Jake but was looking at Amanda.

"This is Miss Sloane," Jake said. "From New York. She's going to take a look at Great Granddaddy's painting. She pulled in here to get out of the hail. Miss Sloane, this is Luke Slate, our ranch foreman. And that's Julie Decker." He nodded toward the cowgirl sitting next to Luke. "Julie is in charge of our equine breeding program." The cowgirl leaned forward and looked across the cowboy, nodding hello to Amanda.

"How'd it go with Dolly and Rocket?" Jake asked.

"They're both just great," Julie said. "Come next April, you can bet on a baby Rocket. Or Dolly," she said, speaking to Jake but also looking at Amanda.

Luke let the clutch out and the truck rolled down the rutted drive toward the gravel road.

"You follow me," Jake said to Amanda. "We'll get you to the ranch in a few minutes. Sorry about the bad weather. In springtime, you can't tell what it's going to do out here. Least we didn't have a twister."

Amanda walked around the tractor and got in her car. As she started it and pulled out from under the canopy, Jake mounted and spurred his horse into a trot down the rutted drive. She followed slowly in the car, slipping occasionally in the mud but keeping up. Jake looked over his shoulder. *That woman is one damned fine filly,* he thought, standing in his stirrups to adjust the crotch of his jeans. *And damn if she hasn't given me a hard-on.*

Chapter Four

Amanda followed Jake down the muddy drive and out onto the gravel road, thankful that she hadn't gotten stuck. On the gravel road, Jake spurred into a faster pace and she sped up, trying to keep the car close. As she watched him ride, she wondered what in the world he thought of her. First honking like a madwoman at his cows, but then to be caught—Jesus, she couldn't imagine what must be going through his head. *Richard,* she thought, *if the Morgans don't sign with PP&C, it will surely be because you sent a voyeuristic sex-crazed slut to represent you. A slut who got caught with her fingers in the nookie jar.*

At the top of a slight rise, Jake pulled off to one side and waited for Amanda to catch up. As she crested the hill, she slowed down, looking at a sight that took her breath away.

Immediately in front of her, announcing the entrance to the ranch, was a gateway created by two huge tree trunk posts, holding up a massive log crossbeam that stretched to the sides of the road and beyond. In the center of the crossbeam hung the skull of a longhorn steer, its horns stretching out at least six feet from tip to tip. Beneath the skull hung a large, welded metal M.

Once past the open gateway, the road wound down into a shallow valley that was a glistening patchwork of green meadows and fields of wild flowers in various shades of blue and yellow and red. In the bottom of the valley, a stream meandered between the fields of green hay and colorful flowers, disappearing into the distance at the valley's far end. On the side of the valley, she could see forty or fifty white-faced cattle like the ones she had scared the bejesus out of earlier in the day. On the other side sat a cluster of buildings. Some were obviously barns and stables, others she was unsure of.

Set back against thick groves of pines and cottonwoods and overlooking the entire valley, sat a large two-story stone and timber structure that was obviously the main ranch house. It did, indeed, look more like a hunting lodge than the ranch house she'd expected.

The entire panorama looked like a set staged for a Western epic, and Amanda had to stop the car for a moment to catch her breath and take the sight in.

Just when she thought the scene couldn't be prettier, the sun broke through the last of the storm clouds, its late afternoon light casting a golden glow over the entire valley. The stream, now a russet reflection of the setting sun, suddenly burst into a sparkling ribbon of dancing light. A rainbow appeared, faint at first, then in sharp definition as it arched halfway across the sky.

Holy crap, she thought, a bit overwhelmed by the sheer beauty of the valley bathed in golden light. She didn't particularly believe in omens, but she also had never experienced a rainbow in a scene so incredibly spectacular.

Jake nudged his horse over to her car. As he approached, she rolled down the window.

"Everything okay?" He leaned down toward the open window.

"Yes, everything's fine. I'm just admiring the view. It's really very beautiful from up here."

Jake raised back up and looked over the valley. He smiled. "It is pretty, isn't it? I guess you get used to it, seeing it every day." He gazed at the scene for a moment then turned back to Amanda. She suddenly realized he was looking at her in the same way she was admiring his ranch. The realization sent a flutter of butterflies through her tummy.

"Do you mind if I take a picture? I'd like to e-mail a snapshot back to my office in New York."

He smiled. "Help yourself. It is a damn pretty sight." He said this with an appraising gleam in his eye, looking at her, not the ranch. The butterflies in her stomach did a loop. She got out of the car and snapped three quick shots with her cell. Later, she would send the pics to Sarah with the message, "Eat your heart out, city girl."

When she got back in the car, Jake said, "Just follow the road up to the lodge. Justin should be there waiting on you. I'll be up as soon as I take care of Ginger." He slipped a pocket watch out of his vest and glanced at it, then looked over his shoulder at the sun, now an orange ball in the Western sky. "We can put you up in a guest room for as long as you like. We've got six or seven. I'll have our housekeeper, Rosita, see to it."

Before she could say thanks, he reined his horse and trotted down the road toward the ranch. After a moment, he spurred the horse into a gentle lope, heading toward a long, low-roofed barn similar to the one where she had seen the stallion and mare being bred.

She wasn't sure how long it might take to authenticate the supposed Randell painting, but she hoped she could do it in a day and spend no more than one night at the ranch. But it was important to get it right. She needed plenty of time to study the painting. This was only a preliminary authentication and she wanted to be sure of the advice she offered to the Morgans.

Amanda drove down to the lodge and parked the car next to a red pickup. She took her carry-on from the trunk, leaving her suitcase in the car. Her carry-on was just big enough for her laptop and cowboy hat, which she had brought along even though she was sure she would never wear it. She was already out of her comfort zone wearing cowboy boots instead of her usual pumps, knee boots, or running shoes.

Up close, the house—or lodge—was even bigger than she had thought. Wide stone steps led up to a large front porch that wrapped around the front and two sides. A balcony to the second floor rooms also wrapped around the front and sides, forming the roof of the porch. The heavy front door of the house was open, covered only by a Victorian-style screen door. Amanda had just reached the top step when she heard yelling and the sounds of a scuffle through the open door.

Suddenly, the screen door burst open and a heavyset man in a black cowboy hat and gray Western cut suit burst out backward, his boot-clad feet backpeddling rapidly as he tried to maintain his balance. Another man, taller and younger, was up in his face, propelling him backward with quick jabs of a pointed finger in his chest. Even though the second man's face was contorted in anger, she knew immediately that he must be Justin Morgan. He looked so much like Jake that the two men could be twins. The man backing up was almost at the edge of the porch, just a few feet from her.

"Goddammit," the man was shouting. "It's mine, Justin! It's never been yours or your daddy's or your granddaddy's."

The younger man's eyes, more gray than deep green like Jake's, were blazing with anger.

"And you're full of crap, Winslow! Granddaddy hung that painting on the wall a hundred years ago and it's been there ever since."

"It's mine, you son of a bitch! You give it up, you goddamn thief!"

"You get the hell off our property, Winslow, or I'll kick your ass from hell to Sunday!"

By this time, the man walking backward had reached the edge of the porch. Amanda had to leap to one side to keep from being run over. She made it, but her rolling carry-on didn't. Just as she tried to jerk it out of the way, the heavy set man stepped down, his boot smashing the center of the bag.

"Watch out," Amanda cried as she pulled the handle of the bag, trying to get it out of the way. Her effort pulled the man off his feet and he fell sideways, landing in the mud at the edge of the porch.

The younger man gaped at Amanda in openmouthed astonishment. He had been totally unaware of her presence and now, as she looked in dismay at her crushed roll-on, he forgot all about the man he'd been arguing with.

Winslow, covered in mud and livid with anger, lunged at Amanda and her carry-on, apparently thinking she had tripped him on purpose. "You goddamn bitch! I'll..."

As she raised her hands and jerked back in fear, almost falling off the porch herself, an arm shot past her shoulder, propelling a fist into Winslow's nose. Once again, he went down, this time on the steps, blood flowing from his nose onto his muddy suit.

Amanda turned to see it was Jake Morgan who had slugged the man. Two other cowboys appeared from nowhere and in seconds had the injured man up and stumbling toward the red pickup she had parked next to.

"Jesus!" The younger brother held her by one elbow. "I'm damn sorry about that."

Jake, holding her other arm, helped her up onto the porch, guiding her to the open front door. "Let's get you inside." He reached down to grab the handle of her carry-on.

As they reached the doorway, both men called out, "Rosita," A beautiful, middle-aged Mexican woman appeared. She was wearing jeans and an off the shoulder peasant blouse decorated with colorful embroidered flowers. The woman immediately took over, guiding Amanda to a large wingback leather chair.

"I'm okay," she said as she sat down. "Really, I'm just fine..." In fact, she was trembling and tears were beginning to well up in her eyes. It had been a day of intense emotions, from getting lost, to the frightening hailstorm, to witnessing the stallion breeding the mare. Then getting caught finger-fucking herself while she spied on the cowboy and cowgirl in the barn. Her nerves were on edge and the unexpected argument and fistfight had finally sent her over the brink. Noticing splatters of blood on her tank top, she began to cry. She tried to hold back the tears, but they came in torrents. At least it was a quiet cry, and she wasn't sobbing hysterically.

The two men stood watching her, their hands dangling uselessly at their sides. Neither man seemed quite sure how to comfort her. The Mexican woman shoved the helpless men out of the way and brought Amanda a glass of water. Before she handed it to Amanda, the woman retrieved a bottle of brandy from a side table and added several ounces to the glass.

"Drink," she insisted, handing Amanda the glass. Tears still running down her cheeks, she took a sip and made a face. "Drink," the woman urged. "It will help."

Amanda took another sip, then tipped the glass up and drank it all. The smooth burn spread through her tummy and she realized she had stopped trembling. She held the glass out, sniffling loudly. The Mexican woman smiled and poured another three inches of brandy into the glass. Amanda sniffed again as she downed it, hoping that her mascara wasn't running too badly.

As the warmth of the second brandy spread through her, she wiped her eyes with tissues the Mexican woman had provided and took a deep breath. She looked at the two men staring at her. Both still appeared clueless about how to deal with an emotional woman.

Jesus, they're both handsome, Amanda thought, looking from one to the other. Finally, she sniffed loudly and smiled. "I'm fine." She took a deep breath. "If I could just use your restroom."

"Sure. You bet." The men both answered at once and, once again, the Mexican woman pushed them aside. She extended her hand to Amanda, helping her from the chair.

Jake stepped forward. "Justin, Rosita, this is Miss Sloane from New York. She'll be spending the night. Maybe a few nights. Rosita, please show her to one of the guest bedrooms."

"I'll get her bags." Justin quickly stepped back out onto the front porch.

Amanda followed Rosita up a wide staircase to a hallway that branched in two directions. Rosita opened a door and ushered her into a large bedroom with French doors that opened onto the balcony above the front porch. The room, filled with golden light from the setting sun, was tastefully decorated with a large four-poster bed and a collection of antique Western-style furniture. A small side table held bottles of sherry and brandy, along with crystal snifters. A beautiful handmade patchwork quilt covered the bed, which sported a stack of pillows against the headboard.

Rosita opened the door to a large bathroom, also tastefully decorated, with big fluffy guest towels and an assortment of soaps and lotions. Shelves by the clawfoot tub were stocked with candles, matches, and bubble bath. Just the place she needed to spend the next couple of hours.

Rosita stepped aside to let her into the bathroom. "Please, *señorita*. If you'll give me your top, I will try to remove the bloodstains. And if there is anything at all you need, just ask. I'll be downstairs in the kitchen."

Justin appeared in the bedroom doorway with her carry-on and overnight suitcase, which Rosita took from him and arranged on the large chest at the foot of the bed. After Justin left, Rosita waited as Amanda slipped out of her flannel shirt and tank top. She took them both, quietly closing the bedroom door as she left.

Now wearing only her bra and jeans, she took a deep breath and studied herself in the bathroom mirror. *Damn*, she thought, looking at her running mascara and red, swollen eyes. Her nose was red, too, but she didn't know if that was from crying or from embarrassment. She wet a washcloth and began to wash her face. *Amanda girl,* she thought, *you've got to get a hold of yourself.* A wry smile tugged at the corners of her mouth. Maybe she should rephrase that. She had already gotten a hold of herself once today and had been caught doing it.

As she washed her face, she thought of Jake Morgan watching her at the barn. She looked at her breasts in the mirror, her nipples easily visible through the thin lace of her bra. Getting caught had been horribly embarrassing, but now the thought of it had her nipples as hard as pebbles again. Maybe she was a voyeur *and* an exhibitionist.

Had watching her turned on Jake Morgan? He hadn't indicated as much. So far, he hadn't indicated much of anything, other than an obvious interest in her breasts. And being a bit pissed off for scattering his cattle with her frantic honking. Otherwise, he had been the stereotypical stoic cowboy. And a damn good-looking one, too. But so was his brother, Justin. Talk about doubling your pleasure. Of course, Justin Morgan had been anything but stoic when he'd thrown that Winslow man off the property.

What was that about? Taking her makeup bag from her suitcase, Amanda began to repair the damage that had once been her face. Was there some dispute over ownership of the painting she had come to evaluate? She glanced at her watch. It was seven-thirty in New York. Richard must be pacing the floor waiting for a phone call. She slipped her phone out and scrolled to Richard's number.

"Mandy! Sweetheart. Is it real?" Richard almost screeched.

"I don't know Richard. I haven't seen it yet. I just got here. My flight was delayed by the weather. And then I got caught in a hailstorm."

"Oh dear! Are you all right?"

"I'm fine and here at the ranch for at least tonight. I want to hold off looking at the painting until tomorrow so I have fresh eyes. God knows my eyes are not fresh right now."

"Whatever you think best, sweetheart." His disappointment was obvious to Amanda even over the phone. "But if you change your mind, and want to look at it tonight, call me whenever you do. Any time, okay?"

"I'll call you tomorrow, Richard, as soon as I have anything to report. And tell Sarah I'm fine and I'll call her tomorrow." She considered saying something about the possible question of ownership, but decided not to worry him until she had more information.

Doing the best she could to hide her puffy eyes and red nose, Amanda stepped into the bedroom and unzipped her carry-on. Her new cowboy hat was crushed, just as she feared, but her main concern was her laptop. Taking it out of the case and turning it on, she was relieved that it seemed to be working fine. She opened her files on Charles Randell and everything looked okay.

She returned her attention to the crushed hat. She popped the crown back out, but it would always be a little worse for being stepped on. She tried it on, standing in front of the large mirror that topped the antique dressing table. She adjusted the brim down a bit on her forehead and struck a hands-on-hips pose, tilting her head at an angle and thrusting her bra-clad breasts out.

"Howdy, partner," she said with a drawl, then made a playful quick draw, shooting "bang bang" with her forefingers. Blowing imaginary smoke from her fingertips, she smiled and slipped the pretend guns back into their holsters.

She checked herself in the mirror again, thinking she didn't look half bad in her cowboy hat. She lifted it off for a moment and tucked her hair up beneath the crown. Even better, she decided, wondering if she would ever actually have the nerve to wear the hat in public. "Not yet," she said aloud, setting the hat on top of one of the high posts at the foot of the bed.

She took a clean pink tank top and lavender plaid shirt out of her suitcase and slipped them on. She had planned on this being an overnight trip, but she'd packed for a two-night stay just in case. She had also thrown in a handful of sexy lingerie. Even if she had to stay a week, Amanda would have clean panties.

After running a brush through her hair, she made her way downstairs and back to the lodge's main room. Jake and Justin Morgan sat in two leather club chairs in a corner, their heads close as they talked quietly. She took a moment to study the room before she entered.

The space was huge and filled with Western-style furniture arranged in various conversation areas. A large stone fireplace filled one wall and a massive set of elk antlers was mounted above the mantle. A small painting hung to the right of the antlers and, even from this distance, she could tell it was the painting she had come to see.

The rest of the room was decorated in hunting lodge chic, with trophy heads of deer and antelope displayed throughout. She didn't like the idea of animals being shot for sport, but she wasn't here to judge anyone's lifestyle. There were a few other paintings in the room and some Native American artifacts, but nothing close to the value of a Charles Randell oil. As she stepped into the room, Jake and Justin both rose from their chairs. Seeing them together, she could tell that Jake was the older brother, perhaps by three or four years. They were both over six feet tall and ruggedly built with amazingly handsome faces. They both looked at her the way a woman wants to be looked at by an attractive man.

She smiled and stood a little straighter, angling her breasts up and out, her nipples firm against the pink tank top. She walked across the room, extending her hand. "Maybe we should do introductions again. I'm Amanda Sloane, with Peabody, Patterson & Cope." She shook each man's hand. "I'm sorry about what happened earlier. It's been a somewhat eventful day for me." She looked at Jake Morgan as she said this and caught just a hint of a smile at the corners of his mouth.

"We're the ones who are sorry." Justin Morgan shook her hand. "I'm sorry you had to witness that business with Winslow. It's embarrassing."

"So would you like to look at the painting now?" Jake Morgan gestured toward the fireplace.

"Absolutely," she said. "That's what I've come eighteen hundred miles to do. But I must tell you,

I'm only going to give it a quick look tonight. I'll need to study it in detail tomorrow when I can look at it with fresh eyes."

"Fair enough." Jake led the way to the painting.

The painting was a vertical oil on canvas, about twenty by thirty inches, of a cowboy riding on a horse and lighting a hand-rolled cigarette. At first glance, everything about the painting screamed Randell: The color palette, the brushwork, the subject, and especially the signature—a small M for his middle name Marion tucked inside the C for Charles and his trademark buffalo skull painted in outline below Randell.

She studied the painting intently for a few minutes then turned to look at Jake and Justin.

"Well, what do you think?" Justin looked at her expectantly.

She smiled and said nothing. Now it was her turn to be stoic.

"Well?" Jake asked. "Any thoughts about it at all?"

"I really can't say anything positive or negative about the painting until I have some time to study it in detail. Plus, it really needs a good cleaning. The fireplace is probably the worst place to hang a painting like this. It must have a hundred years of soot and smoke residue on it."

Jake and Justin both frowned.

"Don't worry. A good conservator can bring it back pretty quickly and at not much cost. Tomorrow, maybe I'll be able to tell you if we need to take that step."

The Morgans stopped frowning and Justin said, "Okay. That's that until tomorrow."

"One other thing." She looked from one man to the other. "I'll need you to sign a contract making Peabody, Patterson & Cope your brokerage firm in the event you do want to eventually sell the painting. Regardless of whether the painting is an actual Randell or not."

"No problem," Jake said. "Just show us where to sign. Right Justin?"

"Absolutely," Justin affirmed. "You're the broker."

"You'll also have to provide the provenance and proof of ownership."

"We can do that," Jake replied. "No problem."

Rosita appeared in the doorway and announced that supper was ready. The two men escorted Amanda to a large dining room paneled in knotty pine. An eight-foot diameter pedestal table filled the center of the room. Jake and Justin took places on each side of her, and Rosita brought in large platters of enchiladas, tacos, and tamales.

She had enjoyed Mexican food in New York and on her trips to Santa Fe and Taos, but she had never tasted anything equal to this. The enchiladas and tamales were accompanied by bowls of spicy rice and refried beans, which, following the Morgans' lead, she scooped up with pieces of rolled flour tortilla. Washed down with cold Mexican beer, the meal was beyond delicious.

As she wiped refried beans from her plate with a piece of tortilla, she looked up to find Jake and Justin looking at her with amusement.

Suddenly realizing she had been stuffing food into her mouth like she was starving, she blushed. "Sorry I'm eating like such a little pig. I'm afraid I missed lunch, and this is delicious."

"No problem." Justin grinned. "Enjoy. We're used to eating with ranch hands. Rosita is the best cook in Texas. But save room for sopapias. She makes the best. And we have wild honey from the ranch. The bees love the bluebonnets."

The flaky, sugarcoated sopapias were even better than Amanda expected, and she ate three, liberally coated with bluebonnet honey. As she finished the third sopapia, Rosita placed a bottle of chocolate liqueur on the table, along with cups of dark, rich coffee.

As the trio sipped chocolate-laced coffee, Amanda asked how the Morgans came to own the painting. At some point, she would have to ask about Winslow's claim. Proof of ownership would be critical if PP&C were to broker the sale.

****

Jake leaned back and hooked a boot heel over the rung of his chair. He looked at his brother. "Jump in Justin, if I leave anything out." He looked back at Amanda. "Family history," he said, "says that our great granddaddy, Odel Morgan, who built the first house on the ranch in 1890, went on a cattle drive from Texas to Montana with Charlie Goodnight in 1886 or 87. He was sixteen at the time and drove the chuck wagon for the drive. Odel stayed in Montana a couple of years. He wrote back to his mother in Fort Worth that he had met an artist called Kid Randell, who gave him a picture of a cowboy on a horse in exchange for a piece of blank canvas Great Granddaddy cut from the back flap of the chuck wagon."

"We've got that letter in a safety deposit box at the bank," Justin interrupted.

"Anyway," Jake continued, "Odel Morgan came back to Texas around 1890 and started the ranch. At that time, it was called the Morgan spread with an M for the brand. He built a log cabin to live in, which is still on the property about two miles up the creek. We use it as a line shack during roundup."

"Teddy Roosevelt camped there one night on a bear hunting trip," Justin said. "That was before he became president."

Jake continued, "Around 1910, Odel had twin sons, Bartlett and Bethel. By that time, he had built the first barns and buildings where we are now. Bartlett Morgan was our granddad and Bethel was our great uncle. When the twins were born, Odel changed the name of the ranch to the Double M and made a brand that looked like four mountain peaks. We suspect Odel thought it would be a ranch built on brotherly love, but it was far from it. Bartlett and Bethel fought about every damn thing you could think of, from what kind of cattle to raise to who was going to marry what girl.

"In 1930, our dad, Boots, was born. A couple of years later, Bethel and his wife had a son they named Weston. Bartlett and Bethel continued feuding about everything on the ranch until they finally decided to split the place and everything on it. Uncle Bethel even got a hack saw and cut the Double M brand in half, turning it into two single Ms.

"Great Granddaddy Odel's only will was a handwritten note to Bartlett and Bethel, telling them to share and share alike, otherwise they would just have to tough it out."

"Which they did," Justin said, "through five years of probate and legal wrangling."

"In the end, about 1940, our granddad, Bartlett, got the six thousand acres of working ranch and Great Uncle Bethel got four sections of property with oil wells."

"And the painting by Randell?" Amanda asked. "If it is a Randell," she added.

Jake and Justin both smiled. "Spelled out in court documents." Jake said. "It was put in Granddaddy Bartlett's half of the split and passed on down to our dad, then to us."

"Winslow," Justin said, "the man who stepped on your suitcase, is Bethel's son and our cousin. Even with the oil income, which is a lot, he and his dad think we got the better half of the split."

Jake scowled. "The man is a snake. A goddamn sidewinder, even if he is our cousin."

"He's a son of a bitch," Justin agreed, "who will do anything to get what he wants. He's got more money than Midas, and he doesn't think it's enough."

"That's enough about Winslow." Jake turned to Amanda. "Just know that we have solid proof of ownership of the painting. It's ours. Winslow probably never even thought of that painting until he heard we were going to sell it."

Amanda looked at the two brothers. "If you don't mind my asking, why do you want to sell it if it's been in the family so long?"

Jake looked at Justin, hesitating. Finally, he said. "Frankly, we need the money. The ranch is self-sustaining, but three years ago our dad, who died last year, took out a loan to finance a couple of wildcat wells on our property. Uncle Weston was making money hand over fist, just two miles away, and Dad was sure we must have oil underneath our place, too. Anyway, we didn't know anything about it until last month when we got a notice from the bank that a balloon payment of four hundred and eighty thousand dollars is coming due next month—less than four weeks. Except for the land and the lodge and our cattle and horses, that painting is the only thing on the ranch that has any value. At least we think it might have some value.

"Do you think it might?" Jake looked at Amanda, an eyebrow raised.

"Maybe," Amanda said. "If it's a genuine Randell. If it has never been cataloged, it could be worth a lot of money."

"Best case, if it's real..." Justin asked. "How much?"

Amanda looked at both men. "Haven't you looked on the Internet?"

The Morgans looked at each other, then at Amanda. "Not really," Justin responded. "We just thought that it could be worth something since Randell was a famous painter. So what kind of price range are we talking?"

"If it's real and authenticated as such, and if we get some avid collectors watering at the mouth, it might go for ten or maybe even twelve. But that's a lot of ifs."

Jake looked at Justin. He knew his expression registered the same look of disappointment as his brother's. "Twelve thousand is a lot of money," he said. "But that's not even close to what we need."

She smiled. "You misunderstand. I didn't mean ten or twelve thousand. I meant ten or twelve million."

Jake looked at her, wondering if she could possibly be serious. She just smiled.

"Son of a bitch," he said, looking at his younger brother.

"Amen." Justin added.

Chapter Five

Amanda poured herself a snifter of brandy from the bottle on the side table in her room. She ran a tub full of hot water and took a long bubble bath, soaking for almost an hour in the big tub with bubbly water up to the tips of her breasts. Using vanilla scented soap, she washed her body slowly, lingering over her breasts and inner thighs and finally her pussy, teasing herself with the soap and a slippery finger. As the aroma of the soap filled the room, she remembered reading somewhere that the scent of vanilla turned men on. Would that include Jake Morgan?

As her finger teased her pussy lips, the tingling sensation expanded as she remembered the scene at the barn: The blonde cowgirl bending over for the cowboy's big dick, yelling "Fuck me Luke! Fuck me hard!"

God, would she ever overcome her inhibitions enough to tell a man to "fuck her hard?" She thought of Jake Morgan watching her. She had been so embarrassed. And frustrated at not having an orgasm. But, she smiled to herself, she had her trusty battery powered friend in her suitcase, and the night was still young.

Maybe she would fantasize about Jake when she used her joy toy. Damn, the man was good looking. And sexy. She couldn't wait to share some of the details of her Texas adventure with Sarah. If she dared to.

Amanda shaved her legs and underarms then carefully trimmed her pubic hair into a small neat triangle above her clit. She shaved her labia smooth and rinsed off with the hand held shower nozzle as she drained the bubbly bathwater. She dried off with a giant fluffy towel, then slipped into a long-tailed cotton T-shirt, her nightgown of choice when she was traveling. It was not particularly sexy but very comfy.

The big featherbed was amazingly comfortable, and Amanda was certain that after the wonderful meal and relaxing bubble bath she would be asleep in no time.

Forty-five minutes later, she was still wide-awake, staring at the ceiling. Her mind was filled with events of the day and kept rerunning the scenes that had been so outrageously beyond her normal day-to-day existence. Underlying all her thoughts about the cattle and hailstorm and the horses and lovers in the barn was the distinct and exciting possibility that the painting downstairs just might actually be an unknown Randell. Her first look had been cursory, but the damn thing looked like the real deal.

She slipped out of bed and opened the shades of the French doors leading to the balcony. The sudden appearance of what seemed like billions of stars took her breath away. Never in her life had she seen the sky so filled with stars, so many that their light filled the room, casting sharp shadows across the big feather bed. She opened the door and stepped out onto the balcony, moving to the railing for a better look at the sky.

The storm clouds had moved on. Now the vault above her was an inky canvas filled with diamond points of light, scattered like seeds in every direction. She walked slowly to the corner where the balcony turned to run along the side of the lodge. From here, looking northward, she could actually see the Milky Way. She could just make out the Big

Dipper and its constant companion, the North Star. She ambled along the side balcony toward the rear of the house, totally enchanted by the star-filled sky. The closest most of her fellow New Yorkers would get to such a sight might be a photo or postcard.

As she reached the end of the balcony and turned to go back, she became aware of noises coming from the corner room. A light suddenly came on and Amanda found herself staring into a bedroom similar to the one she occupied. Except the curtains were open and two very naked people were in it—Luke and Julie, the couple she'd seen in the barn. Now, with the light on, she could see that Luke was tall and lanky, but very muscular. The man also sported a cock that rivaled a porn star. Julie was more cute than beautiful, and she had small breasts tipped with light pink nipples. The young woman was completely shaved, her pussy a smooth pink slit.

Not again, Amanda thought, as the couple climbed onto the bed. Close your curtains, you idiots!

She realized that the couple would never suspect anyone to be standing on the balcony outside their room. If anything, she should hustle her voyeuristic ass back to her own room. In the few seconds it took to register that thought, Julie had risen to her hands and knees on the bed and Luke was kneeling behind her, rolling a condom over his large cock.

She had almost turned away when Luke started sliding his cock into Julie's bare pussy. Amanda was momentarily mesmerized by the ecstatic expression on the young woman's face.

In spite of herself, her pussy grew wet beneath her T-shirt and she felt her nipples harden and pucker against the white cotton cloth. Determined to not let her baser instincts take control, she took a deep breath and started to turn away.

Just then, Julie lifted one arm, beckoning. Another man suddenly appeared and slid onto the bed, positioning himself so that his cock was in Julie's face, close to her begging mouth.

"Oh Jesus," Amanda whispered, stopping in mid-step. The man who had suddenly appeared had his back to the window, and she could tell only that he was tall and well built with broad shoulders and a tight, sexy butt.

With Luke gripping Julie's hips and sliding his cock slowly in and out of her pussy, Julie leaned forward and took the second man's cock into her mouth. At first, she could only manage to get her lips around the bulbous head, but keeping the cock wet with saliva, she soon had several inches of the thick shaft down her throat.

The sensible, modest part of Amanda's consciousness, the part that wanted to turn away and scurry back to her room, was quickly overcome by a more sensual, erotic impulse. She stood transfixed by the sight of the couple fucking, doubly transfixed because two men were pleasuring Julie at once. And "being pleasured" was an understatement, she thought, as she watched the woman writhe in passion while both men fucked her mouth and pussy.

Amanda's own consciousness was now swimming in the wet channel between her legs. Her pebble-hard nipples were tingling with arousal, begging to be caressed.

In the bedroom, Julie had stopped sucking her second lover's cock and was leaning up to kiss him. The kiss was passionate, deep and sensual, ending when she broke away to turn her head back so she could kiss Luke. Somehow, seeing Julie kiss both men one after the other seemed more erotic than fucking them both. She felt a sudden surge of liquid heat coursing through her core. With all her attention concentrated on the sexual energy spreading through her body, it surprised her that she could be aware of anything else. But suddenly she was aware—aware that she was not alone on the balcony.

****

"Does that turn you on Miss Sloane? Watching Julie make love to two men at once?"

She jerked around to find Jake standing not more than two feet away. Barefoot and shirtless, he stood wearing only a pair of jeans. The starlight gave his body a luminous glow, defining his ripped pecs and abs.

"Oh God," she whispered, staring up at him in shock, unable to move.

"Does it turn you on?" He repeated, obviously aware of her arousal.

A loud moan from the bedroom caused Amanda to blink. He glanced past her shoulder and smiled. "It's amazing how much pleasure two men can give a woman." He reached out and put one hand on the back of her neck, pulling her close.

She raised her hands, pressing her palms against the smooth muscles of his chest, trying to push away. Slowly, deliberately, he leaned down and kissed her, his hand behind her neck keeping her lips turned up toward his. With his free hand, he held the small of her back, pulling her closer. Then his hand slid up to caress her breasts, his fingers pinching and twisting her nipples, sending currents of electricity straight to her pussy. For a long moment, he continued the kiss, his tongue probing deep, searching. His kiss ignited a desperate need and she kissed him back, her limp arms finding life, lifting to encircle his shoulders and grasping urgently at his neck.

He slid his hand down over her breasts and tummy, then up under the tail of her T-shirt to the moist V between her legs. At his touch, her knees buckled and her pelvis jerked forward, wanting more, wanting his fingers deeper inside her.

But she couldn't! She couldn't let this happen.

She unwrapped her arms from his neck and pushed on his shoulders, struggling, breaking the kiss, breaking the connection of his hand between her legs, whimpering as his fingers came free of her wet channel.

"Jake..."

Before she could complete the sentence, Jake reached down with one smooth motion and swept her up, cradling her in his arms. As he strode across the balcony, Amanda knew she should resist. But she was beyond resistance. Clinging to his neck, she cast one last look over his shoulder at the trio in the bedroom. She wasn't surprised to see that the second man in the ménage a trois was Justin Morgan.

****

In half a dozen strides, Jake was across the balcony, pushing a door open with his foot. As he stepped into the room, he turned and tossed Amanda on the king-sized bed. He stood looking down at her.

She stared up at him, her brown eyes wide, her expression one of desire mixed with fear and uncertainty. When he tossed her on the bed, her T-shirt came up around her waist and she tried to pull it down to cover the bare flesh between her legs. She scooted back on the bed toward the headboard, grabbing a pillow to hold in front of herself like a shield.

Jake smiled, amused at her attempt to hide behind a feather pillow. She looked into his eyes, then let her gaze drift down over his chest to the front of his jeans. When she saw the bulge of his fierce arousal, her eyes opened even wider and she held the pillow tighter to her breasts. He saw that she was visibly trembling.

"I've wanted you since this afternoon at the barn, watching you stroke that sweet pussy. I think you want this, too, Amanda," he said. "As much as I do. If you don't, all you have to do is say 'No.'" He could sense her arousal, could see the desire behind the fear in her eyes.

He waited, knowing she could stop him with a single word. "'Yes' or 'No' Amanda. It's your choice." In her expression, he saw her wrestling with desire, possibilities, consequences.

Finally, she lowered her eyes and whispered, "Yes."

He smiled and unsnapped his jeans. "Get rid of the pillow and take off your shirt."

Amanda complied. She was still trembling nervously but she tossed the pillow aside. For a moment, she just stared at him. Then she stripped the T-shirt up and off. She lay back on the bed, naked, and willing. The fear in her eyes had begun to fade and her expression was now one of intense desire. He smiled at her eagerness as he stripped his jeans off. As his denim and underwear hit the floor, his cock sprang into view. He opened the nightstand drawer and took out a condom, quickly rolling it on. Laying down beside her, he propped his head up one with one arm, studying her face in the shadowy light, his sense of urgency suddenly reined in. A moment went by, then another. He just looked at her, admiring what he saw.

She looked at him a bit uneasily. "Don't you want me?"

"Oh yes. I want you. And I'm going to show you just how much. But when I close my eyes and slide my cock inside you, I want to remember just what a beautiful woman I'm fucking."

She smiled and leaned up on one elbow to face him. With her free hand she reached out and touched his shoulder, then let her hand slide slowly down, feeling the firm definition of his muscular chest and abs. At his taut belly she paused, then moved her hand down to his groin.

"Oh my." She looked down in admiration. "I'm definitely going to have something to visualize while you...while you do it to me."

Jake could see her struggle with the words. "While I do what to you, Amanda? What do you want me to do to you?" He caressed the insides of her thighs with one hand, his fingertips lingering briefly over the wet slit of her pussy, then pulling away to caress her breasts.

"You know. While we do it...have sex..."

"No. You know what I want you to say." He rolled over until he was on top of her, holding himself up with stiffened arms. His cock, big and hard, lay nestled just at the entrance to her pussy. She shifted against his heat, urging him to slide forward. He let the head slip into the mouth of her core, then pulled back. "Say it Amanda. What do you want?"

"Oh God," she whimpered, lifting her hips, her body begging for his cock. "Don't tease me. Do it. I need it."

"Need what Amanda? Tell me." He slid in a few inches, stretching her tight sheath with his thick cockhead. He pulled back then thrust in deeper, filling her with his thick length.

"Please," she whispered. "Fuck me." She spread her legs wider, opening for him.

"What do you want?" he demanded. "Tell me."

"Fuck me. Oh God, fuck me!"

"How, Amanda? Like this?" He grasped her thighs, tilting her hips up so she could take his full length, then drove his dick into her, deeper, faster.

"Yes! Oh God, yes!" The words came quickly now. With urgent moans, she unashamedly told him what she wanted. "Fuck me hard! Deeper, Jake!"

"Do you like this Amanda? My cock in your hot sweet pussy?" He could feel her quivering, her pussy clenching at his cock.

"Yes, yes! Fuck my pussy. I want it. I want your cock!" The words tumbled out in a salacious plea, unchecked by her previous inhibitions.

"Where Amanda? Where do you want my cock?" He was relentless now.

"In my pussy. My hot pussy. Oh God! It's so good. Fuck me, Jake. Fuck me. Fuck me! Fuck me!"

Fueled by the desperate need of the woman writhing in passion beneath him, Jake fucked Amanda with a ferocity that he had never felt before. His plunging jack-hammer thrusts quickly had her moaning in unrestrained passion

"Oh God...now," she cried. "Now, Jake. I'm going to come now!"

Chapter Six

Amanda's orgasm erupted in the warm wet flesh between her legs, ignited by the friction of Jake's cock plunging deep and then pulling away. As she surrendered to her climax, the spark blazed white-hot, then spread down the insides of her thighs and up through her abdomen, spiraling up her spine with incandescent brilliance.

Her neck arched and her pelvis lifted. Amanda closed her eyes and clutched at Jake's shoulders, locking her legs around his thighs as if holding on to him was the only thing that kept her from flying off the bed and disintegrating in ecstasy.

"Ohhh...my...God!" Her cry became a moan and finally a scream she couldn't control. She couldn't control anything. She was lost in the moment and knew only that this was what she had been searching for, what she needed so desperately. At its apex, her orgasm lifted her out of her body.

She came back to reality slowly, her nerve endings still thrumming with electricity. Jake's weight shifted as he rolled to one side, his erection sliding out of her still throbbing pussy. She finally opened her eyes and looked at him. Once again, he was propped on one elbow looking down at her, smiling. She took a deep breath and smiled back at him. "That was...incredible."

"It was for a fact. You are an incredible, beautiful, sexy woman."

She blushed at the compliment. Glancing down, she saw Jake's cock was still hard, a thick shaft angling up from his groin. "I was out of it for a little while. Did you...I mean..."

"Did I climax? Not yet. But don't worry, I will once you enjoy as many orgasms as you want."

She started to reply, but hesitated. How much could she share with this man? She barely knew him. But he had just fucked her to the threshold of oblivion. "You know, I've never had an orgasm like that. It was amazing."

He grinned at her. "Orgasms like that are habit forming. Once you have one, you just want more."

"I'm sure that's true." She stretched, releasing the tension in the muscles that had clinched during her climax. "In fact, I may be ready for another one."

She could hardly believe she was telling a man she had known for a few hours that she was horny enough for another mind-blowing orgasm. But this was the man who had teased and cajoled her into telling him to "fuck" her and "shove his cock in her hot pussy." She felt very naughty, but pleased to have actually voiced her desires.

Amanda studied Jake's features. The man was not only impossibly gorgeous, he was an incredible lover. As if reading her thoughts, Jake reached out and cupped her breast, squeezing the nipple between his thumb and forefinger.

"Are you ready for more, Miss Sloane?" He rose up on his knees and scooted between her legs.

She spread her legs, giving him more room. "I'm ready for you to fuck me senseless." It was easy now to tell the man what she wanted. "Fuck me with your big hard cock."

Jake grinned at her new-found lack of inhibition. He placed his hands on her upraised knees and spread her legs farther apart. "I don't think so," he said, leaning down toward her pussy. "I need to see just how delicious you taste." As he lowered his head, Amanda was glad she had shaved and trimmed her pubic hair. Then Jake's tongue swiped up the length of her slit and settled on her clit. Further thought became impossible.

"Ohhh God!" No one had ever done that before. Not like this. A shudder of pleasure swept through her body. Amanda reached down and clutched Jake's head with both hands, entwining her fingers in his hair. "Oh! Oh! Oh my God!" Her cries rose in a crescendo of moans as her pelvis bucked against his churning tongue. She pulled him closer then pushed him away, her clitoris and pussy so sensitive she could barely stand the exquisite torture of his touch. She had become so needy with arousal, she wanted him to do nothing less than devour her.

This time her orgasm came in waves, small sensations at first, building into a crashing surf that swept her up in a tsunami of pleasure. Jake held her bucking hips, keeping his mouth and tongue tight against her pussy, sucking and teasing her swollen, wet flesh. Her moans became a wail, a cry of rapture. Finally, the uncontrollable contractions of her climax waned, the intensity of the flooding current ebbing away to a quiet calm. Amanda lifted her head and looked down between her legs. Jake grinned at her, his chiseled lips and masculine chin glistening with her juices, his eyes twinkling mischievously.

Oh God, what have I done, she thought, letting her head drop back on the pillow. *I've just had sex with a client. Twice.*

****

Jake wiped the evidence of her passion from his face, then sat on the edge of the bed looking down at her.

She scooted back against the headboard and shook her head. "I'm afraid I haven't been very professional. I want you to know that this...what we've done...won't affect how I evaluate your painting. Or any business agreement we might come to."

"I wouldn't expect it to," he said. "What we just enjoyed is totally extracurricular to any business I have with Peabody, Patterson & Cope." He leaned forward and kissed her gently.

"And that goes for anything we might enjoy in the future," he continued. "Agreed?" He held out his hand. She stared at his extended hand and then looked up into his eyes.

"Agreed," she said.

As he shook her hand, he wondered if she knew just how much "future enjoyment" he had in mind. He thrived on being an instrumental part of a woman's sexual awakening and, from Amanda's reaction to the last hour and a half of love making, he was certain she was experiencing sex in a whole new way.

And, he thought with a smile, *the little minx is certainly multi-orgasmic. Now, however, it's my turn.*

Jake lay down on his back, his condom-clad cock angling up from his groin. Amanda grinned and straddled his hips, holding his cock upright as she lowered herself onto the rigid shaft. "So now I get to take my first Texas pony ride."

Jake held her hips as she worked her pelvis back and forth, grinding against his groin then sliding up until just his cockhead was captured between her labia. She was leaning slightly forward, her palms pressed firmly against his pecs. He reached up and cradled her breasts in his palms, lifting the smooth round globes to feel their weight. Her nipples were large and, as he pinched and twisted them, he heard her sharp intake of breath.

For several minutes he stared up at her face as she fucked him, her hips rocking back and forth as she slid over his cock. Her eyes were closed, her lips compressed in determination, her concentration seemed totally focused on giving him the same pleasure he had given her. She moved faster and he closed his eyes, dropping his hands to her hips. She began to make a circular motion with her hips on each down-stroke and he tightened his grip.

He felt his own need ignite, a spark of white-hot heat spreading out from his groin to every nerve ending in his body. His cock, wrapped in the tight, slick sheath of her pussy, ached for release. Finally it came and he erupted in orgasm, his head tilting back as he groaned loudly. With a deep guttural moan he spurted again and again, his cock jerking in spasms inside her pussy, his hips jerking reflexively with each pulse.

Amanda came again, too, her pussy pulsing tightly as she cried out in pleasure. He reached up and pulled her head down, guiding her lips to his for a passionate kiss, fueled by the ecstasy of his orgasm.

As their climaxes faded, she collapsed on his chest, sweaty and trembling, trying to catch her breath. Finally, she rolled to one side. "God, I never knew sex could be so good."

"I knew it would be good with you," he said. "Ever since I saw you at the barn."

Amanda blushed, heat spreading up her neck to her cheeks. "I was so embarrassed when you saw me. I'm normally very inhibited about sex. I've never done anything like that before."

"Never?" Jake got up and discarded his condom, then slid back onto the bed beside her.

"No. Never. But now I'm glad it happened. It made you want me."

"You haven't been too inhibited tonight. Far from it."

She giggled. "That's because you have shredded all my hang-ups." She reached down to grip his cock, still large even in its flaccid state. "You unlocked my libido and unleashed my inner slut. Aren't you ashamed of what you've turned me into? And all in a matter of a couple of hours."

Jake chuckled and squeezed her breast, tweaking her nipple. "God your nipples are sexy. And I don't feel a bit guilty. You'd gotten yourself pretty worked up on the balcony."

Her blush deepened. "Okay. I admit it. Watching Luke and Julie turned me on. I swear, I'm not a voyeur. But watching them had me dripping wet." She hesitated, then said, "Especially when Justin joined in."

They lay quietly for a moment, Amanda holding his penis while he caressed her breast. Finally he said, "Have you ever been in a threesome?"

"Not really. Although, I once watched my roommate in college with two boys. It was pretty erotic."

"Would you like to be? In a threesome, I mean."

****

Amanda blushed, a rosy heat spreading up to her forehead and down over her breasts. In the shadowy starlight, she couldn't see the change but her body heat had risen several degrees. She couldn't believe Jake was actually asking if she would like to participate in a ménage a trois. But then, she could barely believe they had just spent two hours having passionate, uninhibited sex. And, she wondered, if the sex was this good with Jake, how much better would it be with Jake and his brother? Or Jake and Luke?

"It's a popular fantasy for a lot of women. Have you ever thought about it?"

She hesitated, felt the tingle stirring between her legs again. "Well, since you've already discovered how wanton I can be, I'll admit I've wondered about it."

"Maybe we should make it happen."

She rose up on one elbow and studied Jake's

face. There was a wickedly devilish slant in his smile. "Are you serious?"

"Totally. If you wanted to spend another night here."

She looked at him without speaking, trying to read the expression in his eyes. His cock was growing hard again under her touch and she could feel her own arousal increasing.

"Why don't we play it by ear? Let me do my work tomorrow before making any commitments for tomorrow night. Okay?"

"Fair enough. And if you decide to stay another night, I'll assume you want to explore the possibilities of…doubling your pleasure."

She smiled seductively. "Speaking of pleasure, if you've got another condom, I believe I'd like to saddle up and give this big boy one more ride." Taking the lead in initiating sex made her feel deliciously wicked.

Jake grinned, reached over, and opened the nightstand drawer. Donning the condom took but a moment, but the passion in his eyes spoke volumes.

After straddling him and riding his cock for several minutes she crawled off and knelt on her hands and knees, inviting him to fuck her from behind. It was a position she would now call stallion style, remembering how Rocket had mounted Dolly, ramming his huge cock into her. As Jake knelt behind her, she dropped to her elbows, tilting her ass up to give him a better angle for penetration. He stroked the smooth globes of her bottom, caressing them gently before squeezing them as he nudged forward.

Finally, his cockhead was at the entrance of her upturned slit and he pushed in, shoving his cock in to the base in one powerful stroke. At her long wail of pleasure, he slid one hand up the firm skin of her belly and over her breasts, reaching up to touch her lips with his fingers.

She immediately opened her mouth, sucking three of his fingers inside, swirling her tongue around and between them, sucking them as if they were another cock. Behind her, Jake uttered a guttural moan and began to fuck her harder and faster, jamming his cock deep into her pussy with each thrust. Imagining that she might actually have Jake's cock in her pussy while Justin fucked her mouth was an intense turn on. She could feel Jake's arousal increase as well, his free hand tightening on her hip, his cock shoving even deeper. She came hard, slamming her ass back against him as he orgasmed in a forceful rush, flooding her core with heat.

****

Amanda awoke in a big featherbed similar to the one in her room. But it was not her bed or her room. It was Jake Morgan's and, with that realization, she immediately recalled all the naughty, delicious, sexy, outrageous things she had done with the rancher the night before. She especially remembered the invitation to participate in a threesome. Thinking about it gave her a nervous knot in her tummy, but it also made her pussy tingle and moisten.

She got out of bed and picked up her T-shirt from a chair and slipped into it. Jake had left a note on the dresser that he had chores to do and would be back for breakfast at eight. *Jesus, I wonder what time it is?* She opened the door to the balcony to go back to her room and ran smack into Justin.

"Oh, sorry." She blushed, closing Jake's door as she stepped out onto the deck. Justin was now wearing jeans, chaps, and a flannel shirt. Spurs jingled on his boots and he wore a weathered grey cowboy hat.

As he stepped aside to keep from bumping into

Amanda, he grinned and tipped his hat. "Morning Miss Sloane. Hope you slept well."

She turned redder, hesitating, unsure whether she should step back into Jake's room or walk beside Justin to her own. She opted for the latter and, a moment later, she was inside her room, leaving the grinning cowboy to his own lascivious thoughts. Considering that his nighttime activity had involved two other people, he certainly had no right to judge her for sleeping with his brother.

The memory of the threesome she had seen gave Amanda an instant tingle between her legs. *What will it be like?* she wondered, having both nipples sucked at once, having four hands caressing her, having cocks in her mouth and pussy at the same time. It sounded so erotic.

Thinking about it now, she wondered if she would dare accept Jake's invitation to spend another night at the ranch. A threesome! She assumed it would be with Justin, although Jake hadn't actually said so. Maybe it would be with Luke. That would be okay she supposed, although Justin was more handsome. But Luke was definitely well endowed. Her imagination was filled with thoughts of Jake and Justin and Luke and the inhibitions she had shed in her short time at the ranch. *Thank you Jake,* she thought. *I don't know how you managed to find my "on" button so quickly, but that is one switch that's going to stay flipped.*

Chapter Seven

Amanda e-mailed the photo of the ranch to Sarah, then spent thirty minutes on the phone with Richard, giving him a quick summary of her trip and an initial reaction to the painting's possible authenticity.

"But don't get too excited," she said. "It was only a quick look. I'll call you again this afternoon when I've had more time to study it."

Since the Morgans said they had proof of ownership and some documents regarding provenance, she didn't mention the altercation between Justin, Jake, and their cousin, Winslow. If necessary, she would bring that up later. She did discuss what Jake said about needing the money at the end of the month.

"That's a problem." Richard said. "If it's an obvious fake, you'll know pretty quickly. But if it's authentic, it might take weeks or months for our Randell experts to sign off on it. And no collector is going to pay top dollar for an unknown Randell without some independent verification."

"I know. What do you think we should do?"

"I don't know. But the first thing we have to do is determine if the painting is actually a genuine Randell. If you think it is, we will have to get some independent analysis as quickly as possible."

"I'll let you know what I think as soon as I can."

"I'll be waiting to hear from you, Mandy."

Amanda dressed in jeans and a tailored white button-up blouse. Completely buttoned up, the blouse looked very businesslike. With a few buttons undone, it looked very sexy. Still under the influence of her extremely satisfying romp with Jake, she chose to go for sexy, leaving the top three buttons undone and showing ample cleavage and a peek of her lace bra. Sexy but not slutty. Slutty, she thought, can come later. She thought of Jake's invitation to stay another night, possibly fulfilling her fantasy of a threesome. Would she dare?

Amanda followed the wonderful aroma of bacon and eggs and biscuits down to the dining room. The large table was already half full with Jake, Justin, Luke, Julie, and a Mexican rancher introduced as Jorge Sanchez. She noted that when she walked in, all four men looked from her cleavage to her face and back to her cleavage. For half a second, she thought maybe going sexy was a mistake. But from the smiles on the men's faces, she decided it was the right choice after all. Even Julie gave her a smile.

After her night with Jake, Amanda knew she was glowing. A wet rag couldn't have wiped the grin off her face. She caught a glimmer of a conspiratorial smile in Jake's eyes, but it lasted just a moment before he returned his attention to Mr. Sanchez.

Justin was equally circumspect, giving no indication that he had seen her coming out of Jake's room wearing nothing but a T-shirt.

From what she could make out, Jake, Julie, and Mr. Sanchez were negotiating the price of a half-dozen Quarter Horses the Morgans wanted to sell, and the stud fee for a stallion the rancher wanted to bring up from El Paso. The conversation was all in Spanish, of which Amanda had only a rudimentary knowledge.

Once breakfast was finished and the table cleared, Luke and Julie escorted Mr. Sanchez outside while Jake and Justin lingered over coffee with Amanda. Neither she nor Jake hinted in any way that they had spent most of the night together.

But from the looks she got from Rosita, she was certain the housekeeper could see she had the glow of a well-fucked woman.

Amanda had brought a folder with the PP&C brokerage contract downstairs and presented a copy to Jake and Justin after breakfast. Justin thumbed through the ten-page document quickly then slid it back across the table to Amanda.

"Jake's the one to sign this. He's the lawyer in the family. And he has power of attorney on my behalf."

She looked at Jake in surprise. "You're a lawyer?"

Jake gave his younger brother a quick scowl and then turned back to Amanda. "I got my jurist doctorate in Austin, but never took the bar. I just wanted to be able to deal with legal issues on the ranch. If Granddad and Great Uncle Bethyl had understood half of what the probate lawyers were doing, they might have avoided this goddamned feud that's been going on for decades. Just give me a few minutes to read your contract. I'm sure the terms will be fine, but I do want to read it."

"Of course. If you agree to the terms and can prove ownership, just sign on the dotted line and I'll take the copies back to New York for Richard's signature. We'll next-day ship a copy back to you."

"All right." Jake took an envelope from the buffet table and handed it to Amanda. "Here are copies of the settlement specifying that Granddaddy was to get the painting, and a copy of Granddaddy's will leaving the painting to our dad. There's also a copy of the letter from Great Granddaddy to his mother, telling how he got the painting in the first place."

As she took the envelope, Justin got up from the table. "I'm going to make sure Julie cuts out the right horses," he said. "We don't want to ship Senor

Sanchez the wrong stock."

Amanda looked at Justin, wondering what he would be like as a lover. He was definitely handsome and well built. He certainly seemed nice enough. He could be aggressive, as he'd demonstrated with Winslow the day before. But an aggressive lover might be a good thing.

She suddenly realized she'd been staring intently at the slight bulge in the front of Justin's jeans. She looked up to find the man staring back at her with a bemused look on his face. *Oh God*, she thought. *Caught looking again.* She blinked and blushed, turning away. If Jake had mentioned anything to Justin about the threesome, the younger Morgan was not letting on.

Justin walked out and Amanda rose from the table, walking into the lodge's main room. She laid the envelope with the painting's provenance on her laptop and walked over to look at the painting, giving Jake a chance to study the PP&C contract. Essentially Peabody, Paterson & Cope would have the exclusive right to sell the painting, with a twenty percent commission on the selling price paid by the buyer. If the painting proved authentic, the commission itself would be a small fortune. If the painting was not authentic, that twenty percent might be a commission on nothing.

The contract also stated that if the PP&C representative, namely Amanda Sloane, felt reasonably sure the painting was a genuine Charles Marion Randell, the firm would cover additional authentication, with the fees deducted from the seller's total gain.

Jake read the contract, and then stepped into the main room where she was studying the Randell. "This looks fine," he said. "My only concern is how long it will take for authentication. We need four hundred eighty thousand by the end of the month."

"I'll be honest," Amanda said. "Fully accepted authentication by a community of Randell collectors will take time. The collectors don't want another unknown painting showing up. It decreases the value of the works they already have. And the odds are not in favor of it being genuine. In the past fifty years or so, there have been at least eighteen paintings surface that have been proved forgeries. And only three that have been authenticated as genuine Randells. One of the three is still in dispute by some collectors. The problem with your painting is that there isn't any reference to it in Randell's notes or ledgers or letters. No bill of sale, no mention of it of any kind."

Jake's expression had become somber.

"That doesn't mean it isn't a Randell," she continued. "There are hundreds of works that aren't specifically mentioned anywhere. If the painting is authentic and gets a green light by the Randell authorities at the Montana Museum of Western Art and a couple of independent experts we work with, there will be a few collectors who will have to have it. I wasn't kidding when I said it might bring twelve million."

"And if the painting is a fake?"

"PP&C walks away and you have a nice piece of art for your mantle."

Jake looked at her seriously for a moment. "Do you think it's real?"

"It looks like it might be. I'll need a lot more time with the painting and my laptop. And there is no guarantee we can get independent verification within a month. But I can't go forward without a signed contract."

"Then it's a deal," Jake extended his hand.

Amanda shook it, keeping her grip firm and businesslike. She couldn't help remembering that she was holding the same hand that had caressed her breasts and slid between her legs just a few hours earlier.

Jake signed the contract and Amanda put it in her folder.

"Great," she said. "Now I'll get to work. I want to take the painting outside so I can see it in daylight."

Jake lifted the painting from the mantle. He handed it to Amanda but held on as she tried to take it from him. With the painting separating their bodies, he leaned in close, looking down at her over the top of the painting's frame. "I want you to know how much I enjoyed being with you last night. You are an amazing woman."

She blushed at the compliment, then looked up into his beautiful eyes. "I enjoyed it, too. More than you know. And I want to reiterate that what happened last night will not influence my analysis of the painting."

"Or what might happen tonight?"

She felt her blush deepen but she held her gaze steady. "Not at all. I would never let personal issues interfere with my work. Ever."

"I believe you. But I would like to interject with one more thing."

She raised an eyebrow but, before she could speak, Jake leaned down and kissed her, softly at first but with such increasing intensity that she had to hold tight to the painting just to keep from falling down. Whatever point Jake Morgan was making with this kiss involved more than just sex, no matter how delightfully free and fun the sex might be.

As he pulled away and released the painting, Amanda said, "Wow." She looked into his eyes, wondering what was there besides desire.

He smiled and stepped away, lifting his hat off the deer antler rack by the lodge's front door. As he started out, she studied his denim-clad butt admiringly, holding the painting tight against her chest to ease the tingling in her rock hard nipples.

As he opened the screen door to step outside, he looked back over his shoulder. "Have you considered spending another night with us?" He didn't emphasize the word "us," but there was no doubt what he meant.

She looked at him, still holding the painting tight against her breasts. "Yes, I've considered it."

"And?"

"And I think I'm going to need more time with this artwork than I planned. So maybe I better stay one more night."

He looked at her a moment and then smiled and tipped his hat.

As he left, she was smiling, too.

****

Jake caught up with Luke and Justin loading a bay gelding into a horse trailer at the north end of the corral. "So what do you boys think about our New York City art appraiser?"

The two men looked at each other and grinned, then looked back at Jake. "On a scale of one to ten," Luke said, "I'd give her a twelve."

"Oh, hell," Justin said. "Her tits alone are worth that. She's a fifteen at least. She is one damn fine looking filly. She can cowgirl up on my pony any time."

"I think she wants to do just that." He grinned at Justin, then at Luke. "You too, fence post." Luke and Justin's grins faded and they looked at Jake seriously.

"She saw you last night with Julie." Jake said.

"I know," Luke said. "We saw her, too. Thought we might put on a show. Let her see how we rodeo in Texas. Then you came along and swept her off her feet."

"Literally," Justin added.

Jake smiled. "I haven't done that with a woman

in a hell-of-a long time. But Amanda is choice. And whatever she saw the three of you doing, she was as turned on as any woman I've been with."

"We know," Luke said. "You left your window open and we could hear her moaning for hours. I don't know what you were doing, but she sure seemed to be lovin' it."

"What's up, Jake?" Justin said. "You usually don't talk about your ladies."

"This woman is very special. I think she is just starting to understand what a sensuous, sexy woman she can be. Last night, she told me she was letting go of some inhibitions that have kept her sexually repressed for a long time, and she wants to shed some more. I think we can help her explore some of those boundaries."

Luke and Justin looked at Jake, waiting for him to continue.

"She got really turned on watching the three of you last night. Said a threesome had been a fantasy of hers for a long time. I told her we could arrange something if she would stay another night. She wants to stay.

"So what do you boys think? Can we help her out?"

Luke and Justin were both grinning now. "Hell yes," Justin said. "I definitely want a ride in that rodeo."

"Count me in," Luke added. "I'm always ready to help out a damsel in distress."

"One thing though," Jake said. "Amanda may be a wildcat in the sack, but she has a sweet soft side and I don't want her to get hurt. In any way. Understood?"

Both men looked at Jake seriously again. "Understood," Justin said.

"Totally," Luke added.

"Alright," Jake said. "I'll let her know. Nine

o'clock tonight."

As he walked away, both cowboys were grinning from ear to ear.

Chapter Eight

Amanda took the painting out onto the front porch, along with her camera, laptop, Jake's envelope, and her magnifying glass.

It was a clear bright May morning, warm enough that she didn't need a sweater or jacket. She propped the painting up on a windowsill and pulled a wicker porch chair up so she could sit and study it in detail. After taking a dozen digital photographs, she started to open up her laptop, then decided to first read the documents Jake had given her.

The documents were boilerplate legalese, basically claiming that the painting had been handed down to Jake and Justin, who were to split the proceeds if it were ever sold. In a smaller envelope, she found a photocopy of a hand written letter dated 1889.

Amanda had no doubt that Odell Morgan's letter was authentic. Or that Charles Randell had given him a painting. But if the painting on the windowsill was *the* Randell, or *a* Randell, the proof would be in the painting itself.

Amanda returned the letter to the manila envelope and opened up her laptop. She had already done extensive research on Randell and had downloaded all the information about the artist. She now needed to revisit every bit of data so she could to compare it to the Morgans' painting. She focused on the probability that the painting was a forgery and would study every detail that could prove her right.

Four hours later, she'd found nothing to

convince her that the painting was a fake. If it was a forgery, it was a damn good one.

At one o'clock, Rosita brought her a lunch of chicken tacos and an ice-cold beer. Amanda paused just long enough to wolf down a couple tacos and half a bottle of beer, then returned to an article about common mistakes forgers made when they copied Randell.

Often the style of cowboy hat was wrong. Or the signature didn't match a particular period. She continued through the afternoon, comparing the painting to hundreds of others on the Internet, looking for any anomaly that might indicate a forgery. For the Morgan's sake and for the sake of PP&C, she hoped the painting was a genuine Randell. Still, she tried to maintain a strong degree of skepticism.

Intently studying the work with her magnifying glass, she was startled when a voice behind her said, "Pardon me, ma'am."

She turned quickly to see Justin on horseback. He had ridden up close to the porch and was smiling at her startled expression.

"Sorry." He tipped the brim of his hat. "Didn't mean to scare you. Just thought you might like to take a break and go on a quick ride. You've been at that quite a long while."

Amanda looked at Justin, then at the horse. The animal was solid black and looked huge, even though she was looking down on it.

"I...I don't think so. I've never ridden a horse before."

"Nothing to it. You can sit behind the saddle and hold on to me."

Holding onto Justin Morgan wouldn't be a bad thing under any circumstances, she thought. Amanda wondered if Jake had already arranged the threesome. He probably had, considering the grin on

Justin's face.

"Put that painting back on the wall and hop on. We'll take it slow and easy. I'll make sure you enjoy the ride."

Pun intended, Amanda thought, looking at the cowboy's sly smile.

"You can't come to a Texas horse ranch without riding a horse, can you?"

What the hell, Amanda thought, admiring Justin's slim waist and muscular chest and shoulders. "All right. Give me a minute." She took the painting and her laptop back into the lodge, returning quickly to the porch. "How do I get on?"

Justin nudged the horse near the steps. "Come down about halfway. You can grab my arm and swing your leg over his back. This is Cricket." He patted the horse's neck. "He's gentle as a lamb. Just climb on up."

Amanda stepped down a few steps then grabbed Justin's arm. As she expected, his bicep was hard and muscular. The swing up was easy and, in seconds, she was straddling the horse's back, her crotch just behind the back of the saddle. She held Justin's shoulders for a moment, not sure where to put her hands. Finally, she slid them down to his waist.

"Ready?" Justin looked back over his shoulder.

"Ready," she called, with just a bit of apprehension.

Justin reined the horse away from the porch and walked him toward the stream that ran behind the stables. The stream was barely twenty feet wide at this point and they crossed with Cricket wading next to a narrow wooden bridge that spanned the quickly running water. On the opposite bank, they started up a fairly steep slope. Amanda held on tighter, worried about sliding off the back of the horse. At the top of the rise, the ground leveled out and she relaxed.

As Justin guided the horse up the gentle slope, he said, "I reckon you're looking at the painting out on the porch because of the natural light."

"Yes. Makes it easier to more accurately judge the color and brush strokes."

"Well, I don't want to scare you, but you should be cautious. Winslow is such a snake, I wouldn't put it past him to come back and cause a bit more trouble."

"What kind of trouble? Do you think he might try to steal the painting?"

"There's no telling what he might try to do. Just be cautious. We once beat Winslow on a bid for a stallion we wanted to put to stud. Winslow bitched and moaned for a week. Then one day, we found the stallion dead in the south pasture, which butts up to Winslow's property. There was no healthier horse on this spread. We had the vet do an autopsy, and he said the horse died from a snakebite. But based on the amount of venom he found in the horse's system, the rattlesnake would have to have been fifty feet long. We've got some big rattlers in Texas, but none quite that big."

"So you think your cousin injected the venom into the horse?"

"The vet couldn't find any bite marks. And a snakebite usually swells up at the puncture wound. There's no doubt in our minds that Winslow decided if he couldn't have that horse, neither could we."

"That's horrible! How could anybody do something like that?"

"Just be cautious. Winslow knows we can't be around the lodge all the time. So if you see that red pickup of his come through the gate, take the painting inside and lock the door."

"Yes. I will. Of course."

Justin's warning about Winslow was

disconcerting. Watching out for a nutcase was not in her job description. But then, so far, nothing about this project had been either. *For God's sake,* she thought. *Here I am riding across the Texas prairie with a man I've barely met and will probably be fucking in a few hours.*

Jake turned, speaking over his shoulder. "Ready to trot?"

Before she could say yes or no, he spurred the horse and she suddenly found her butt bouncing up and down on Cricket's back.

"Hey...could we...slow down...a bit?" She had wrapped her arms around Justin's waist and was clasping her hands tightly in front of his belt buckle. Justin reined back and slowed the horse to walk.

Amanda tried to admire the hills covered in wildflowers, but it was difficult to ignore the issue with Winslow Morgan. Justin solved that problem when, after another hundred yards, he said, "The stars were really beautiful last night, weren't they?"

"Yes...they...were," she stammered. Had he seen her outside on the balcony?

"We saw you on the balcony last night. Watching our little rodeo."

She felt herself turning as red as the Indian paintbrush they were riding through. *Oh my God,* she thought. *I can't believe I'm sitting on the back of this horse holding onto a man who's telling me he caught me spying on his threesome. Thank God he can't see my face.* "I...I didn't mean to..."

"It's okay," Justin said. "Julie really gets off on it." They had ridden through a thicket of red cedar and come out on a hilltop in a clearing that offered a panoramic view of the land to the west. The landscape flowed from rolling hills for several miles to butte-like mountains in the distance. The sun was angling down, looking like it was going to make a beautiful sunset. Justin stopped the horse and swung his leg over the saddle horn, turning halfway around toward Amanda. She'd let go of his waist and was resting her palms on her thighs.

"Jake said you might be interested in a threesome. Is that so?"

Amanda knew she was blushing deeply. It was one thing to casually discuss a threesome when you're lying in bed, naked and sweaty from just fucking one of the possible participants. It was quite another to discuss it in the clear light of day with a possible participant you've barely met. Even if the man was pussy-melting hot.

She glanced at his expectant smile then turned her head away, looking at the distant mountains. "God, I can believe we're talking about this. That I even..."

"But it is what you want isn't it?"

"Yes," she said softly. "If it's something you want, too."

"Are you kidding? Any man in his right mind would want to. You are drop-dead gorgeous. And smart. And sexy!"

He quickly slid down to the ground, then he reached up and grabbed Amanda's waist, helping her down. They stood next to the black stallion, facing each other, his hands still on her waist, holding her close.

They stared at each other, his eyes glowing with desire, while she couldn't help but compare Justin to Jake. Justin was younger, fairer, and a little softer around the edges than dark-complexioned Jake. She had seen Justin with Luke and Julie for only a few minutes, but she had no doubt he would be an amazing lover to broaden her sexual horizons. It could be an especially erotic experience with Jake and Justin both factored into the equation.

She studied Justin's face and felt her desire growing. She licked her lips as her pussy moistened beneath her jeans. "Do you think I'm totally wanton? For wanting to have sex with two men at once?"

Justin smiled. He slipped his hands behind her back and pulled her up against his body. She could feel her nipples against his hard chest, could feel his cock against her tummy. His erection was growing harder by the second. She tilted her face up, looking into his steady gaze. His eyes were lighter than Jake's, more gray, but equally beautiful.

"I think you are a beautiful, sexy woman with a desire to indulge in an erotic adventure that many women fantasize about but few ever have the opportunity to experience. And I'm very happy that I get to be part of that experience. I hope we can make it as enjoyable as you deserve." Justin lowered his head and kissed her, his lips opening quickly, his tongue slipping into her mouth.

For a moment she kissed him back, letting her own tongue curl past his into his mouth. As the passion of the kiss increased, she slid her arms around his neck and pressed her body tighter against his. One of his hands slid down to her buttocks, the other around to her front. He pulled his hips back slightly, making space for his hand to explore. As his hand moved to the front of her jeans, she spread her legs, inviting him to cup her pussy. His palm pressed against her throbbing core, sending a hot current through her body.

Suddenly she thought of Jake, how he'd made love to her the night before. She lifted her hands to Justin's chest, pushing back. "As much as I enjoyed that kiss and would love to try it again, I think we might want to wait until later. We'll have plenty of time tonight."

Justin slid his hands to her ass and pulled her close again, pressing his hard-on against her tummy. "Are you sure? Sometimes an appetizer can make the main course even better."

She smiled at him. "I'm sure. Let's wait until tonight."

He looked disappointed but mounted Cricket and helped her swing up behind him. They got back to the lodge just as Rosita was ready to serve supper. This time, it was only Jake, Justin, Julie, and Amanda at the table. She ate more slowly than she had the night before, taking time to savor the delicious chile rellenos Rosita had prepared. Jake and Justin tried to get her opinion about the painting's authenticity, but all she would say was that she hadn't seen anything yet that showed it to be an outright fake.

"But I'm not ready to say it's authentic either. I need to spend a bit more time with it. I'll make a decision tomorrow about calling in more experts."

After supper, Amanda went to her room and called Richard, reporting what she had and hadn't found in her research. "It's looking good, Richard. But I'm not ready to commit to anything yet. Give me until tomorrow, and I'll let you know if we need to move forward. I'll be bringing the signed contracts and the proof of ownership back to the office with me. I also have a letter the Morgan's great granddad wrote in 1889, saying a cowboy named Kid Randell gave him a painting of a cowboy on a horse. The letter looks authentic, but it doesn't necessarily establish provenance either."

"Thanks Mandy. I hope you don't mind staying an extra night."

She smiled, thinking about what the night held in store. "I don't mind, Richard. I don't mind at all."

Amanda was already very aroused by the prospect of a ménage a trois , but she also had a slightly unsettling feeling about that last kiss with Jake. It had knocked her a bit off-balance and left her feeling that the kiss meant more than a prelude to another night of delicious, uninhibited sex. She wasn't ready to deal with feelings yet. Romance played no part in this situation—pleasure without jealousy, giving herself to two men at the same time, and enjoying what they could give her in return.

As long as Jake wasn't jealous about sharing her with another man, whether it was his brother or Luke or whoever, why should she worry? Jake had freed her from some sexual hang-ups that had inhibited her all her adult life. Now, she intended to explore just how unfettered her libido could be.

Throughout supper, neither Jake nor Justin indicated that they had anything planned for the evening, particularly not a threesome. As she went to her room after the meal, Amanda was unsure how events would unfold. But on her pillow sat a note that read, "Justin's room, nine o'clock."

It was just past eight when she found the note, which gave her an hour to shower and wash and dry her hair. She also trimmed her already smooth pussy and spritzed her wrists and neck with perfume.

She dressed in a simple tank top and jeans, nothing else. With no underwear or shoes, getting undressed would be simple. But if she decided to back out at the last minute, at least she could dress quickly.

At nine sharp, Amanda stepped through the French doors onto the balcony. The sun had just set, and the darkening sky was beginning to fill with bright diamond points of light.

Chapter Nine

Amanda walked around the balcony past Jake's corner room to the room at the far end where she had seen Justin, Luke, and Julie. Jake's curtain had been drawn and, as she passed his room, she wondered if he was already waiting for her with Justin.

When she reached Justin's room, she discovered his balcony door was standing partway open, an invitation to enter. She hesitated just a moment, then took a deep breath and stepped inside. A bedside lamp lit the room with a soft glow, and a row of votive candles flickered on the dresser. Amanda smiled. Maybe these rough-edged cowboys had romantic streaks she hadn't seen yet.

Jake was sitting in a side chair, a half empty glass of brandy on the dresser beside him. He was barefoot, wearing only jeans and a freshly ironed western shirt, unbuttoned and the shirttails untucked. His hair was damp. When she walked in, he stood and walked toward her, smiling broadly.

"I'm glad you came."

"Did you think I might not?"

"No. But I'm glad you are here. Would you like something to drink? A glass of wine? Whiskey?"

"I had a brandy in my room. Two, in fact. I'm fine."

"You are at that." He stepped closer. "Extremely, outrageously, amazingly fine." He reached out and cupped one of her breasts in his palm. She didn't pull away. Her hard nipples pressed against the fabric of her shirt. The thin material couldn't hide the size of her nipples.

He cupped her other breast and lifted them both, tweaking her nipples with his thumbs and forefingers, pinching them lightly. She felt her knees go weak, and her pussy begin to moisten.

"You have incredible breasts. I love your nipples. They're very sexy."

She blushed. "They can be embarrassing sometimes."

"But not now."

"No, not now." She felt a current of energy flow straight from her nipples to her pussy.

"I haven't done this before. A threesome." Or will it be a foursome, she wondered.

"I know. That makes it very special for all of us. Maybe we should take these off." He reached down and unsnapped her jeans.

Slipping her thumbs inside the waistband, she wiggled them down over her hips. When they reached her ankles, she stepped out of them and kicked them aside.

Jake looked down at her neatly shaved pussy and smiled. "I like this look," he said. He slid his hands up under her tank top to caress her breasts once more, this time against her bare flesh.

She closed her eyes and sucked in her breath. When she opened her eyes, he was leaning toward her for a kiss. She hesitated, looking up into his eyes. "Jake...tonight...it's just sex, right?"

He looked at her seriously for a moment, then smiled. "Of course. Tonight is just sex."

He leaned down and she lifted her lips to his. The kiss was gentle at first, not too eager. It was a kiss that said, "We'll take it slow and easy. We've got all night." As she returned the kiss, Amanda felt herself grow wetter. Jake's hands were still squeezing her breasts and nipples as the kiss became firmer, more insistent.

The bathroom door opened and Justin stepped out, a towel wrapped around his waist. She was pleased the threesome included Jake's handsome brother. She couldn't forget their kiss on the hilltop earlier in the day.

As Justin approached, Jake turned her toward him and backed away. Justin took her in his arms, pulling her close. "You're trembling,"

"I'll be okay." She lifted her lips toward his. He leaned down for a deep probing kiss that made her pussy moisten even more. He tasted of mint and had a masculine, soapy scent, similar to Jake's.

She raised her hands and placed her palms against his chest. She let one hand slide down over his stomach and inside the towel. She was not used to being the aggressor and her actions made her feel bold. Her searching hand loosened the towel and it dropped to the floor, leaving him naked. She continued kissing him, her tongue searching, needy now. They might have all night, but she didn't want to waste a minute of it. She reached down and grasped his cock. He was rigidly erect, thick and hot in her palm.

Suddenly, she thought of Jake watching as she kissed Justin and held his cock. Knowing he was there, watching, was tremendously exciting. She felt as if the sparks in her pussy might burst into flame. Her kiss became more urgent and she pressed her body tighter against Justin's. *Amanda,* she thought, *you are a wanton exhibitionist.*

She felt Jake again behind her, his hands on her waist, his lips on her neck and shoulders. What an incredible sensation, kissing one man while another man's lips were on her flesh at the same time. Liquid heat seemed to surge from her pussy, spreading throughout her groin and filling her with desire. Four hands caressed her breasts and her ass. Two pairs of lips were trailing wet kisses over her shoulders and back and the tops of her breasts. With a whimper, she turned, wanting to kiss Jake on the mouth.

But it wasn't Jake. "Oh!" she gasped, looking up into Luke's dark eyes. Her confusion lasted only a moment and then Luke, already naked, was kissing her mouth. A hand explored the crevice between her thighs, a finger searching the wet slit. She surrendered to Luke's mouth, kissing him back, kissing him passionately.

She still held Justin's cock in one hand. Now, she reached down for Luke's cock. Her hand closed around it and she realized just how big he was. The shaft seemed impossibly long and so thick she could barely wrap her fingers around it.

As the two men moved to stand on each side of her, she looked again to where Jake sat, watching the trio and sipping his brandy. When he caught her gaze, he smiled and lifted his glass in salute. She glanced down and saw that Jake had the fly of his jeans open and his cock in his hand, stroking it slowly. *Maybe he will join in later,* she thought. Or maybe he's just going to watch. She returned his smile. Being watched, she just discovered, could be extremely erotic, too.

She turned her attention back to Justin and Luke, who were both caressing her breasts and ass and the warm wet flesh between her legs. She kissed Justin deeply, hungrily, for a long moment, then turned to kiss Luke with equal passion. After several minutes of alternating kisses, Amanda pulled away to catch her breath. She glanced over at Jake again. He was still stroking his cock.

He smiled and said "Why don't you take off your top, Amanda? Show the boys your magnificent breasts and your amazing nipples."

Amanda was trembling nervously but she returned his smile and then slowly, teasingly, stripped her tank top up and off.

Facing Luke and Justin, she palmed her breasts and lifted them, then tweaked her nipples between her thumbs and forefingers. She gave a sideways glance at Jake and smiled when she saw his attention, like Luke's and Justin's, was focused intently on her breasts. Naked now, she stepped backward and lay back on the bed. She was still trembling, but was ready for whatever came next. Luke picked up two condoms from the nightstand and tossed one to Justin. They rolled the condoms on quickly and, a moment later, were lying on the bed, each sucking a nipple between his lips.

Luke paused and looked at her. "This is what you want, isn't it? Two men at the same time?"

"It's exactly what I want." She reached down and grasped both of their cocks. Justin's was impressive, but Luke's was much larger. Would she actually be able to take it in her pussy? Julie seemed to have no problem.

She was quiet for a moment then said, "I have to ask. What about Julie? Will she be jealous?"

"Not at all." Luke shook his head. "If she wasn't in a truck hauling horses down to El Paso, she would probably be knocking on the door begging to join in."

Amanda raised an eyebrow. "Really? Would she want to...I mean, is she bisexual?"

"You might say that," Justin said.

"I'd say," Luke added. "She's every kind of sexual there is. Although, she certainly favors men. Sometimes two at a time."

"If she was here, we could have invited her to join us," Justin said.

Amanda blushed and looked at the two men, then over at Jake. "I think I've got all I can handle right here." She gave both of their erections a squeeze then lay back, her head on the pillow.

Justin and Luke went back to sucking her

nipples and she felt a surge of electricity spread upward from her groin. Amanda reached down past her tummy, letting her fingers slide over the small triangle of pubic hair to her clitoris. The pink bud was engorged and tingling, so sensitive she almost climaxed at her first touch. She looked at Jake, wondering if he would give her more direction.

"I think our girl is ready for a cock," he said. "Aren't you, baby?"

"Yes," she whispered, her voice suddenly hoarse. "Please. I need a cock. A hot, hard cock. Now."

Luke and Justin both smiled at her request. "You are a naughty girl, aren't you?" Justin said. "Begging so sweetly."

She lifted her finger, wet with pussy juice, and sucked it into her mouth. She licked it off and looked at Justin shyly. "Yes. I am naughty."

Luke rolled to one side and picked up a bottle of lubricant from the nightstand, then moved back to position himself between her legs. "How about we see just how naughty you can be?" He dribbled oil on her slit, then she felt the large bulbous head of his cock teasing her pussy entrance. "Yes!" She whispered breathlessly. "That's what I want." She reached down, using her fingers to spread her pussy lips, arching her pelvis up and welcoming Luke's penetration.

Amanda's slick passage had become wet from her first kiss with Jake and her pussy now seeped with the evidence of her arousal. Even so, she was glad Luke had provided lube to help her accommodate his huge size. Even then, he had to go slow, letting her get used to his thickness and length as he shoved the rigid shaft in inch by inch.

"Oh...My...God!" Her pussy stretched with each inch of Luke's amazing dick. "Oh God. It's...so...damn...big!" She continued to whimper as he pushed in deeper. She lifted her hips, giving him a better angle. "Ohhh fuck," she moaned, as his pulsing cock pushed in deeper, stretching her, filling her. Justin knelt next to her, caressing her breasts. She glanced up at him, then looked at Luke kneeling between her legs. Both men were smiling down at her, knowing she was undoubtedly being fucked by the biggest cock she'd ever had. She glanced at Jake, still stroking his cock. He was smiling at her as well, but his eyes blazed with hot desire.

Luke flexed his pelvis and pushed another two inches of thick cock into her pussy. Amanda closed her eyes and moaned loudly, her back arching up as her head tilted back. Justin moved up to kneel by her head and slid his erection into her open mouth. The moment she felt the head of his cock slide between her lips, she sucked him eagerly into her mouth, her tongue swirling wetly around his shaft.

The sensation of having a cock in her pussy and another in her mouth was intensely erotic. Amanda adjusted the angle of her head so she could suck Justin's cock and still see Jake, who was now sitting at the end of the bed, giving himself a better view of the three lovers. She could see that the head of his cock now glistened with pearly drops of pre-come. Knowing that Jake was watching heightened every sensation and her body responded to Luke and Justin with abandon.

Luke was fucking her hard and deep now, his thick cock filling her completely. Justin pulled his cock out of her mouth and lay down beside her, leaning over to suck a nipple between his lips. Lathing the nipple with his tongue, he pinched and twisted her other nipple between his thumb and forefinger, sending hot currents of electricity straight to her pussy. She could feel the energy of her building orgasm spreading in a spiraling heat that grew brighter and brighter. Luke suddenly pulled completely out of her pussy and she whimpered in desperation. Then his tongue was sliding through her creamy folds and she sighed, feeling her pleasure once again rising in her core.

****

Jake moved to the edge of the bed, leaning in to whisper to Amanda. "How do you feel, Amanda? Do you like what Luke and Justin are doing to you?"

"Yes!" Amanda's eyes were closed, one hand wrapped around Justin's erection, while the other twisted the sheet into a tight knot. "It's good. Oh God, it's so good!"

Jake could see Luke's tongue sliding into her wet slit and then out again to lick up her pussy lips and flick rapidly over her clitoris. From the way her body was writhing, Luke's lips were setting her on fire.

Jake could sense the depth of her passion. "You do like it, don't you, Amanda? Do you want to come? Let go, Amanda. Let yourself come."

She turned her head to look at Jake's face, just inches from her own. Her eyes held a glazed, helpless look. Suddenly, Luke's probing tongue had her at the edge, then forced her over it. Jake smiled as he watched her eyes roll back and close tightly as she climaxed. As her head arched back against the mattress, twisting from side to side, she cried out, half moan and half scream. Both of her hands gripped Luke's head, pulling him tight against the wet flesh of her pussy as her hips bucked and jerked in orgasm.

When her cries reached a crescendo and began to fade to a breathless, contented sigh, Jake moved close to whisper in her ear again. "I love watching you come, watching you enjoy the pleasure sex can give you. You are an incredibly erotic woman. Did you enjoy your climax Amanda? Do you want more?"

She looked at him through half lidded eyes. "I don't think I can take any more."

Jake chuckled. "You'll be surprised at the body's capacity for pleasure."

****

"Come here sugar," Justin said. "I think you need to take this pony for a ride."

Amanda turned over to see Justin lying in the middle of the bed, his cock angled up like a bowsprit. She glanced back at Jake, who was sitting back down in his chair. Justin reached for her and she swung one leg over his waist, straddling his hips. She smiled down at him and rubbed her pussy up and down the length of his straining cock. She was wet from her climax with Luke and her pussy lips slid easily along his shaft. After a moment, she rose up on her knees and held his cock upright, guiding it into her needy slit. As Amanda slowly lowered her pussy over his dick, she rotated her pelvis back and forth, fucking him as she worked his cock deeper and deeper.

She slid up and down on his cock, exhaling in short breaths on each down-stroke. Justin gripped her ass in his hands, guiding her movements as she rocked up and down on his cock. After several minutes of thrusting, Justin held her waist and rolled without removing his cock from her pussy. Now on her back with Justin between her legs, she lifted her pelvis to meet his thrusts. Glancing at Jake, Amanda could see he was watching her intently.

Luke discarded his condom and knelt next to her face, the velvet smooth head of his cock stroking her cheek. She looked up as the corona caressed her lips to see him smiling down at her. She opened her mouth and extended her tongue. Luke slid his cock over her tongue and into her mouth.

Once again, she felt filled with cock, filled with arousal, desire, need, pleasure. Justin was fucking her hard and fast, his cock a piston driving her to the brink of ecstasy. She looked up at him, saw his muscular chest and forehead covered with a sheen of perspiration, his eyes scrunched tight, obviously ready to come. She let Luke's cock slip out of her mouth for a moment to encourage him. "Yes, Justin. Do it. Let me feel you come."

Justin grabbed her ass, clutching her almost desperately as he lifted her hips, pushing into her as deep as he could. Holding her by the waist, he pulled her tight against his pelvis, his cock as deep in her pussy as possible. His body grew rigid and, for a moment, he held perfectly still. Then with a deep guttural moan, he surrendered to his orgasm.

As Justin came in heated spurts, she opened her mouth to take Luke's cock once again. The thick bulbous head had barely slipped between her lips when Luke's cock spasmed in her mouth, the splash of his cum salty on her tongue as he climaxed.

"Ahhhh God! Yes! Yes!" Luke growled as she tried to swallow spurt after spurt of his creamy ejaculate.

Luke's and Justin's orgasms sparked her own and her moans became a keening wail, blending with the grunts and groans of the men fucking her.

It took the trio several long moments before they could move and extract themselves from the connections of cocks in pussy and mouth. It took even longer for their post-orgasmic bliss to finally fade. They lay quietly next to each other, each trying to catch their breath and regain some semblance of consciousness.

****

Jake got up and walked over to the bed. He stood looking down at Amanda, smiling and waiting for her to open her eyes. She was coated in sweat, her thick dark curls a matted mess, her lips and breasts and labia swollen and rosy from the kisses and caresses of her two lovers. When she finally opened her eyes, she looked up and gave him a wan smile.

"Did you enjoy that, Amanda? Was it everything you wanted?"

She stared up at him. Her lips moved but no words came out. Finally, she nodded and lifted her arm toward him. He took her hand, cradling it in his. As he held her hand, she sighed and closed her eyes.

Luke and Justin lay on the bed, unmoving, their eyes closed as well. "That was fucking incredible," Justin said.

"Totally fucking amazing," Luke added.

"It was damn sure incredible to watch," Jake said. "But I think this woman has had enough of you two stallions for one night." He reached down and picked her up, cradling her in his arms. Her eyes still closed, she lazily wound her arms around his neck. He pushed the balcony door open with his foot and stepped outside. Unlike the night before, this time he carried her to her own room.

Laying her on her bed, Jake got a damp cloth and gently washed her face, brushing stray locks of hair away from her cheeks, then tucked her under the top sheet and pulled the quilted comforter over her. Only then did she open her eyes.

"Thank you, Jake," she whispered. "It was...it was everything I fantasized about, and more."

He smiled and leaned close. "I'm glad you enjoyed it. You were amazing to watch."

He leaned closer and kissed her, a gentle sweet kiss goodnight. She sighed and closed her eyes again. He knew by the time he got in his own bed, she would be sleeping peacefully.

In his own room, Jake lay in bed thinking about how intensely arousing it had been to watch Amanda spread her sexual wings and soar. It had taken all his will power to keep from joining in as

Justin and Luke took her on that erotic ride. Even now, he was rigidly erect, his cock still as hard as Texas granite.

When he fucked her again—if he ever got the chance—he wanted it to be just him and her. Not that he couldn't share a woman with Luke or Justin, or even with both men at the same time. It had certainly been no problem with Julie. But there was something special about Amanda, something that made him feel there could be more to their relationship than pure sex. It was a feeling that caught him by surprise and was simultaneously exhilarating and disquieting. He wasn't sure he liked the feeling, but didn't know how to do a damn thing about it.

As he drifted to sleep, he knew he could never get in Amanda's way as she continued her journey of sexual awakening. Trying to keep her corralled would be a big mistake. But he couldn't help wondering what it might be like to have a special relationship with her that involved more than sex.

Forget it, Jake, he finally said to himself. *In a couple of days, the woman will be out of your life forever.*

Chapter Ten

Amanda awoke slowly. Dawn was just breaking and, somewhere in the distance, a rooster crowed, welcoming the day. She opened one eye and glanced at the clock on the nightstand—six a.m. She wasn't sure how long she'd been in bed. At least in this bed. She had spent several hours in Justin's bed being fucked. Kissed and sucked and fucked and fondled and fucked some more, in more ways than she'd thought possible.

The rooster crowed again and she thought of cocks. Good God, she'd had cocks! In her hands and mouth and pussy over and over again. More cock in one night than she'd had in the ten years since her senior prom, when she'd given up her virginity to a boy she could barely remember. As a result, her pussy was sore, even her jaw ached. But it was a good ache. A delicious, amazingly pleasant ache that reminded her of just how much she had enjoyed the hours with Justin and Luke. And Jake.

She lay still, wondering how she would feel when she woke up completely. Would she feel guilty? She smiled. No. Not at all. She felt absolutely no guilt about her night with Luke and Justin. She had fantasized about a threesome for years, had wanted it, and she had enjoyed it immensely. So much that she knew if an opportunity arose, she would do it again in a heartbeat.

Amanda stretched and slid her hands down over her breasts. Jesus, even her nipples were sore. They had been playthings for Justin and Luke, receiving an extraordinary amount of attention during her introduction to sex with multiple partners. She reached down and slid a finger between her pussy lips. Not surprisingly, she was still wet. Even though she was physically sated, the memories of how well she'd been fucked stimulated her arousal. If Justin or Luke or especially Jake walked into her room at that moment, she would welcome any one of them with open arms. Or any two of them for that matter.

She still wasn't sure why Jake had set her up with Justin and Luke and not joined in. He had apparently been content to just watch while the two cowboys fucked her, first with sensitive sweetness and then with a balls-to-the-wall ferocity that had her screaming through her orgasms.

What, she wondered, *did Jake think of her?* Was she simply a woman exploring a newly found freedom from her inhibitions? Or did he think she was an insatiable nympho? He had assured her that last night had been about sex and sex only. But that kiss when she'd told him she would stay...It was definitely a kiss with more meaning than she had expected. Or asked for. Did she really want to deal with any emotional involvement, especially with Jake?

Amanda put those confusing thoughts and questions aside and concentrated on the Randell painting. At that thought, she smiled. She was already thinking of the work as "the Randell painting."

Sunlight was spreading like golden butter over the tops of the hills and across the valley to the west when she got up and took a quick shower. As she was toweling herself dry, a knock sounded at the door. Wrapping the big towel around her body, she answered hesitantly. She was surprised to find Rosita standing in the hallway. The housekeeper was holding up a beautiful Mexican-style dress.

"*Senorita,*" Rosita held the dress out toward

Amanda. "This is a present for you from all of us at the ranch. I'm afraid I was not able to get the blood spots from your blouse, and we know you are staying longer than you planned. So please, this dress is a token of our thanks to you. We would be so pleased if you would wear it. It was handmade by my cousin in San Antonio."

"Oh no, Rosita. It's too much. I can't take this."

"But you must. You will make us all very happy if you wear it. I think it should fit you perfectly." Rosita smiled and turned away, walking back down the hallway to the stairs.

Amanda closed the door and held the dress up at arm's length. It was fine cotton in a rich turquoise with an elastic off-the-shoulder neckline and short gathered sleeves. The dress was trimmed with a beautiful row of flowers embroidered in silver and gold all around the bodice.

Another row of flowers was embroidered around the bottom of the full skirt, which came a few inches above her knees.

She laid the dress across the bed and finished drying off. The garment was beautiful and she actually had worn her last change of clothes the day before. She had intended to ask Rosita to wash her white blouse or one of her tank tops, but in all the night's excitement she had completely forgotten. Her choice for the day had been to wear a pair of jeans and a tank top for a second time.

She slipped on a white thong but decided against a bra. With the off the shoulder bodice, her bra straps would show. She stepped into the dress and pulled it up over her hips. As she slipped her arms through the sleeves and pulled up the elastic waist, she saw that the dress fit perfectly. She studied herself in the mirror, delightfully surprised and pleased at how well the dress fit and how much the turquoise color complimented her dark brown hair and eyes. The color also worked well with the new cowboy boots she had bought for the trip. The boots, a rich chocolate brown almost the same color as her hair, had an eagle with uplifted wings hand-stitched in gold thread across the front and sides.

She studied herself in the mirror, pleased with her appearance. She headed for the door, hesitated, then looked at herself in the mirror once more. On a whim, she took her new cowboy hat off the bedpost and set it on her head. *What the hell,* she thought. I've ridden a horse and three different cowboys. I deserve to wear my hat. Posing with her hands on her hips, Amanda decided her outfit needed one more adjustment. Grasping the elastic top she pulled the bodice down another two inches, leaving the sloping tops of her breasts exposed almost to her nipples.

Considering how much Jake seemed to admire her breasts, this look would certainly capture his attention. She grinned mischievously and started down the stairs to breakfast.

Rosita was in the kitchen busy preparing *huevos rancheros* for breakfast. When she saw Amanda she stopped, her face breaking into a broad smile. "Oh *señorita*, it is *muy bonita! Es* very beautiful on you."

"It's a beautiful dress, Rosita. And beautifully made. Your cousin is a real artist."

Two simultaneous wolf whistles made her turn around. Luke and Justin had come in through the back door and were looking at her with big grins.

"That's one damn pretty dress, don't you think, Justin." Luke looked at Amanda as if she were a confection ready to be gobbled up.

"And sexy, too," Justin agreed.

She smiled and blushed, even though it had been the reaction she had hoped for. The embroidered flowers around the bodice looked like they had been custom sewn to encircle and emphasize each breast, leaving just enough unembroidered fabric to highlight her nipples as they pressed against the thin cotton. The sight held the cowboys totally entranced.

"Hope you had a good night sleep, Miss Sloane." Luke grinned at her.

She blushed again and glanced at Rosita. The housekeeper, who seemed to know everything, rolled her eyes and winked.

"I slept like a baby." Amanda quipped.

Just then, Jake walked in and looked at the grinning faces. When he saw Amanda, he did a double take. "Nice dress," he said, staring at the significant amount of bare bosom she was revealing. His gaze lingered on the peaks of her barely covered nipples. "I like your hat and boots, too." He managed to pull his eyes away from her cleavage and up to her face.

She tried to read the expression behind his emerald eyes. They held each other's gaze for a moment, and then Rosita was chasing everyone from the kitchen to the dining table.

During breakfast, Justin and Luke joked and laughed good-naturedly without making any remarks about sharing her through most of the night. Jake acted as if nothing had happened. Remaining his silent, taciturn self, he made polite conversation. She still couldn't figure the man out, although she was pleased to see him sneaking admiring glances at her several times during the meal.

After breakfast, Jake excused himself to go to his office just off the lodge's main room. Justin and Julie were driving to Austin to pick up some supplies, while Luke headed toward the stables to take care of various ranch chores. Amanda took the painting and her laptop back out onto the porch for further study. She had taken her hat off during breakfast, but now put it on again.

Less than an hour into her examination, she came across something in the painting that gave her a sinking feeling in the pit of her stomach. Ten minutes later, she discovered another problem, one that twisted the feeling in her tummy into a tight, hard knot.

"Fuck." She murmured softly, studying the painting. "Fuck! Fuck! Fuck!" She re-read her Internet research, then read it a third time just to make sure. Finally she sighed, wondering how in the world she was going to tell Jake. First, she decided, she would get confirmation of what she had found from Richard. Her discovery was too important to rely on her suspicions alone. There was too much at stake, from her reputation to saving the ranch.

She picked up her phone and called Richard. He answered with a cheerful, "Howdy Mandy. How's Texas? And the Randell?"

"I'm not so sure it is a Randell, Richard. I've found a couple of things that bother me."

"That's not what I had hoped to hear. Have you said anything to the Morgans?"

"No, nothing yet. And I won't until I'm absolutely sure. I need you to confirm what I've found, all right?"

"Of course. Just tell me what I need to be looking for."

She told Richard what worried her and he said he would get back to her as soon as he had any information—good or bad. "I'm keeping my fingers crossed that it will be good."

"Me, too. But right now I don't have much hope." As she hung up, Jake walked out onto the porch. He was wearing chaps and spurs, ready to be on horseback. He was smiling broadly. She took a deep breath and returned his smile, hoping hers didn't look too forced.

He grinned. "So did you enjoy last night as much as you seemed to?"

She felt herself blush. "I would say so, thank you very much." She paused. "I guess everyone on the ranch must think I'm a nymphomaniac."

Jake shook his head. "Not at all. And my understanding is that nymphomaniacs keep seeking sex because they can't be satisfied. Haven't you been satisfied?"

A big grin lit up her face. "Oh yeah. Over and over again."

Jake returned the grin. "Good. I'm glad." He stepped closer and reached out, laying a hand on her bare shoulder. "I really am glad."

"I am too. But I was wondering…"

"Yes?"

"I was wondering why you only watched and didn't join in. Not that it wasn't great with Justin and Luke. But I wanted you."

He looked at her intently, still holding her shoulder. "I wanted you, too. I'm not sure why I didn't join in. Maybe I wanted to watch you test your boundaries. Or test my capacity to share someone that I…" He looked away.

Someone what, she wondered. *Someone he cared about?*

"Someone what?" She asked, even though she wasn't sure she wanted to hear his response.

He looked into her eyes. "I'm not sure. It just seemed like you needed to experience a night of pure sex. I knew Luke and Justin could give that to you."

"Does that mean you care—"

He cut her off. "I'm not sure what it means. But, since you will probably be leaving tomorrow, maybe you would consider spending the night with me." He let the hand on her shoulder slide down to cup her breast. They were out in the open on the porch, but she didn't pull away. She took a deep breath, lifting her breasts, pressing her nipples against his palm. With his other hand, he gently tilted her chin up. Leaning down, he kissed her, softly at first, then more passionately.

Amanda returned the kiss with equal passion, pressing her crotch against his leg. After several minutes, she pulled back, breathless, panting, and wet between her legs.

"We definitely have a date for tonight."

He smiled, gave her another quick kiss on the lips, and then backed away. As he walked down the steps, he said, "I'm eager to hear what you think about the painting."

She was glad he didn't turn around to see her expression change.

Chapter Eleven

Amanda stood on the porch with conflicted feelings. She was sad about the possibility—or probability—that the painting was a forgery, but excited and aroused about spending the night with Jake. Perhaps she liked him for more than just sex. Regardless of any emotional or romantic feelings they might have, she had a great deal to thank him for. During one night of passionate lovemaking, he'd stripped away inhibitions that had kept her bottled up her whole life. For that, she would always be grateful.

She turned back to the painting, almost certain now it was not a genuine Randell. How, though, did it end up here? Had Randell given Odel Morgan a forged work?

A voice behind her gave her a start.

"Oh!" She turned around to find Luke standing in front of the porch. "You startled me. What were you asking?"

"Just wondering if that little picture could really be worth a ton of money."

She hesitated. "If it's a genuine Charles Randell, it could be."

"Is it genuine?"

"I'm not sure yet. I need to study it some more. Although, I've looked at it so much I'm about cross-eyed."

"You need to take a break. Come with me and I'll show you something that's just as pretty as that picture. Prettier even."

"You're not going to show me a stallion and a

mare getting it on, are you?"

A wide grin spread across Luke's face. "Nope. Something much better. Come on down here. It'll only take a couple of minutes."

"All right." She pulled her hat firmly down on her head before taking the painting back inside and placing it on the mantle. Laying her laptop and phone next to the painting, she locked the door and hurried down the steps. "Let's go," she said to Luke. "I'm ready to see something pretty."

She had to hustle to keep up with Luke's long strides, but she managed. They walked to a small barn about a hundred yards from the lodge. Luke ushered her through the door.

The barn was much nicer than where Luke and Julie had bred Rocket and Dolly, with banks of overhead fluorescents and clean concrete floors. There were six stalls in the barn, but only one was occupied.

"Over here." Luke beckoned her to the occupied stall. She stepped forward and looked over the top rail.

Inside the stall stood a beautiful reddish mare with white stockings on all four legs, a sorrel like Jake's horse, Ginger. Behind her, half hidden, a newborn foal stood on spindly legs.

"Oh!" Amanda moved around to the other side of the stall. "It's a baby. He's beautiful." She turned to look at Luke. "How old is he?"

"How old is *she*," he said, looking at his watch. "Right now, she's about five hours old. Julie got back from El Paso just in time to play midwife. I'm babysitting until she and Justin get back from Austin. She is pretty isn't she?"

Amanda stared at the foal over the stall's top rail for several minutes. Her heart was filled with joy at the miracle of new life. For an instant, she felt tears well up, then she sniffed them away and smiled. The foal, her legs still wobbly, tucked its head beneath her mom to suckle. Luke moved up behind Amanda, standing close, looking over her shoulder at the mare and the foal. She stared at the newborn filly for a long moment. "Thank you for showing me the foal, Luke. She's beautiful."

Luke moved an inch closer and lifted his hands to Amanda's waist. "You're welcome. And speaking of beautiful, you've got the prettiest neck and shoulders of any woman I've ever known." He leaned forward, tucking his face under the brim of her hat. His breath was warm on her bare neck and shoulders.

She turned her head halfway toward him, not quite sure what she should say. This was the man, one of them at least, that she had begged to fuck her just hours earlier. She felt his lips on her shoulder and a little shudder traced its way up her spine.

"Luke. We really shouldn't..."

His hands moved from her waist around to her stomach and up to cup her breasts. Her nipples, already hard, grew even more erect. "Oh, Luke. We shouldn't..."

His fingers found the elastic top of her neckline. With a gentle tug, he pulled the bodice down, baring her breasts. He palmed them, his thumbs teasing her nipples. Amanda's mouth went dry and her pussy flared with heat. She turned her head, trying to look over her shoulder as she grasped the top rail of the stall.

Luke ran his tongue from her neck to her shoulder, and then lifted his lips to kiss the corner of her mouth, her cheek, her ear. "Relax, sweetheart," he whispered. "I know you want this."

"I think you're right, Luke. She does want it." Jake's throaty voice came from close by.

Amanda glanced to one side and saw Jake standing next to the stall. He nodded at her approvingly, the hot gleam in his eyes saying, "You want what Luke can give you. Don't you?"

She did want it. With Jake looking on in approval, Amanda wanted whatever they could give her. She wanted it so badly her pussy was on fire.

Jesus, how could she be so aroused so quickly? Luke pushed his hips forward, his crotch pressing against her bottom. She felt the large bulge under his jeans through her skirt, remembered his big cock fucking her so eagerly the night before. God, how he had filled her, stretched her. Now, she wanted to feel that magnificent shaft filling her again.

She looked at Jake, saw his eyes narrow as his gaze traveled from her face to her bare breasts and back again. He licked his lips and she smiled. Knowing Jake was watching, seeing he was aroused, only made her hotter. With her eyes locked on his, she slowly leaned forward, grabbing a lower rail. She pressed her ass back, arching her back and lifting her bottom. At her blatant invitation to Luke, Jake grinned. "You are a horny little minx, aren't you? You just can't wait for some more of that big cock."

She glanced down, saw that Jake had a large bulge under the fly of his jeans. She grinned. He was obviously just as turned on as she was, She looked over her shoulder, saw Luke unzip his jeans and lift his cock out. Her eyes widened and a shiver swept up her spine.

Luke took a condom from his pocket and quickly unwrapped it. He rolled it on, then lifted the back of her skirt, revealing her ass and core. Reaching between her legs, Luke pulled the thin straps of her thong aside, revealing her shaved pussy lips.

"No," She said over her shoulder. "Take my thong off."

He grabbed the thin waistband of her thong and stripped it down, kneeling behind her as he worked it down her legs and over her boots. Kneeling put him eye level with her pussy, which was already swollen and moist with arousal. Leaning forward, he ran his tongue slowly up her slit, causing her knees to buckle.

Luke grabbed her hips to steady her. "Damn you taste sweet. And you're dripping wet and ready." He leaned forward and licked her slit again, this time taking a moment to tease her clit with the tip of his tongue.

"Oh God," she whispered, tilting her head back and closing her eyes as she held on tightly to the railing. When she opened her eyes again, Jake was standing next to her, leaning against the railing of the stall.

"You do want this, don't you Amanda?" Jake asked quietly. "I can see how wet you are."

When she answered, her breath was shallow, her voice dry and raspy. "Yes. I want it."

"You want Luke's big cock in your tight pussy?"

"Yes."

"Fucking you?"

"Yes."

"Making you come?"

"Yes! Yes, yes, yes! Fuck me. I want it. So bad."

Amanda looked over her shoulder again, her eyes wide, her breath coming in shallow pants. Luke's mouth was driving her insane with desire. She pushed back against his tongue and lips, silently begging him for more. She felt wantonly salacious but somehow Jake being there made it okay. Even better than okay. She stared at him, knowing he could see how eager, how hungry she was for Luke's cock. She glanced over her shoulder again. "Fuck me, Luke. Fuck me now."

She looked back at Jake. As much as she wanted Luke to fuck her, she wanted to perform for Jake. Jake smiled and nodded and she arched her back and stiffened her legs, spreading them apart. She knew what an erotic sight she must be presenting to the two men, with her boots on and her legs spread, her skirt at her waist, framing her round bottom and swollen pussy. She wiggled her bottom seductively. She looked at Jake, heated by his approving gaze. "I hope you enjoy this."

"Oh. I will," Jake said. He reached over and put one hand behind her head, tangling his fingers in her hair. Turning her face toward his, he leaned in and kissed her. It was a hard, passionate kiss that sent heat surging through her body.

Luke stood up and grabbed her hips, positioning the large head of his cock at the entrance to her slit. Jake continued the kiss, holding her lips tight against his as his tongue swirled in her mouth, probing deep, searching each wet crevice. When he finally ended the kiss, leaving her breathless, she was fully impaled on Luke's cock. "My God, you are hot," Luke groaned, his hands holding her waist, his cock deep in her core. "I've never known a woman so eager to fuck."

Once again, she was stretched by the thick shaft, her pussy completely filled with cock. "God your pussy is sweet," Luke muttered. "It's so fucking tight." Then he was fucking her, his cock stretching her wide, his length going deep, filling her until she moaned in pleasure.

He fucked her slowly at first, letting her feel every inch of his thick shaft as he slid in and out of her pussy. She tried to hold still, tried to savor the feeling of his cock filling her completely. But the sensation of Luke's balls slapping against her clit as he shoved himself deep was too intense. Having Jake standing next to her made it even more erotic. She couldn't hold still. She had to fuck back, had to pump her ass up and down, had to squeeze her pussy tight around his cock as he plunged in and out.

As he fucked her faster, deeper, harder, she felt herself slipping closer and closer to the fire of an orgasm. Luke was growling in raspy breaths, panting hoarsely each time he shoved his cock into her. Suddenly, his grip tightened on her hips and she knew he was close as well. Reaching down between her legs, she raised the front of her skirt to caress her clit. She momentarily caressed Luke's thick shaft filling her pussy, and then she rubbed the swollen bud of her clit, urging herself toward her climax. Then Jake was there, his hand under her skirt, pushing her fingers away. She caught her breath as he found her clit, then moaned as her climax began to build.

Amanda heard Luke groan and mutter, "Ahhh, God, yes! Fuck me, Amanda. Give me your hot pussy." She pressed backward, bucking her ass up and down. The head of his long thick cock stroked her G-spot, and the sensation, coupled with Jake's fingers on her clit, intensified second by second until she was tearing toward orgasm. Luke's grip tightened even more. He let out a loud guttural groan and she felt his cock jerking as he climaxed. Her pussy was so tight around his cock she could feel every twitch and spasm as he ejaculated into the condom.

Luke's climax and Jake's fingers flying over her clit sent her over the edge. She closed her eyes and wailed in ecstasy. "Oh, oh God! I'm coming!" Her orgasm swept through her in a rush of pure bliss, spreading from her clit and her cock-filled pussy to every nerve ending in her body. At the peak of her orgasm, her knees buckled and she grabbed Jake's arm, holding herself up with his hand still in place on her throbbing pussy. Finally, the intense pleasure faded and she sighed, opening her lust-glazed eyes to look at Jake, then over her shoulder at Luke. Luke stared at her, dazed, staggering as he stepped back, his cock sliding out of her pussy.

She almost felt embarrassed by her wanton behavior, at how eagerly she had begged for Luke to fuck her. She turned toward the wall, away from Jake, almost timidly pulling the elastic bodice of her dress back up over her breasts. As she smoothed down the skirt, she wondered just what Jake thought of her. Was she the biggest slut in Texas? Or was she simply a sensuous woman trying to overcome her inhibitions and discover her sexual self? A journey that Jake had offered to help her with.

She turned back toward him, a shy smile on her face. "So did you enjoy..."

Jake was gone.

A minute ago, he was not ten feet away. Now, he was nowhere to be seen. She looked at Luke, who simply shrugged his shoulders.

"Well fuck." She said, pushing past Luke as she walked to the door of the barn. "What the hell was that all about?" She saw Jake fifty yards away, walking toward the corral. She turned toward Luke, her eyes flashing anger. "Did you and Jake plan this fuck-fest, or did it just happen?

Luke lifted his hands up, palms toward her. "It just happened, Amanda. I didn't know Jake was anywhere around."

She glared at him, not quite sure she believed him. After a moment, she turned and stalked toward the door.

"Don't worry," Luke said. "Jake will be okay."

"Then why did he walk out like that?" She hurried out of the barn, holding her hat to keep it from flying off.

Jake was at the stable paddock unhitching Ginger from the fence rail. The horse was already saddled, ready to ride. He swung up into the saddle and turned the horse, spurring the filly into a trot before Amanda got halfway there.

"Damn," she muttered. "Damn, damn, damn." She was standing with her hands on her hips, watching Jake ride away when Luke walked up. He held out her thong. She jerked it out of his hand, turned, and stormed away. Two cowboys working with horses in the paddock stared at the scene, their expressions brightened by wide grins.

"Wait!" Luke ran to catch up with her. "Where are you going?"

"I need to take a walk. Alone." She turned past the stables and headed down toward the creek she and Justin had crossed on their ride the day before. Crossing the wooden bridge, she started up the rise on the opposite side.

"Wait." Luke had to hustle to keep up with her. "Let me go with you."

"No!" she sped up. "I want to go by myself."

Luke stopped, as she walked on. "Well don't go far. It's going to storm again."

She glanced up. The sky was clouding up, turning darker. Just like her mood. Still, rain didn't look imminent.

"And watch out for rattlers!"

The last warning almost stopped her but she kept walking, her strides long and purposeful.

Fuck the snakes, she thought. I'll stomp on them with my fucking new boots!

She took long, hard strides, trying to work out the frustration she felt at Jake's sudden defection from what should have been a very fulfilling experience, one he had helped create. Had Jake and Luke planned the tryst in the barn? *Damn Luke,* she thought, then instantly rescinded the curse. It wasn't his fault. After all, she'd spent half the night enjoying his sexual favors. Favors that Jake had arranged for her. But it was her fault for being so goddamned horny.

Well, she thought, *that's Jake's goddamn fault, too.* He's the one who helped her shed her inhibitions. Now it seemed there was nothing she wasn't willing to do. But what she really wanted was to spend another night with Jake.

Why, she asked herself, was that so important? Despite the spoken—and unspoken—agreement with all three men that the sex was only sex, there had been something more developing between her and Jake. Was that why he had walked away so quickly? Because he was also feeling that pull?

Amanda kicked at a prickly pear cactus with the toe of her boot, sending one of the spiny pads flying. Her involvement with the three cowboys at the Morgan ranch was becoming just about as thorny and complicated as a patch of cactus. And it pissed her off that she couldn't control her erotic desires or her emotions long enough to keep from getting tangled up in ways she wanted to avoid. Especially now that she suspected the painting was not a Randell but simply an excellent forgery.

On the other hand, if the painting was a fake, there was no ethical or professional reason for her to back away from exploring her sexual boundaries.

Who was she hurting? Certainly not Luke or Justin. Jake maybe? If so, he certainly didn't seem willing to share his thoughts. And if there was jealousy on his part, it was an emotion he had no right to feel. And it was damned unfair of him to stir up feelings she didn't want to deal with.

Chapter Twelve

Amanda continued walking briskly through the fields of grass and wildflowers, letting the exercise and beauty of the landscape calm her. She took the path she and Justin had ridden on Cricket, across a swath of Indian paintbrush and through thick stands of red cedar.

She had expected to come out on the hilltop in the clearing, but after several minutes of walking through the trees, she realized she must've taken a wrong turn somewhere. On the ride out, her attention had been focused more on Justin than on the trail, and now she was not sure which direction to go. Backtracking, she tried to find her way out of the grove of cedars. Finally, the trees began to thin out and she found herself in a clearing. But it definitely was not the clearing she and Justin had been in the day before. She kept walking, skirting the thick, bushy trees, not wanting to go back into the confusing growth. She saw a building in the distance, perhaps a half a mile away. It looked like a log cabin of some kind, but it was too far away to tell.

A sudden boom of thunder made Amanda look up. The sky was much darker now, with rain clouds lowering and streaks of lightning flashing in the distance.

"Damn," she muttered, remembering how quickly the storm had built up on her arrival. *Damn and double damn.* What if it hailed? She'd get knocked senseless out here in the open. She continued around the edge of the stand of cedars, keeping the clearing in sight. There was another crack of lightning and boom of thunder, closer now. She didn't want to get struck by lightning up here on this hilltop either. *Fuck,* she thought again, not in total despair but damn worried. She couldn't be that far from the ranch. Someone would surely come find her.

The rain hit just as she skirted another cluster of cedar trees and came to a wide cattle guard protecting the opening in a barbed wire fence. She wasn't sure if she and Justin had ridden across a cattle guard.

The rain was not a downpour. Yet. Just a smattering of drops, big ones, and cold. But if she didn't find her way back soon, she would soon be soaked to the skin. Her thin cotton dress offered no protection at all, and she didn't even have underwear on. Amanda stopped and looked at her hand. She was still clutching the tiny white cotton thong she had jerked out of Luke's hand. Lifting her skirt, she quickly stepped into the panties, then looked around wondering just what she should do.

The fence stretched in each direction for what looked like miles. Maybe, she thought, I should just follow the fence line. It's bound to lead somewhere. Maybe it runs to the entrance road of the ranch. The only other options were to head off across the hills or go back into the growth of cedar trees. Given how dark it had become in the thicket of trees, Amanda ruled that out completely. *I'll follow the fence,* she thought, leaping over the two dozen links of round pipe that formed the cattle guard. But which way?

Picking a direction at random, she started walking. She had walked less than a hundred yards when she topped a gentle rise and saw a cluster of buildings in the distance. She studied the buildings carefully, her heart leaping when she realized it was the lodge and barns and stables of the ranch.

"Thank God," she said, delighted that she wasn't completely lost. She was, however, a hell of a lot farther from the ranch than she should be. *Jesus. How did I get so far away?*

As if to dampen her elation, the sprinkles of rain came quicker, the drops bigger and colder. *Doesn't matter, at least I know where I am.*

The lightning and thunder had been sporadic, but now was growing in intensity. The sky was darker also, spreading a gray pall over the colorful fields of wildflowers. Still, she could at least get back to the ranch, even if she did end up looking like a soggy rat. And if she ever wanted to take another walk on the Texas prairie, she damn sure wouldn't do it alone.

Amanda had just topped another small hill, when she realized she wasn't alone. A dozen cattle, the same brown-bodied white-faced beasts she'd honked at, were grazing in a shallow valley off to her right. She was unconcerned about the cattle until she saw the large one halfway up the hill she was standing on. This one, she realized, was not a cow but a bull. His huge testicles were hanging low enough to touch the top of the grass the cattle were grazing on.

The bull didn't have horns, but if the fearsome thing decided to just bump her, it could probably break her back. Or worse. As if reading her thoughts, the bull turned her way and lifted his head, sniffing the air. She wasn't sure how far away the animal was, but she could see his nostrils flare, could see the slobber dripping from his mouth.

Fuck! That son of a bitch is huge. "Double fuck," she muttered when the bull turned and walked toward her. This was not good.

Amanda turned and looked at the fence. The cattle guard was too far back. Her only hope, if the damn thing decided to charge, would be to hop over the barbed wire fence. And it looked like coming after her was just what the bull was going to do. The animal had lowered its head, still looking at her, as it pawed the ground with one hoof.

She backed slowly toward the fence, keeping her eyes on the bull. It was coming, not running but moving faster. She turned away from the bull with the fence just feet away. For a moment, she considered grabbing a fence post and swinging both legs over. But the top strand was too high. She would never make it. Her only chance was to climb. By the time she had her hands on a fence post, she could feel the ground tremble under the bull's pounding hooves.

Lightning cracked and hit a tall cedar a hundred yards away, splitting it like kindling. Thunder exploded across the plain, rumbling away in all directions. The splattering sprinkles of fat raindrops suddenly came faster, building toward a drenching rain. Amanda grabbed a wooden post with both hands, lifting her right boot to step on the middle strand of wire. The slick sole of her boot hit the wire and slid sideways, finally catching on a sharp barb. *Oh God,* she thought. *There's no way I'm going to make it.* As she attempted to swing over the top strand, the high boot heel locked onto the middle wire.

"Damn!" A barb on the top strand sliced through her dress and stabbed the inside of her left thigh. She held tight to the post, trying to lift her leg up as the barb pushed deeper and another punctured her right thigh.

She screamed in pain, unable to move without the barbs stabbing deeper. She knew the bull was close, running at her with its head down. A thousand pounds of terror in full charge. She felt a sudden rush from behind—more hooves pounding, a loud yell. She glanced over her shoulder to see Jake on

Ginger, cutting the bull off ten yards from the fence. A quick leap and the mare avoided the bull's charge, turning the animal just enough that it crashed into the fence post next to her. The entire section of fence tilted over, leaving her hanging at an angle. Screaming as the barbs dug in deeper, her face ran with rain and tears.

In seconds, Jake tossed the loop of his lariat around the bull's neck and had the other end of the rope tied off on the saddle horn. The strong Quarter Horse immediately backed up, pulling the animal away from the fence. Leaving Ginger to restrain the bull, he leapt from the saddle and rushed to Amanda. She was crying now, as much in relief as from the pain of the barbs in her thighs.

"It's okay," he said. "You'll be okay. Hold on just a minute." Stepping between the wires of the slanted fence, he grabbed her waist and lifted, letting her lift one leg off the stabbing barb. Still sobbing, Amanda managed to work her inner thigh free of the second barb. As Jake led her away from the fence, her legs gave way and she collapsed in his arms.

"It's okay, Amanda." He slipped his arms under her knees and back to cradle her against his chest. He held her for several minutes, letting her cry, her face buried against his shoulder. They were both soaked from the downpour.

Finally, her sobs eased to a soft cry. Jake carried her to Ginger, who was still tied to the bull. The bull, head down and legs stiff, was trying to back away from the horse.

Jake swung Amanda up onto Ginger, causing her to cry out as her inner thighs came down hard on the horse's back. "Ouch!" She cried. "That really hurts."

"Sorry. We need to get you out of the rain. I should've brought my slicker." He looked up at the clouds, now turning an eerie electric green. "It looks like it's gonna hail. Might even blow up a twister."

Looking up at the sky, she watched the ominous thunderstorm build higher and higher. She didn't care what happened. Jake was here, and she felt safe.

Amanda had lost her hat when the bull crashed into the fence and Jake picked it up and handed it to her. He remounted and flicked his lariat off the bull's neck then untied it from the saddle horn. The bull leapt sideways and ambled off, heading down the hill toward his herd.

As he settled into the saddle, small pellets of hail began to fall. "Damn," he muttered, glancing over his shoulder. "We'll never make it back to the lodge without getting beaten all to hell."

Amanda had scooted forward again, whimpering as her wounded thighs pressed against Ginger's back. "Should we go up into the trees?"

"No. I know where we can go. Hang on." As he turned and spurred the horse, she held on tightly, locking her hands around his waist.

Jake spurred Ginger into an all-out run. Amanda had never been so scared or excited at the same time. Her head rested against Jake's shoulder with the brim of her hat tucked just under his. Surprisingly, with the horse running flat out, her butt didn't bounce and the pressure on her injured thighs was bearable.

Jake guided the horse away from the ranch, cutting across the cattle guard in a leap and then turning down the hill toward the lone building Amanda had seen earlier. The rain had almost stopped, but the hail was coming hard now, the balls of ice growing in size. By the time they reached the cabin, they had both been bruised several times by hailstones. Jake guided Ginger under a lean-to and dismounted to help Amanda down. The cabin door was padlocked, but he quickly pried it open with a rusted metal rod he'd found lying near the lean-to.

Inside, the cabin was dark and musty. Two small windows on either side of the front door were boarded up with solid wooden shutters. Jake swung the shutters open, letting some light and fresh air into the cabin. Rain and hail slashed against the dirty glass windowpane so hard Amanda thought it might break.

The cabin was a single room with a black pot-bellied stove centered on the back wall. Sets of bunk beds sat against two walls. Jake hung both their hats on a rack of antlers on the wall by the door. He took an old-fashioned kerosene lamp down from a shelf, along with a can of matches. He pumped the plunger to get oil to the wick and lit the lamp. The soft golden glow quickly lit up the small room. A small table with two rickety wooden chairs filled the middle of the cabin. Amanda pulled out a chair and sat down. Lifting her ripped dress, she examined the punctures on the inside of each thigh.

Jake moved the lamp closer, giving her more light. The punctures were deep and bled out large spots of crimson on her dress, but had scabbed over quickly.

"Still hurt?" He looked at the bloody holes just inches from her thong-covered crotch.

"Like a son of a bitch. They don't look like much, but they hurt like hell." She looked up at Jake, who was still holding the lamp. "Thank you for rescuing me. That was close. Too close."

"You're welcome," he said softly. "Maurice, our bull, can get a little protective of his ladies."

"Like a lot of males," she said. She sat with her arms around her knees, shivering roughly.

"You're soaked," Jake said. "Let me get a fire started. Maybe find a first aid kit, too, but I doubt it."

He set the lamp on the table and tossed sticks of

kindling in the door of the stove. Amanda looked around while he got the fire started. The bunk beds were covered with heavy woven Indian blankets and striped ticking pillows. One wall sported several shelves of tin plates and cups and half a dozen hand-thrown clay pots in various shapes and sizes. The clay pots were simple but elegant designs that seemed familiar but she couldn't quite place. Old wooden chests sat at the end of each bunk bed.

"We only use this place occasionally." Jake turned up the lamp. "During spring roundup, one or two of the extra hands we hire will stay up here. This was the first home Great Granddaddy Odel built on the place. Not much, but it beats living in a tent."

"Or being out in a hailstorm," she quipped, still shivering.

The fire in the stove was blazing and Jake left the hinged grate open, releasing more heat into the room. As Amanda pulled her chair up close to the stove, Jake rummaged around in the chests, looking for a first aid kit.

"Eureka!" he finally said, holding up a bottle of iodine.

From the look of the label, the antiseptic could have easily been fifty or sixty years old. He shook the bottle then twisted with all his might to unscrew the cap. Finally, it came loose. She stared at the ancient bottle uncertainly, but lifted her dress and spread her thighs as he knelt down in front of her.

"We'll tend to these properly when we get back to the lodge, but I'm afraid this is the best we can do right now."

"Ouch!" She cried as he daubed the reddish orange antiseptic on her wounds. "That stings."

"That's good. Maybe it's not too old to work."

He daubed the puncture holes a second time. She winced but didn't complain. When he finished, she edged her chair closer to the stove. Anything to break the bone-deep chill.

"You're soaked to the bone, Amanda. You need to get out of that wet dress. You can wrap up in a blanket."

She studied his expression. He glanced down at her breasts. The wet dress was plastered to the full round globes and her large nipples were easily visible beneath the thin cotton. Jake glanced back up to her face, a hint of a smile on his lips. He pulled a blanket off one of the bunk beds and held it up, arms outstretched.

She stood and quickly stripped out of the wet dress and thong, carefully pulling the garment over her thighs. Naked now, except for her boots, she backed up toward him. When he wrapped the blanket around her shoulders, he held her for a moment, then let go. Clutching the blanket close, she sat down again in the chair next to the stove.

He knelt down next to her, reaching for her boots. "Let me take these off," he said. "They're soaked, too."

She lifted her legs one at a time, letting him take her boots and socks off. When he was finished, she tucked her feet back under the blanket. Amanda was already warming up from the thick blanket and the waves of heat coming off the stove.

Jake still knelt beside her, not saying anything, just studying her face. She met his gaze. They were quiet for a moment, then she said, "Jake. About Luke, in the barn...did you plan..."

He gave her a slight smile. "No. I just happened by at an opportune moment. I probably should have left the two of you alone, but you just looked so damned hot and sexy..."

"Then you weren't upset? Or..."

He reached out and put a finger gently against her lips, stopping her in mid-sentence. "Jealous? No.

I don't have my brand on you."

She looked at him for a long moment. "Then you aren't...angry or anything? At me? Or at Luke?" *Do I want him to be? Maybe I do. Maybe that's why I got so mad when he walked away.*

He smiled. "No. You and Luke are both adults. Both free to do whatever you want with whoever you want. I think from what you've already seen and experienced, you know we have a pretty liberal attitude about sex around here. We all feel that it's something to be enjoyed."

She blushed, the heat blending in with the rosy glow from the pot-bellied stove. "Is that why you walked away? Because I was enjoying fucking Luke so much?"

"Partly, I guess. We had already agreed you would spend the night with me. I thought you might want some time with just Luke." He smiled. "You definitely looked like you were enjoying yourself.

"But you being there was what made it so hot. And when you started rubbing my clit...I swear I saw fireworks."

Jake grinned. "I must say, I do love watching you orgasm."

She blushed again. "You must think I'm very easy. Ready to spread my legs and tilt my ass up for anybody, anytime."

"What I think is that you are a beautiful, sensual woman, waking up to certain erotic pleasures. I'm glad to be a part of that. I don't want you to feel guilty about anything you do on this ranch."

She studied his face for a moment. Nothing in his expression said that he was being disingenuous.

"Does that mean you still want to spend the night with me?" Amanda smiled at him, watched his smile grow into a broad grin, his eyes twinkling.

"Absolutely. If you haven't changed your mind."

She grinned and hugged the thick wool blanket close. "It's still a date as far as I'm concerned. But in the meantime, you really should get out of those clothes. You're as wet as I was, and the storm doesn't seem to be dying down."

Jake looked down. His leather vest and chaps had offered some protection from the rain and hail, but his jeans and flannel shirt were soaked.

The storm outside was increasing in strength, rattling the shutters and whistling around the eaves of the cabin.

"I think we're going to be here for a while," he said. "Maybe I should get dry."

Amanda smiled. "Yes. I think you should."

Chapter Thirteen

Jake took off his spurs and laid them on the table. As he undressed, taking off his boots and vest and unbuckling his chaps, Amanda picked up the spurs to examine them. The spurs had large wheels, maybe two inches in diameter, each with a dozen sharp spikes. They looked to be solid silver, intricately hand-carved with delicate roses and intertwined vines. The leather strap that wrapped over a boot was hand-tooled with the same floral design as the metal part.

"These are beautiful," she said. "For something that looks so dangerous. Do you actually poke Ginger in the sides with these?"

He grinned. "Not hard enough to hurt her. This style is Mexican. They're a lot bigger than American-style spurs. My granddad wore these eighty years ago. They mean a lot to me." He unknotted his bandanna and took it off, then dropped his chaps to the floor and sat down on one of the chairs to slip off his socks. Jake rose again to unhook the silver oval buckle of his belt.

She grinned. "Finally getting to the good part. Took you long enough."

He returned the grin. "I don't usually strip without music." He unbuckled his belt then unbuttoned his jeans.

"Da-dah-dah-dum, da-dah-dah-dum..." She hummed the classic stripper's tune, watching him shove his jeans down over his hips and legs. His soaked underwear did nothing to hide the thick shape of his cock. She was pleased to see he was hard and erect.

He took off his leather vest, then unsnapped the pearl snaps of his soaked flannel shirt. Once open, he took it off and hung it on the back of a chair, before sliding his underwear over his legs. Finally, he stood naked in front of her. Reaching out, he brushed her hair back and looked into her eyes. "I could get my own blanket." He smiled. "Or we can share this one."

She smiled warmly and held the edges of her blanket wide, revealing her own naked body and inviting him in.

****

God she's beautiful, Jake thought, stepping forward as she wrapped her arms and the blanket around his back. In the soft light from the coal oil lamp and the wood-burning stove, her skin was glowing. He pressed his eager cock against her abdomen. He felt it growing harder, as her nipples pressed like pebbles against his chest. He slid his arms around her back, lifting her to her toes and kissing her hard before finally coming up for air.

"You do know how to take a girl's breath away," she gasped against his mouth.

He grinned. He wanted to rekindle the fiery passion that had consumed her in the barn with Luke, but intended to take his time getting there. He kissed her again, barely touching her with his lips and the tip of his tongue, lingering over her lips before moving slowly up to kiss her cheeks and eyelids. Jake lowered his head and kissed her chin, then under her chin. With a soft moan, she arched her head back, giving him better access to her neck. His kisses became wetter, more urgent as he caressed her back, sliding his hands from her shoulder blades to her waist and down to her ass and back again. Caressing her naked body was an erotic experience that made his erection harden even more.

When his lips reached the smooth hollow where her neck blended in to her shoulder, he gently nipped at her with his teeth. He smiled at her delicate shudder. "God, you are sexy. You have no idea how much you turn me on."

She pressed closer, pushing her belly against his erection. "I may have some idea." She grinned. "I don't know if you've noticed, but this place is full of empty beds. If you are interested in doing something about it."

"Oh, I'm interested. But first, I want to make sure your beautiful breasts and sexy nipples get the attention they deserve." He picked her up by the waist and sat her on the edge of the table.

She was still holding the blanket around his shoulders. He could feel her body heat blending with his, warming them both. He caressed her breasts, cupping and lifting them in his palms, admiring their perfect shape and fullness. Lifting them higher, he leaned down and flicked his tongue over each nipple. He smiled at her sudden sharp intake of breath. It was all he could do to keep from tossing her onto one of the bunk beds and shoving his cock into her. He had no doubt she would respond eagerly, her pussy wet and open for him. But she deserved, and he wanted, more than a quick fuck. Much more. He kissed and licked her breasts, moving his lips and tongue over each full round globe. He lathed the smooth flesh, purposely skirting each nipple and the dark pink areola surrounding it.

"Please," she whimpered softly, clutching the blanket as she arched her chest to him.

"Please? Tell me what you want, baby."

"Kiss my nipples. Please."

"Like this?" He leaned down and circled the tip of his tongue around one nipple, wetting the areola, causing it to shrink and pucker as her nipple grew and hardened. He sucked the firm tip into his mouth, then gripped it between his lips, pressing hard.

"Ohmygod" She dropped the blanket and clutched the back of his head, pulling him tightly against her breast. He felt her shudder and gasp her pleasure. As she moaned, he moved to the other nipple, circling it with the tip of his tongue then squeezing it tightly between his lips.

"Ohh! Oh my God!" She arched her back toward him, but quickly pulled away as if unable to bear the pleasure. As her body quivered, Amanda looked at him with a bit of awe, her eyes wide. "My God," she said breathlessly. "You almost made me orgasm!"

He chuckled. "Sugar, I intend to make you come many, many times." He had committed to helping this woman explore her erotic boundaries, and he intended to introduce her to as much sexual pleasure as he possibly could. He wrapped her in the blanket and carried her toward the bunk beds. "Top or bottom?"

"Whichever one you're in. Otherwise, I don't care."

He placed her gently on the bottom bunk, then reached for where his jeans had been tossed carelessly. Retrieving a condom from the pocket, he quickly rolled it over his raging cock. As he crawled in beside her, he pulled the second blanket over them. Snuggling close, he slid a hand down over her breasts, lightly circling his palm over each nipple. "You have really sexy breasts and amazingly sensitive nipples."

"I had no idea how sensitive until I met you."

Jake stroked over the taut muscles of her tummy to the neat triangle of curls above her pussy. He paused and then slid his index finger over her clit and into her creamy folds. Her hips jerked back, but then lifted with need into his hand.

"You're wet," he said.

She looked into his eyes. "I want you."

"I want you, too," he said, shifting to one elbow and looking down at her. "More than you know." *And a lot more than I should,* he thought. Somewhere near the edge of his conscious awareness a voice whispered, "Be careful. This woman isn't some slutty cowgirl out for a Saturday night fuck." He hesitated a long moment, gazing down into her beautiful dark eyes. She returned his gaze, waiting. Finally, he rolled to cover her and settled between her open thighs.

"Ouch!" She whimpered as his hips rubbed her punctured thighs."

"Sorry. I'll try to be careful."

"Just make love to me. I'll worry about being careful."

He took her at her word and pressed his pelvis forward, holding himself up on his elbows as he slid his cock into the wet flesh between her legs. God, she felt good! He loved feeling her body under his, his hands stroking her flesh and his cock pulsing in the tight channel of her pussy. He hadn't felt this way with a woman in a long time. If ever.

****

Amanda winced as his thighs rubbed against her wounds, but she reached down to clasp his buttocks, urging him deeper.

"Oh my, yes!" She felt his cock slip in between her pussy lips. She moaned and clutched at his back as he pressed deeper, moaning louder as he thrust into her. "Oh God! You feel so good."

"Is this what you want? My cock in your hot pussy? Me fucking you?"

"Yes. Please...yes!" Her voice was husky, her throat now as dry as her pussy was wet.

From the moment Jake had first entered her, Amanda had closed her eyes and tilted her head back, enjoying the sheer physical pleasure of their union. Now she opened her eyes to see that Jake was staring at her intently, his eyes just inches from her own. This close, with his pupils enlarged in the shadowy lamplight, his eyes seem to be twin pools of deep water, deeper than she could fathom.

She held his gaze, letting her body register the pleasure he was giving her, trying to use her hands and legs and thrusting hips to give him pleasure in return. Reaching up, she tangled her fingers in the curls of his hair, then slid her hands down over his muscular shoulders to his back and waist. She dragged her nails lightly across his back then lifted her arms, twining her forearms above her head. It was a gesture of complete surrender and she smiled at the flash of sexual hunger in his eyes. Then his body took control, and he was fucking her hard, fast, a runaway stallion unable to stop or be stopped.

"Oh God," he groaned, his hips slamming into her. She sensed his need to climax and the friction of his cock ignited her own orgasm, sending her spinning into a blinding ecstasy.

"You...are...so...beautiful," Jake's gaze was still locked onto her eyes. Then he gave in to his pleasure, tilting his head back and closing his eyes as he erupted in a roaring climax.

Amanda clutched at his back and wrapped her legs around his hips, her body desperate to become one with his. She felt him release and spasm deep in her core and her own climax swept over her, lifting her on wave after wave of rolling pleasure. She moaned, her cries of passion filling the cabin and echoing off the log walls. As her orgasm swept her away in a bliss more intense than any pleasure she had ever known, Amanda felt tears well up in her eyes. This depth of emotion during sex was unexpected and disconcerting.

She wanted to wipe the tears away but Jake had

collapsed, his broad chest resting on her breasts, trapping her arms. Amanda lay quietly, waiting for him to come back into his body. She was still reeling from her orgasm, a climax so intense it had triggered what she could only describe as an out of body experience.

Finally he stirred, lifting himself to his elbows. As he opened his eyes and looked at her, a frown crossed his face. He reached up and gently wiped a tear from her cheek. "Was it that bad?" His concern was sincere.

"No." Her smile sent another cascade of tears down her cheeks. "It was that good. I couldn't tell where my body stopped and yours began. I didn't know it could be like that."

Jake smiled and leaned down to kiss the tears from her cheeks and lashes. "It was pretty incredible. I've never experienced anything quite like it myself. Maybe that's what Jung calls 'the blending of souls.'"

Jesus. The man is cowboy, a rancher, a lawyer, and he reads Jung.

"I'm not sure what it was." She smiled up at him. "But it was damn good."

Jake rolled out of the bunk to discard his condom, then quickly crawled back in to nestle beside her.

They lay still for several minutes as she studied the ruggedly handsome features of his face. Her eyes suddenly brightened. "Oh my. Is that what I think it is?"

Jake was stirring again against her thigh, almost at full erection. "I believe it is ma'am. I don't have much control over it. At least not when I'm laying between the legs of a beautiful, sexy woman."

He lifted his chest, then bent down and took one of her nipples between his lips. The pressure of his mouth sent a surge of electricity from her nipple straight to her pussy. Amanda squeezed her thighs tight around his hips, mindless of her puncture wounds.

****

After several minutes, Jake stopped kissing her nipples and swung his legs out of the bed. "Just a minute," he said. "Don't go anywhere. I want to try something."

She grinned. "As if I'm going anywhere."

A minute later, he was back, a new condom sheathing his dick. "Roll over onto your tummy. I want to see that sweet, tight ass of yours."

She looked at him curiously for a moment, and then he saw awareness dawn in her expression. "Jake...I've never..."

"Don't worry. We'll take it nice and slow. It's an experience you should at least try." If Amanda was ever going to lose her anal virginity, he wanted it to be with him. "Just roll over, baby."

She hesitated a moment more, her look uncertain. Finally she rolled over, arching her bottom to him. "Damn, your ass is fine." He caressed the smooth globes with both hands. "It's perfect."

As he knelt behind her, she looked over her shoulder. "Please...be easy..."

He stroked the cheeks of her ass with his palms, spreading them to reveal the puckered rosebud of her anus. "I'll go slow," he said. "If it's too much, just say so and I'll stop."

She glanced back over her shoulder. "Yes. Okay." She lay with her head sideways on the Indian blanket, her bottom tilted up. Jake wet the tip of a finger with saliva and circled her anus for a moment, then gently pushed inside the tight orifice. He felt her flinch and then relax against his hand. He pushed his finger deeper and this time she moaned softly.

He pulled his finger out and then slid it in

132

again, even deeper. As he slowly stretched her delicate tissues, he used his other hand to stimulate her pussy, teasing her clit with gentle circles of his index finger around the sensitive bud. "How does that feel? Good?"

"It feels...tight. And naughty. Naughty sexy."

"Are you ready for me to fuck your pretty little ass?"

"Yes," she murmured softly, almost self-consciously. "I think so."

"I don't have any lube, but your pussy is wet for me."

He slid the head of his cock between the wet flesh of her labia, coming away coated with her glistening juices. Holding his shaft at the base, he pressed the bulbous head against her rear opening and slowly pushed, stretching the rosette until the plum shaped head slipped inside. She cried out with a squeal of pain-laced pleasure, followed by a low moan. He gazed down at the connection of his hard shaft in her ass, feeling the tight grip of her anal muscles squeezing his cockhead. It was an erotic sight and he had to restrain himself from driving into her with full force.

Amanda lay with her head sideways on the bed, her mouth open and her eyes closed. She was gripping the blanket tightly in both hands, but was not resisting Jake's penetration of her ass hole.

"Push gently against my cock. It will open you up to me." He pushed again, felt her relaxing to his invasion. He drove in deeper, eager for full penetration. Almost half his cock was now in her ass.

"Ohh...God! That feels...incredible!" She was panting in sharp breaths, twisting the edge of the blanket into tight knots.

"Do you like my cock in your ass, Amanda? Does it feel good?"

"Yes! It feels good. Give it to me slow and easy." She shifted her hips, giving him a better angle. Jake was surprised that she not only accepted this new sexual experience, but seemed to be enjoying it. He pushed in deeper, driving the full length of his cock into her. As his cock slid all the way into her ass, her moan turned into a sigh.

He fucked her ass with slow, deliberate strokes, letting her get used to this new sensation. After a moment, he felt her ass moving, fucking back against his thrusting cock. Her moans were coming in short sharp breaths and he could sense she was nearing her climax.

Jake was at the precipice, too. The tunnel of her ass around his cock felt so good, so tight, so erotic. He grabbed her hips and held her bottom tight against his pelvis, letting his climax erupt into her ass with spurt after spurt of liquid heat. As his orgasm swept through him, he reached around and stroked her clit, his fingertips flying rapidly over the swollen, sensitive bud. Suddenly, her hips jerked back and forth, and he knew she was also climaxing. She screamed, trying to muffle her wail with the twisted knot of the blanket.

Finally, her spasms subsided and she relaxed beneath him. His cock slid out easily and he leaned down to look at her. Her face was peaceful, her eyes closed. He blew a lock of dark curls from her neck and ear and then leaned down and kissed her, nuzzling his lips against her earlobe. "That was amazing, Amanda. Did you enjoy it?" He traced a wet trail down to the hollow of her shoulder with the tip of his tongue.

"Yes. Yes, I did." She shuddered at the wet touch of his tongue. "It was much more erotic and less painful than I thought it would be." She opened her eyes halfway and looked back over her shoulder. "Was it good for you, too?"

He grinned. "Sweetheart, it was amazing."

****

Amanda sighed and relaxed against the blanket, enjoying the feel of Jake's weight on top of her and the warmth of the blanket underneath her. As she surrendered to post-coital contentment, a vague memory flirted with the edge of her consciousness. She opened her eyes, trying to recall what it was. Suddenly her eyes focused on the blanket she was laying on. She grabbed a corner of the thick wool and her head jerked up.

"Jake! Where did you get this blanket?"

Jake looked at the corner of the blanket she was holding. The blanket was tightly woven wool with stripes of blue and burgundy on a natural background. In the corner, a small red triangle was woven into a blue stripe.

"Hell, I don't know. It's been here for as long as I can remember. I used to wrap up in it on cold nights when Grandpa and Daddy and some of the hands would sit by the stove and play dominoes. Why?"

"Because..." She had to bite her tongue to keep from saying what she was actually thinking. She would not get his hopes up. Not yet. "Because I think it might be worth something. I saw one similar to it in Taos a year or two ago. Sold at an auction."

"Really? For how much?"

"I'm really not sure. But it was a nice price. We should check this one out." She knew exactly what the winning bid had been. One of her clients had bought the blanket for four hundred and sixteen thousand dollars.

She turned to lie facing him, then leaned forward and kissed him quickly. "Let's get up. I think the storm is dying down. I want to take this blanket to the ranch and photograph it. There's someone I know in Santa Fe I want to send it to."

Jake got out of bed and discarded the condom in

the hot stove. He turned to help Amanda but she was already up, pulling the blanket off the bed. She held it up by one corner, handing him another corner. As they stretched the blanket between them, her pulse quickened. *Christ! This looks exactly like the one in Taos.* PP&C dealt primarily in paintings and sculpture, not artifacts. But a blanket worth almost half a million dollars had caught her attention.

She'd been at the auction to sell three Southwestern School paintings to a Santa Fe client. She'd been afraid his purchase of the blanket might mean he would back off on the paintings. But he hadn't. The man was among the newly rich Chinese industrialists and had bought all three paintings, the blanket, and half a dozen Hopi pots.

Pots! The pots on the shelves behind the stove! She handed her corner of the blanket to Jake. "Hold this just a minute," She said, stepping over to look at the clay pots.

"Maybe I should fold this up." He nodded at the blanket.

"Yes. But be careful."

He chuckled. "Well, I don't think I'm going to break a blanket. What are you looking at now?"

"These pots. They might be valuable, too." The pots on the shelves were nicely designed, elegant with minimal decoration. She had no idea if they were worth anything or not. But she would take one back to the ranch and send a picture of it to Santa Fe as well. She selected the one she thought was the nicest example and turned to Jake. "Okay," she said excitedly. "Let's get dressed and head back."

He grinned and shook his head. "Amanda darlin', it's stopped hailing but it's still raining like hell out there. We can't go back yet."

She looked at him for a minute then smiled broadly. How had she not noticed? The wind and rain were still raging, rattling the shutters and howling over the cabin roof. He had laid the folded blanket on a top bunk and was standing facing her, his legs apart and hands on hips. She looked at his grinning face then down to his cock. It was impressive even soft and resting against his thigh.

"Well, we're still naked," she said, putting the pot back on the shelf. "Maybe we can find something to do until the storm does die down." She continued to eye his cock, licking her lips with a sensual I-want-to-eat-you swipe across her upper lip.

"Sounds good. But I get to go first." He shoved his spurs off the table, then turned and picked her up by the waist. He sat her on the empty surface with her bottom just at the table's edge, her legs hanging down. When he knelt between her legs, she smiled, then leaned back on her elbows and spread her knees. Jake lifted her legs and rested them on his shoulders as he gently kissed the iodine coated puncture wounds. His tongue traced a wet path higher up, finally reaching the smooth, swollen lips of her pussy. She was already wet from her other orgasms, but he soon had her dripping with arousal.

Over and over he licked up and down her slit, varying the pressure of his tongue, using the tip to slip between the slick folds, then flattening his tongue for an upward swipe. At the apex of each stroke, his tongue and lips played with her clit, circling it wetly or nibbling and sucking it with his lips. In minutes, she was close to orgasm, but he kept her at the edge, not letting her slip over into climax.

After interminable minutes of Jake's tongue and lips teasing her, he slid one finger into the wet folds of her pussy, then another. Shoving his fingers in and out, he sucked and licked her clit vigorously. Now nothing could pull her from the edge, and she cried out with the force of her orgasm. Her fingers clutched his dark curls, holding him tightly against the throbbing flesh between her legs as she bucked her ass up and down, fucking the fingers he had buried inside her sheath.

As the fiery waves of her orgasm subsided, she lifted her head from the table and looked down at Jake. He was smiling mischievously, his lips and chin glistening in the lamplight from her copious juices. With great effort, she uncrossed her ankles, which she had unconsciously locked behind his back.

"Oh my." She sighed contentedly "Was that me screaming and moaning? Or was it the storm?"

He grinned. "I'm not sure. Your thighs were so tight on my ears, I couldn't hear.

Blushing, she said, "Sorry. It's just...Well, it's never been that good for me. Orally, I mean. That was incredible!"

He smiled and stood up, wiping his lips and chin with his bandanna. "Happy to be of service."

She grinned. "Any chance we could have an encore tonight?"

"Amanda darlin.' You can have anything you want tonight." He stood up and stepped back, helping her off the table. As her feet hit the floor, he took her in his arms and looked intently down at her face. "I mean that," he said. "I want you to have everything you want tonight. Or anybody."

She studied his expression, the steadiness of his gaze. She looked at him just as seriously. "The anybody I want is you. Just you. We'll work out the anything and everything later." She reached down and wrapped her hand around his cock. "In the meantime, you're definitely going to need a hand with this."

He grinned. "I'd really like that. But the storm has about passed. We should get back to the lodge. You can suck my cock tonight."

She smiled. That would be something she would

look forward to.

Amanda's attention returned to the Indian pot and blanket. She was eager to send photos to her collector in Santa Fe. In minutes, they were both dressed, their clothes still damp but not terribly uncomfortable.

He closed up the stove, turned off the oil lamp, and closed the cabin shutters. As he brought Ginger around from the lean-to, Amanda carefully rolled the clay pot up in the blanket. She gave him the bundle to hold, while she swung up behind the saddle, then held it tightly in one arm while she held onto him with the other.

In minutes, he had Ginger at a brisk trot headed back toward the lodge. The bouncing hurt but she didn't want to slow down. The storm clouds were drifting off to the east, billowing white now as the late afternoon sun set the wildflower-covered prairie alight with millions of sparkling rain-drop diamonds.

Chapter Fourteen

They had just crossed the cattle guard and started down the slope to the creek when Amanda yelled, "Oh God, Jake! Look."

A puff of black smoke wafted from the front porch where Amanda had been working with the painting.

The second he saw the smoke, he jammed his spurs into Ginger's flanks, surprising the mare into an all-out run. They leapt the creek and were at the lodge in minutes, Ginger kicking up clouds of dirt and mud as he reined her to a skidding halt. The painting was propped up on the windowsill and engulfed in flames.

Jake swung his right leg over the saddle horn and slid off, yelling at Amanda to give him the blanket.

"No!" She refused, holding the blanket tight against her body.

He turned toward the porch. The painting was already half destroyed, only a portion at the bottom not yet burned. Rosita suddenly ran out through the screen door with a fire extinguisher. Jake took the steps two at a time and jerked the extinguisher from her hands. Turning it toward the painting, he doused the flames in seconds.

"How did this happen?" he demanded angrily.

"I don't know, *Senor* Jake. I was in the garden. I smell smoke and come to look. I don't see no one or nothing. Just the painting on fire. So I go to get the *extinguidor de incenddios.*

Jake turned to see that Amanda had managed

to slide off Ginger without dropping the blanket and pot. Still clutching them to her chest, she walked up the steps to stand beside them.

"Oh God, I'm so sorry..." She reached out to touch his arm but he jerked away.

He turned toward her, his face livid with anger. "Goddammit, Amanda! Why did you leave the painting outside and just walk off? A fucking multimillion dollar painting up in smoke!"

"Jake. I didn't leave it outside! I put it on the mantle before I went to the barn. I swear. You can ask Luke."

He wasn't sure if he believed her or not. "I don't need to ask Luke anything. The damn thing is right where you were looking at it this morning."

"Jake, you've got to believe me. I put it on the mantle and locked the door when I left. It was right next to my phone and laptop." She opened the screen door and stuck her head inside. "Look, Jake. My laptop and phone are still there. Right where I left them."

Rosita was wringing her hands, obviously distraught over his anger. "*Es* true, *Señor* Jake. Look. Someone broke the front door. The lock is broken."

Jake almost turned his anger toward Rosita, but eased up when he saw tears welling up in the housekeeper's face. He looked at the door. *Shit! The lock is broken.* And there was a distinct boot print on the door next to the lock where someone had kicked the door in.

"Rosita, did you see anyone?" As if he didn't know.

"No, *Señor* Jake. I was in the garden. Picking tomatoes for salsa. I didn't see nobody."

"It doesn't matter," he said. "I know who it was, and I should have let Justin kill him earlier. Now I'll have to do it myself." He turned and pushed his way through the door.

Amanda followed him into the lodge. "Wait, Jake. About the painting. I need to tell you..." She set the blanket and pot on a club chair and followed him into his office.

Jake unlocked the gun rack and took out a hunting rifle. As he started back outside, Amanda grabbed his arm. He jerked away.

She stepped in front of him. "Jake, please. About the painting. I've got to tell you..."

"What, Amanda? Our insane cousin just destroyed a million dollar painting and our future. What the fuck can you tell me that will fix that? Get the hell out of my way!" He moved to step around her but she blocked his way again.

"Jake. For God's sake, listen to me!"

He looked down at her and saw the sincerity of her plea.

"The painting is a forgery, Jake. It's a fake."

"What? I don't believe you." But he did. He knew she was telling the truth. "Are you sure? Absolutely sure?"

"I will be as soon as I hear from my office. Let me check my phone messages." Jake watched from the door of his office as she walked quickly into the main room and got her phone from the mantle. She read her text messages on her way back. He could see from her expression that the news was not good.

"How do you know it's a forgery? Yesterday everything looked good."

"Come outside and look at it with me. Maybe I can show you."

The painting, or what was left of it, was still sitting on the windowsill.

"There are two things that made me suspect," she said quietly. "You can see them both in the unburned areas."

Jake looked at her, waiting for her to continue.

"Look at the signature here in the lower left corner. See the nine in the 1889. How the down-stroke curls to the left?"

"Yeah. A lot of people make nines like that. I do myself."

Yes. It is common. But not with Randell. His down-stroke was always straight. Never curved."

"Never?"

"Never," she said with certainty. "Now look at the brand on the cow in the background." She wet her finger and wiped soot off the cow's rump. "What would you say it is?"

He leaned forward and looked closely at the brand. It was small but he could easily make out a capital T attached to the lower half of a circle. "I'd say that was a rocker T. Or maybe an anchor."

"Yes. Unfortunately, there was never a ranch in Montana with a brand like this. Especially not in the Judith Basin where Randell lived and worked."

"Never?"

"Never."

"Maybe he just made it up."

"He never made up a brand. He painted everything exactly from life."

"I guess that's not good is it?"

When she answered, he caught the faint glimmer of a smile. "Does it matter much now anyway?"

"No. I guess it doesn't. But why didn't you tell me about this earlier. We've been together almost all day long."

"It was hard not to tell you. But I didn't want to say anything until I was absolutely sure. I wanted to hear from my office first."

"And your office confirmed your suspicions?"

She held up her phone so he could read the text message. *"srry to say u r right. wrng sig—wrng brand."*

He looked at her, his mind in turmoil. He had worked hard not to get his hopes up, but he had, and now he felt like he had been kicked in the gut by a horse. He and Justin would have to figure out another way to save the ranch. And the prospects of that seemed damn bleak. He glanced up at Amanda, saw the sadness in her eyes, saw she was about to tear up.

He put an arm around her. "Don't cry, Amanda. You'll get me started and cowboys have a rule not to cry in front of anybody but their horse."

She sniffed and grinned up at him. "Do you think your cousin did it? Why would he burn a painting that could have been worth a fortune?"

"Of course Winslow did it. Who else? The man is as crazy as a moon-struck calf. He's capable of anything. He'd rather destroy something than let us have it."

As they walked back inside, he said, "Listen, let me tell Justin about what's happened. And I'd better lock the gun cabinet and hide the key."

****

Jake took what was left of the destroyed painting into his office. "I want to show Justin the wrong signature and brand before we toss the damn thing away." At the door to his office, he turned to her and said, "Amanda, I'm sorry I accused you of leaving the painting out. I was just so damned mad…"

"I know, Jake. It's all right."

"And about tonight. I don't think I'll be very good company. Can I get a rain check?"

"Of course, Jake. I understand." She picked up her computer, the blanket, and the pot and went up to her room. She was thankful the madman hadn't trashed her computer. At least she'd kept Jake from putting out the fire with the blanket. She wasn't certain of its value yet, but she couldn't take a chance on the blanket being damaged or destroyed too. No matter how mad Jake got. If only...God, it had to be what she thought it was. *It had to be!*

She removed the pot and unfolded the blanket on the bed. Standing on a chair at the end of the bed, she took several pictures of the blanket with her camera. Using a towel to handle the pot, she set it on the dresser and took several more pictures, turning the artifact so she could show all sides. Looking in her phone directory, she found Chi Long in Santa Fe and sent him the best of the shots she had taken.

Her text simply read, "*Ni hao*, Chi. Interested? Get back to me by e-mail. I am at the Morgan ranch in West Texas and the phone service is spotty at best. I look forward to hearing from you. Amanda."

She sent the pics, hoping that Chi would be in the States and not in China. Rosita had washed and ironed her clothes so she took a shower and put on clean jeans and a tank top. She could hear the housekeeper ringing the triangle chime on the front porch to announce supper, but she had no appetite. In fact, she was numb. Just a sad emptiness when she thought of Jake and Justin losing their ranch. At that level, she couldn't help being emotionally involved, no matter how professionally distant she remained.

The sun was dipping low in the west and she stepped outside to watch the incredible sunset that seemed to follow every rainstorm. As she walked out onto the balcony, she saw Justin and Julie drive up in the ranch's black pickup truck. Julie walked toward the foal barn carrying a large package and Justin walked into the lodge. A moment later, she heard an unintelligible yell followed by the office door slamming shut. She winced. *I'm glad I'm not there for that conversation.*

As the sun finally set, Amanda went back into her room and checked her e-mail to see if she had a response from Chi Long. There was nothing. She poured herself a large brandy and then sat cross-legged on the bed, staring at the open laptop, willing Long to e-mail, willing the e-mail to be good news.

As she tried to organize the mental scramble in her head, there was a knock on the door. To her surprise it was Julie. She was even more surprised by what the young cowgirl was wearing.

Julie's outfit consisted of a faded hip-hugger denim miniskirt so short it barely covered her crotch. The belt loops held a wide leather belt with a large shiny silver buckle. The buckle was engraved with a beautiful horse head and "Quarter Horse Champion—2006." The waist was so low Amanda figured it would barely cover Julie's pubic hair, if she had any. Which Amanda personally knew she didn't.

Several inches above the mini-skirt, a rhinestone-studded horseshoe on a silver chain dangled from her bellybutton. Her top was a V-neck cotton tee with the bottom cut off just below her breasts. The shirt read, "Save a Horse—Ride a Cowboy." It was obvious Julie's small breasts were not covered by a bra. A pair of fancy red boots and a black cowboy hat completed her outfit, which Amanda could only describe as cowgirl slutty.

"What's up, Julie?" Amanda really hadn't had a chance to get to know Julie, except at the dinner table one night. Seeing her fuck Luke in the breeding barn and then fuck Luke and Justin gave Amanda a sense of intimacy with the young woman, but they hadn't really become acquainted.

Julie smiled. "What's up is you, Mandy. You're going to cowgirl up and join us at the Rusty Buckle. You need a night out. And we need to show you a little Texas hospitality."

"I don't think so, Julie. Who's we anyway?"

"We is me and Luke. Luke is just driving. Once we get there, it's every cowboy and cowgirl for themselves."

"Really, I can't go. I'm waiting for an important e-mail. And I don't have anything to wear. Plus, I need to be here for Jake. In case..."

"Honey, Jake and Justin are locked in their office, and it looks like they will be there for a long time. Everybody on the ranch knows the painting got burned. Right now there's not a damn thing any of us can do about it, so you might as well cowgirl up and get on with life. Nothing gets a girl out of a funk like a margarita and a turn around the dance floor with a two-stepping cowboy. You may as well give up girl, cause I'm taking you to the funnest roadhouse in Texas."

"Seriously, Julie, I don't have anything to wear."

Julie grinned as Amanda stared at her outfit. "Sugar, I've got plenty for you to wear. You're a little taller than me, and you've got bigger tits—which look awesome by the way—but I know we can find something that will reveal your inner...sensuality."

Amanda read "slut" into the word and smiled. Maybe it *would* be good to get away from the ranch for a while. There really wasn't anything she could do to help Jake and Justin. Her whole reason for being here had been destroyed by a maniac. Even if she heard from Chi Long, there was nothing she could do tonight. And Jake had asked for a rain check on their date.

Julie must have seen her wavering and pressed harder. "Come on, girl. You can't really say you've been to Texas until you've two-stepped at the Rusty Buckle. And there are so many damn fine cowboys to dance with. The boys are gonna love teaching a big city girl how to dance Texas style."

What the hell. It'll beat hanging out in this room all alone. With a sigh she gave in. "All right, the Rusty Buckle it is."

Amanda followed Julie to the trailer house

where she lived, parked not far from the foal barn. She had never seen quite so much clutter in such a confined space. Half the mess seemed to be ribbons and trophies for horse shows and pictures of horses. The other half was general mess and dozens of garments, which somehow never made it to a hamper or a hanger.

The first thing Julie did when they got to the trailer was open a pint bottle of whiskey and take a long swig. She handed the bottle to Amanda. "Take a good pull, sugar. They tend to water the drinks a bit."

Seems there's just no winning, Amanda thought, taking a long swig and setting her eyes watering and her throat on fire.

"Here," Julie said. "This is just the thing." She was holding up a chocolate brown suede leather skirt that couldn't have been much more than ten inches from hem to waistband. And the bottom three inches had been cut into a deep fringe.

"I don't think so. That skirt will show off my...everything."

"That's the idea, Mandy. A girl needs to show off enough to get a cowboy's attention, but not enough to get arrested. Now lose those jeans and put this on."

Amanda took off her boots and stripped out of her jeans, giving in to Julie's insistence that she wear the tiny fringed leather skirt.

As Amanda's jeans came down, Julie gave a long wolf whistle. "Darlin', those panties are hot! They are gonna love you at the Buckle!"

Amanda blushed and looked down at her white silk panties with the middle slit laced up with satin ribbon. Of her girlfriends, only Sarah knew about her penchant for buying outrageously sexy underwear. She wasn't sure what Julie meant, but she damn sure didn't plan on showing her panties off at some Texas roadhouse.

"Now we just need the right top. Let's try this." Julie held up a long sleeve western style shirt. "It's a little big for me, so it should fit you just fine."

The shirt had a pointed collar with silver tips on the collar points. The body of the shirt was a dusky rose color with a chocolate brown yolk and cuffs. The yolk and cuffs were cut in a Western-style scallop and double stitched with rose-colored thread.

The shirt was fitted, coming to just below her breasts where it tied in a knot. This left six inches of bare waist and back showing.

A row of pearl snaps closed each cuff, but there were no snaps at all on the front of the shirt. Only the knot was holding the shirt closed.

Amanda looked at herself in Julie's dressing mirror, which was surrounded by horse show ribbons in various colors. "Jesus, Julie. This is awfully revealing."

The shirt was tight and fit Amanda's torso like a latex glove. The open V above the knot showed an inch or more of the white silk cups of her bra and the rounded globes of her breasts.

Amanda pulled the V together a few inches above the knot. "Maybe we should pin it here." She let the V open again. "This just looks pretty risqué."

"Honey, risqué is what the Buckle is all about. You look great. Come on. Luke is waiting for us."

"So Luke is just our driver? Not your date?"

"Not tonight," Julie led the way from the trailer to Luke's truck, which was idling quietly next to the lodge. It had turned dark but the moon was almost full, giving the two women plenty of light to see by.

Before they got to the pickup, Julie said, "I know you saw me and Luke in the barn. And in Justin's room. Luke said he saw you on the balcony watching us. For me, that just made it hotter. Around here, sex is fun. Nobody asks for commitments or makes demands. I suspect you might have had some fun with the boys while I was in El Paso. I hope you did, because Luke is hung like a goddamned stallion." She giggled and then said, "Tonight however, Luke is trying to round up a little redheaded filly from the BigEnuf spread. We are on our own."

The conversation left Amanda feeling both embarrassed and aroused, wondering if there were many cowboys in Texas with cocks as big as Luke's.

They reached the truck and found Luke in the driver's seat waiting patiently. Amanda started to crawl into the small backseat of the crew cab, but stopped at Julie's call. Amanda turned to her in surprise.

"Hey, your hat," Julie said. "Where is it? They won't let you in without a hat on."

"In my room. I'll run get it. I need my purse too. Be back in a minute."

"Don't worry about your purse. Just grab a credit card, some cash, and your phone. Put your money and your credit card in your boot. Your phone, too, if it will fit. Otherwise, give it to me and I'll carry it in my pocket."

Amanda nodded quickly before dashing up the steps. As she entered the lodge's main room, she saw that Jake's office door was closed. She felt guilty for going out with Julie when Jake and Justin had such serious problems to deal with. But Julie was right. There was not a damn thing she could do tonight.

She ran up to her room and grabbed what she needed from her purse. She took her hat from the bedpost, put it on, and checked herself in the mirror. "Damn, Mandy Sloane. For a big city girl, you cowgirl up pretty good." Especially when the look is pure cowgirl tramp. She pulled the hat down an inch in front and ran down the stairs again.

Chapter Fifteen

Amanda had once been to the famous cowboy saloon in New York. In fact, she'd gone only because Chi Long, her client from Santa Fe, wanted to go and Richard insisted she take him. The Rusty Buckle Saloon, however, made that New York bar look tame.

The roadhouse was huge, with at least a couple hundred people in it and room for three or four times that many.

"It doesn't get too crowded on weeknights." Julie leaned close and yelled over the music. "On Saturday night, there will be a four or five hundred in here."

As Luke led the women into the saloon, they passed between a pair of six-foot six bouncers who were as massive as tree trunks. The two cowboys nodded and greeted Luke and Julie by name, but their attention was focused on Amanda.

"Mandy," Julie nodded toward the bouncers. "Meet Skeeter and Billy Bob. If any cowboy gets too friendly, just whistle. One of the boys will show up quick."

Skeeter and Billy Bob tipped their hats and then pushed aside the crowd at the entrance to let Luke and Julie and Amanda into the saloon.

The building was two stories tall and almost completely open. Massive support posts divided the space into four sections, each about the same size. The corner in the back held a dance floor where a five-piece band played a medley of Garth Brooks' songs. Thirty or so dancers were doing the two-step, the cowboys guiding their cowgirls backward in a counterclockwise circle around the dance floor. Amanda was amused to see there was actually chicken wire strung up across the corner to protect the band from flying beer bottles.

In the far right corner sat half a dozen pool tables, all occupied by cowboys shooting or waiting their turn. To their immediate right was a restaurant, with swinging double doors opening onto what was obviously a kitchen. Half the tables and booths were filled and it looked as if every plate had a steak on it.

The area to the immediate left was the most crowded and, as Amanda figured, it was where the liquor was poured. The bar must've been forty feet long with every bar stool filled. All the booths and high tables were also filled, with dozens more cowboys and cowgirls milling around.

Once inside, Julie headed toward the bar. "Come on, Mandy. Let's get something to wash down supper."

The smell of sizzling steaks and the mention of food made Amanda realize she hadn't eaten anything since breakfast, and she was starving. Luke said he had already eaten and was off to grab a longneck and wait for an opening at a pool table.

Julie twisted and nudged her way through the packed crowd around the bar, Amanda following close behind. The rough plank floor of the bar was littered with peanut shells from the bowls that sat on every table.

As they passed through the throng, Julie said over her shoulder, "If you want your ass pinched, just walk through here in an hour or so. And if you really want to get felt up, walk through real slow."

She had worried the cowgirls at the roadhouse would all be fresh faced and hard bodied twenty year olds, but their ages ranged from early twenties to women in their forties and fifties. Her concern that their outfits were too risqué was also misplaced. Almost all the women, younger and older, were wearing sexy outfits of every description—acres of bare skin above the décolletage created by pearl snaps that hadn't been fastened and yards of bare midriffs and bare legs thanks to tiny denim miniskirts and cut-off shorts.

Julie finally reached the bar and got them both margaritas in mugs so big Amanda had to hold hers with both hands. As they made their way out of the packed bar, everyone stared, the men mostly admiringly, the women mostly curious, and a few judgmental. She didn't know if it was because she was a new face or because she was a city girl way out of her element. Either way, it was a bit disconcerting. She didn't like being the center of attention. Unless it was in private, in bed, with a handsome man.

Just as they reached the edge of the bar, Amanda felt a rough hand slip up under the back of her fringed skirt. She let out a squeal and jumped, juggling her margarita and spilling some.

Julie looked over her shoulder and smiled. "I forgot to tell you. The boys are more likely to feel you up if you've got a full drink in your hand. They're less likely to get slapped. But take it as a compliment, sugar."

In the dining room, they found a booth and ordered steaks with onion rings and baked potatoes. Julie tried to get Amanda to order lamb fries, but the New Yorker in her staunchly refused. In her pre-trip research about Texas, she'd learned a great deal about this "delicacy" of calf testicles.

Midway through their meal, a shadow covered the table and Amanda looked up to see a handsome, broad shouldered cowboy leaning over them, resting his hands between their steak plates.

"You two fillies look like you need some

company." The man looked at Julie. "I know you. You're from the Morgan Ranch. But who is this sweet thing here?" He looked at Amanda. The man had a smarmy smile and an attitude she immediately disliked. The cowboy turned and tried to sit down next to her. "Scoot over darlin'. Maybe I can help you cut your meat. Soak up some of those hot juices."

Amanda held her place, not letting him sit down. "No thanks. I'm doing fine on my own."

The man stood back up, a surprised look on his face. "Well listen to you darlin'! You damn sure ain't from Texas, are you?"

"Beat it cowboy," Julie waved her steak knife, shooing him away. "We want to finish our supper."

"Well, when you're done, look me up. Just ask for Buck. Everybody knows me. And I'd love to show Miss Yankee Doodle here how to really do a Texas two-step." The man walked away with a swagger.

"He's a prick," Julie said. "Pay no attention to him. He's a hotshot bull rider who thinks he's God's gift to women. He gets all the pussy he wants from buckle bunnies."

"Buckle bunnies?"

Julie grinned. "Buckle bunnies are rodeo sluts that will go down on whichever cowboy has the biggest prize buckle. But don't worry. There are plenty of nice guys in here, too. Just be sure and check out their back pockets first."

"Their back pockets?"

"Yeah. Look at that cowboy over there. See that round bulge in his back pocket?"

"Yes. I see it."

"Well sugar, he ain't Luke and that's not a package of condoms."

Amanda giggled and looked back at the cowboy.

"That's a can of chewing tobacco. And there's nothing quite as nasty as kissing a man who chews tobacco."

Amanda made a face. "God, I would guess so. I won't even date a man who smokes."

"Sad thing is, more than half the men in here have a can of that crap in their pockets."

Amanda looked around, noticing how many cowboys sported a bulge in the back pocket of their jeans. "It's too bad that those *aren't* condoms. That size would make for a hell of a lot of happy Texas gals." Amanda looked at Julie, giving her a conspiratorial grin. "Luke really is big isn't he?"

"Hung like a horse." Julie returned the grin, sharing a knowing look that only two women who've fucked the same man could share.

They finished their steaks and were making their way to the bar for margarita refills when the band started playing a honkytonk classic. Immediately three of the cowgirl bartenders hopped up on the bar and started dancing, their boots amazingly missing the drinks around their feet. All three of the women had on denim shorts cut off to the crotch, so high in back that at least three inches of each butt cheek showed.

The band was getting louder, the crowd wilder. Julie said she had to pee and suddenly Amanda found herself alone. She edged her way to the dance floor to watch the dancers two-stepping. At some unseen signal, the couples formed a line and began dancing facing each other, the woman on one side and the men on the other. Suddenly, she felt a hand on her bare waist. Startled, she turned to see Buck.

"Come on city girl. Let me show you how we dance in Texas." He had managed to turn her around so they were face-to-face. Keeping one hand on her waist, he reached with the other toward the knot of her shirttail just below her breasts. Using his forefinger, he pulled the knot outward. "You know city girl," he said. "I'm really good at knots. Tying them and untying them. And you've got a great rack. I'd love to lay my gun in a rack like yours."

She was holding her drink in one hand and was ready to draw back and slap him with her other hand. But it was crowded, and she didn't want to hit some innocent bystander by mistake. Instead, she looked up at him and smiled. "Well *darlin'*," she said in the best Texas drawl she could manage. "You probably haven't got a big enough gun to fill my rack." Then she tipped her almost full icy margarita down the front of the man's jeans.

Buck's eyes widened as the cold drink covered his crotch and inner thighs. He stepped back away from her, his eyes wide. Then they narrowed in anger. "You fucking Yankee bitch! I should whip your ass!"

"You'd have to get by me first." Julie said. She must have seen Amanda tilt her drink down the front of Buck's pants. "And if we get into a brawl, which might be fine, you can bet your bull-riding ass that I've got more friends in here than you do. So why don't you go home and change? You look like you peed yourself."

Skeeter suddenly appeared, towering over Buck and the two women. "Any trouble here?"

"Nope." Julie looked hard at Buck. "We're good."

Buck gave both women one last angry look that promised revenge then turned and walked away.

"Well done, Mandy. For a city girl, you take care of yourself pretty well."

Amanda smiled. "There are jerks everywhere. So I've had a little practice. Come on, let's get me another drink."

They switched from margaritas to shots of tequila and, half an hour later, neither woman was feeling any pain. For Amanda, the mild numbness from the tequila was a welcome relief from the events of the day.

"Come on, Mandy." Julie tugged Amanda toward the dance floor. "You can't leave Texas without learning to two-step." They stood watching the circling dancers for a few minutes. Then Julie nodded toward a tall cowboy in a white hat. "There's our guy. He's the best dancer on the floor." When the song ended, Julie walked up and spoke to the cowboy she'd picked out.

"Hey cowboy, my friend here is from New York City and she wants to learn to scoot her boots. Could you give her a quick lesson?"

The cowboy looked from Julie to Amanda, his face lighting up with a smile that said he would be happy to give her a lot more than a dance lesson.

"Sure. Happy to oblige."

The band started playing a Willie Nelson song and the cowboy swept Amanda out onto the dance floor with a smooth, gliding step. It took a minute or two, but the step was a simple quick-quick, slow-slow beat and she had it mastered in no time.

Amanda had also quickly picked up switching from the straight backward two-step into the promenade, where she turned and danced in the same direction as her partner. With a smooth dance partner and just enough tequila to loosen her up, she was having a great time. For the next five or six songs, she was on the dance floor continuously, dancing with different cowboys who cut in on each other. Julie was dancing as well, switching partners just as quickly.

When the band finally took a break, Amanda found Julie. "This is fun," she said. "But I need to get some air."

"And I need to pee again. I'll meet you by the front door in ten minutes."

The parking lot was packed with vehicles, ninety percent of them pickup trucks. Amanda walked between two rows of trucks taking several deep breaths. In a few minutes, she was feeling better. She had just turned to walk back to the saloon when the hair on the back of her neck stood up and a chill ran down her spine.

"City girl, I think it's time you learn about southern hospitality." Buck was leaning against the back of an older model pickup, chewing on a toothpick. His hat was slanted down to his eyebrows and his arms were casually crossed over his chest.

She turned away and quickly walked between two trucks into another lane. Buck was quicker and in seconds he grabbed her, slamming one hand hard over her mouth to silence her scream. She bit down hard and tasted blood, but she wasn't sure if it was from her split lip or his bitten hand. She glanced around, hoping for help, but quickly realized she was on her own. Flailing at him with both hands, she tried to hit his face with her fists, but couldn't connect. Opening her fingers, she clawed at him with her fingernails and managed to rake a bloody set of furrows down one cheek.

"You bitch!" Buck growled quietly, slapping the side of her head with his free hand. The blow shot crackles of electricity across her field of vision and she was suddenly too dazed to fight back or even stand up.

Keeping one hand on her mouth, Buck put his other hand behind her neck, literally lifting her off the ground. Swinging her around, he set her on the lowered tailgate of a nearby truck. The pain in her neck and jaw was excruciating. Amanda tried to cry out, but Buck kept his hand tight over her mouth, barely letting her breathe. Pulling her to the edge of the tailgate, he twisted her body until she was bent at the waist over the metal. Shoving one knee between her legs, he pressed her down, pinning her to the bed of the pickup, her legs dangling on each side of his knee.

"Stop wiggling, you little cunt! Wait'll I get my dick in you. Then you can shake your ass all you want."

Buck kept one hand tight over her mouth, while the other reached up under her skirt to grab the waistband of her panties. With a jerk, he ripped the thin silk band in two. The panty split on one side and dropped down her leg to rest on top of her boot.

She was filled with revulsion and fear but she was furious, too. She might not be strong enough to keep Buck from raping her but she was goddamn sure going to try. He let go of her neck and she felt him struggling, trying to get his cock out of his jeans. She grabbed with both hands and pulled his fingers away from her mouth enough to bite him again. He yelled a curse and slapped her on the side of her head again, and this time she knew it was his blood she tasted.

The blows had staggered her, making her dizzy, but she still fought back, flailing with her arms behind her trying to land a blow. Finally she did connect and Buck grunted in pain. "You fucking cunt. Maybe I should wring your neck after I fuck you. He reached forward and grabbed a handful of her thick curls, jerking her head back, stretching her neck as he leaned forward. "You ready, city girl? You ready for a Buck fuck?"

His bloody hand squeezed tighter over her mouth, so tight she worried he might break her jaw. The pain was so intense, she began to cry and soon she could barely breathe, could do nothing more than scream against his flesh. But then it was Buck who screamed, the earsplitting cry of agony of a man who'd been kicked hard in his nuts.

She gasped as Buck let go of her mouth and sucked air as deeply into her lungs as she could, then expelled it in a scream. Free of Buck's clutches, Amanda stumbled away from the bed of the pickup and turned to run, another hysterical scream on her lips. Behind her she heard the sickening sounds of fist against flesh, the crunch and crack of dislocated and broken bones.

She turned, catching her breath, her scream fading to a gasp as she watched blood splatters sparkle in the parking lot lights, spraying from Buck's broken nose and from his mouth highlighting three missing teeth. One eye was already swollen shut and the other had a wild, fearful look.

Amanda expected to see Luke or maybe one of the roadhouse bouncers. But it was Jake. Jake standing with his fists clenched, legs apart, ready to kill the man who was now down on his knees, swaying back and forth, barely upright.

"Oh God, Jake!" She whispered. He glanced at her, and then looked back at Buck, at the bloodied face and the dislocated bones. The man's penis, still hanging out of his fly, was now soft and small. She looked at Jake, suddenly realizing what he intended to do. Before he could follow through, Skeeter grabbed his shoulder and turned him around just in time to save the badly beaten Buck from losing his manhood.

"That's enough Jake." Skeeter held tightly to Jake's shoulder.

"I'll kill him if he tries anything like that again."

"Just take care of the lady. I'll take care of this bastard." Skeeter picked the barely conscious Buck up by his belt and the seat of his pants and tossed him in the bed of a pickup, then dialed his cell. He turned to Amanda. "A County Sheriff's deputy will be here in a few minutes," Skeeter said. "If you want to give me your statement, I can arrest him for assault and attempted rape. The deputy can haul his sorry ass to the hospital and on to jail after they patch him up."

"*You* can arrest him?" Amanda thought maybe

the blow had rattled her brains.

Skeeter smiled. "I'm a Texas Ranger. This is just a side job for extra cash. I arrested Buck three months ago for assaulting a girl over in Travis County. I know he's on probation. This time, I'm sure he'll end up in jail."

Jake stood next to Amanda while she told Skeeter what happened. When she finished, Skeeter asked Jake if he had anything to add.

"Only that the next time I see the son of a bitch, there won't be a Texas Ranger to keep me from kicking his nuts up his asshole."

"I won't word it quite that way," Skeeter said with a grin, slipping his notebook back into his pocket.

Jake turned to Amanda. "Are you sure you're okay? Did the bastard hurt you?"

She blinked back the tears she felt welling up, then shook her head and wiggled her jaw back and forth. "I'm okay. I think he might've split my lip a little." She ran the tip of her tongue over her lips, searching for the cut.

Jake took off his leather vest and draped it over her shoulders. "Sorry I don't have anything warmer. And this looks like it has a bit of blood on it."

"Not yours, I hope," she said.

"No, I'm okay. Except for my knuckles."

She held one of his hands, examining the damage his knuckles had suffered. "We need to get you home and take care of this. How did you know the bastard had me anyway?"

"I saw you walking through the lot when I drove in. By the time I got parked, you weren't there so I came looking for you. Sorry I didn't get here sooner."

"Thank God you got to me at all. Do you realize this is the second time you've rescued me today? First from a bull. Now from a bull rider." She looked at him, her eyes glistening wetly. "I don't know how

161

to thank you."

He studied her seriously for a moment, then smiled. "Maybe we should go find Luke and Julie. Let them know you have another ride home."

"Do I?" She studied his face.

"Of course you do. If you want one."

"I do." She held out her arms.

He lifted her off the truck and held her steady as she stood up. "You okay?"

"Yep. I'm fine. Let's go find Julie."

Chapter Sixteen

Once she assured the concerned cowgirl that everything was fine, Amanda told Julie she was riding home with Jake.

"No problem," Julie said. "If Luke gets lucky, I can always find another ride home."

As they were leaving, Julie handed Amanda her phone. When she checked her messages, she was excited to find one from Chi. "Most interested. Pick me up at the Circle W Ranch tomorrow at noon. Confirm by text or e-mail. Chi." She smiled brightly as she read the message.

"What's up?" Jake asked.

"I can't say yet." *Or won't,* she thought. "I have a client who wants to see me tomorrow. Wants me to pick him up at a ranch called the Circle W."

"That's Billy Walker's place," Julie said. "About forty miles east of us. It's easy to get to."

"My client is Chinese," Amanda said, "but lives in Santa Fe when he's in the States. I don't know why he wants to meet me at the Circle W."

"Well, they've got a landing strip." Jake said. "Maybe he's flying down. Walker lets people use the strip."

"That's it!" She was beaming. "Chi has his own plane. A twin engine something or other. I'll need to drive over and pick him up, if you can give me directions."

"I'll drive over with you," Julie offered. "I want to talk to Walker about our new foal."

Jake obviously wanted to know more about the man coming to visit Amanda, but didn't ask. He just said, "Invite him for lunch at the ranch. And supper, if he plans to stay that long."

"Thanks," she said happily. "I will."

****

As Jake helped Amanda up into the cab of his truck, her tiny fringed skirt rode up, giving him a peek at her bare bottom. An ugly bruise now marred the milky skin on the inside of her thigh, reminding him of just how rough Buck had been with her. He admired the way she had been fighting like a wildcat when he showed up, but there was no way she could have gotten away from the bastard. He would love to have another ten minutes alone with the son of a bitch.

On the ride home, he reached over and laid his hand on the smooth skin of her thigh. She laid her hand on top of his but, at her touch on his ripped knuckles, he winced. She jerked her hand back.

"No, it's okay." He patted her leg. "It's okay."

She laid her hand back, resting it on his as softly as she could. When they parked the truck and walked up the steps to the lodge, he held her elbow as if to steady her.

"I'm okay Jake," she said. "I'm much better now."

Jake unlocked the front door. He carefully steered her through the entry into the main room and then walked beside her up the stairs to the second floor. At the top he took her arm and gently turned her toward him. He looked into her eyes for a long moment, and then leaned down to kiss her gently, trying not to hurt her cut lip. He pulled back and looked at her.

Even in the dim hall nightlight she looked a mess. Her lip was split, her cheek was bruised and her hair was a stringy mop. Her sexy top had been torn and was splattered with blood. His heart ached for what had happened to her. But at the moment, even in the mess she was in, she was beautiful. He had saved her pretty ass from serious danger twice in one day and he could think of nothing he would rather do than take her to his room and wrap his arms around her, protecting her.

She looked up, studying his face. "Thank you again for the rescue."

He smiled, holding her in his arms for a moment. His care and concern for her had opened a door to a room full of feelings he hadn't expected. Feelings that went deeper than desire and physical pleasure. "I believe we had a date tonight." He glanced at his watch. "There are still a few hours left of the night. Don't go to your room. Come with me to mine."

"I thought you wanted a rain-check on our date."

"I've decided to cash it in."

"I'm really a mess," she said, cringing as she touched her face and messy hair. "I need a long, hot shower."

"I've got a shower." Jake hoped his perseverance would pay off.

"I don't have anything to sleep in."

"Get something from your room. Better yet, we'll both sleep naked.

She sighed. "You're about to wear me down. But, honestly, I'm not in a very sexy mood. I'm really worn out."

"I know you are. That's okay. Come to my room anyway."

Amanda stared up at him. He could see the question in her eyes, her hesitation. He knew if she agreed to spend the night with him without having sex, it would mean a major shift in their relationship. It might be a shift to be avoided, a silent declaration of feelings they had agreed not to express. After all, as a practical matter, in a day or two she would be gone. Gone from the ranch, gone from Texas, gone from the swirling maelstrom of uninhibited sex she had stirred up. It didn't matter. At the moment, all he wanted was to hold her in his arms and protect her.

He smiled when she gave in. "All right," she said. "I guess we did have a date, didn't we?"

"Indeed we did," he said, his arms still wrapped around her. *And practical matters be damned.*

Jake let her shower first, watching the stars from the balcony until she was through. When she came out of the shower wrapped in one of his big bath towels, he set her down on the edge of the bed to get a good look at her cut lip.

"I don't think it will scar," he said. "I'd put some antiseptic on it, but I'm afraid you would just lick it off."

She grinned, wincing a bit when the grin stretched her lip. "It's okay. I'll just be careful who I kiss for a while."

Hoping her attempt at humor was a good sign, he left her sitting on the edge of the bed while he quickly showered and then spent some time doctoring the ripped skin on his knuckles. When he came out of the bathroom twenty minutes later, she was curled up on the bed and fast asleep. Amanda had fallen over where she sat, losing the towel and laying naked half on and half off the bed.

He turned down the covers, picked her up, and laid her on one side of the king-size bed. He moved carefully, not wanting to wake her, but he quickly realized how exhausted she was.

Jake slid into bed beside her, lying on his back with his hands behind his head. In the past, the ranch had seen eventful days—like the day the hay barn burned down or the day a twister killed one of his favorite horses. But there had never been a day like this. He looked at the pretty brunette lying beside him, her complexion glowing in the moonlight. How the hell could one woman get into so damn much trouble? In one day?

Of course, the sex that they'd had at the cabin hadn't been any trouble. No trouble at all.

As if she knew he was thinking about her, Amanda stirred, stretching and then turning on her side, her back to him. He felt himself stirring as well, his aching cock growing hard as he remembered how passionately she had responded at the cabin.

Turning on his side, he spooned up against her back. He slipped an arm around her carefully, his hand cupping one bare breast, as his erection pressed against her firm, round ass.

****

Amanda woke up to the crow of a barnyard rooster. Jake was snuggled up against her back, his erection pressing firmly against her bottom. He had one arm over her waist, reaching up to hold her breast, and he was sound asleep. She slowly eased the covers up and off, trying not to wake him as she slid from the mattress for a quick trip to bathroom. When she returned, he had turned onto his back. His cock, hard and erect, tented the sheet. She grinned and opened the nightstand drawer where he kept the condoms. She took one and opened it, then gently lifted the sheet up off his body, careful not to wake him. When his cock was uncovered, she slowly rolled the condom down over his erection. Once the condom was on, she straddled his hips. Grasping his shaft, she used the tip of his cock to gently manipulate her clit, causing her pussy to spasm and her juices to cover his dick's engorged head. When she could take no more teasing, she slid herself down on his cock.

As she slowly impaled herself on her sleeping lover, she reached down and lightly rubbed her clit, making herself wetter and that much closer to climax. By the time she had half of his cock in her pussy, she saw him trying to hide a grin and knew he was awake.

"Good morning," she said, releasing a long sigh as she settled herself completely over his erection and slowly thrust her hips back and forth.

"Oh, it definitely is. A very good morning. One of the best I've ever had." He reached down and grabbed her waist, then let his hands slide down to her bottom, squeezing her ass cheeks as she rocked over his cock. She felt his arousal building with hers, felt him lifting his hips to meet each of her downward thrusts. It was exciting to see him respond to her body, and she shifted her hips faster, unable to maintain a slow, deliberate pace.

They made love passionately, urgently, needing the orgasms postponed the night before. Jake came first, obviously inspired by the sight of Amanda straddling him while she squeezed her breasts and nipples with one hand and stroked her swollen clit with the other. When he came, groaning and erupting into her with pulsing spasms, she ground her pussy down over his cock, needing to feel as deeply connected to him as possible.

As his orgasm subsided, he looked up at her with a sheepish grin. "God, I really needed that. Sorry I couldn't wait for you. You had me so damned aroused."

"Don't worry. My turn's coming." She slid the cum-filled condom from his cock and disposed of it, then reached in the nightstand for a new one. "I'm glad you have a drawer full of these. We may need a bunch before we're through."

"And I may need a few minutes to recharge before I'm ready for another one."

"Maybe I can help out a little," Amanda said, scooting down on the bed until her lips were just above Jake's flaccid cock. She looked up to see him watching her and grinned. "Lay back and close your eyes, cowboy. I'll be busy down here for a minute or two."

Amanda leaned down and swirled her tongue around the head of his soft cock, wetting the velvet smooth corona. She took the head in her mouth, getting it slippery with saliva before sliding her lips down the length of the shaft. By the time her lips touched his pubic hair at the base, she could feel the shaft growing harder. Holding his cock in one hand, she jacked him off while she alternated between sucking the tip and lathing his testicles with her tongue. In a matter of minutes, his shaft was hard as a rock again.

She raised up and grinned at the look of pleasure on his face. "Like that?" she asked.

"Oh yeah. A lot."

"Next time, I want you to come in my mouth. But right now, you need to fuck me." She took the new condom and tore open the foil, then put the unwrapped condom in her mouth. She positioned it over the head of Jake's cock and used her compressed lips to roll it down the full length of the rigid shaft.

She lay on her back and spread her legs wide, an open invitation to Jake. He rolled toward her, positioning his cock at the wet, swollen entrance of her core. Excitement skittered up her spine in anticipation of his cock sliding into her, filling her with its length and thickness. She pressed her heels against the mattress, lifting her hips toward him.

"Fuck me, Jake. Please, fuck me. I need you. I need your cock." She rolled her hips, her body begging for the thrusting shaft that would catapult her into ecstasy. Then he was inside her, inside the warm wet channel of her sex, his cock stroking deep and pulling away, only to slide deep once again. Her own arousal and need seemed to turn Jake on and he fucked her with a frenzy she had never experienced, his body slamming into hers, his hands clutching her ass, lifting her to meet his plunging cock.

Amanda reacted to Jake's ferocity with total abandon, writhing under him and wailing in pleasure as he drove into her. "Ohhh God! Yes. Yesss! Fuck me hard, Jake. Make me come."

Her climax came in a wave of fiery heat. She clutched Jake's shoulders and screamed as rapturous sensations surged through her body.

Between the waves of pleasure that swept through her, she felt Jake tense over her, his hips bucking and slamming into her core with his climax, surrendering to a bliss that blended with hers, uniting them in ecstasy.

As their orgasms faded, they lay facing each other, gazing into each other's eyes as they had done in the cabin. "My God, that was incredible," Amanda said. "How can sex with you just keep getting better and better?"

"Not sure," Jake said. "Practice maybe?"

She giggled. "Well, I must say we've had plenty of that. Thanks to you and a couple of cowboys."

"Any regrets?"

"None at all. On our first night together, we talked about me exploring my sexual boundaries. I can't tell you how much I've enjoyed that journey." She grinned mischievously and circled one of his nipples with her fingertips. "I might be able to show you though."

Jake grinned and shook his head. "Could we maybe get some breakfast first? I'm starving." He got out of bed and put on fresh underwear and a clean pair of jeans from his closet.

"It's sexy, watching you get dressed," she said. "I like it."

"Well, I might like watching you get dressed,

too. I'm usually too worried about getting you undressed."

"At the moment, I don't have anything to put on. I don't want to wear Julie's clothes again. Or even my bra. Not after last night. I can probably make it to my room in a towel."

Jake slid his closet door open and pulled out a clean denim work shirt. Thumbing through the shirts hanging in the closet he took another shirt off its hanger. "Here." He tossed it to her. The shirt was soft flannel with a scalloped yoke and cuffs.

She grinned and slid off the bed. "Oh, I like this. It's the same color as your eyes."

****

Jake dressed quickly as he watched Amanda. She'd slipped on the flannel shirt but only snapped the two snaps at the waist, leaving the top ones undone and revealing glimpses of her breasts as she moved around. The open tail of the shirt, which reached almost to her knees, offered teasing glimpses of her pussy when she sat on the edge of the bed. It was an effect that he admired.

He sat down on a leather footstool and put on his socks. As he reached for his boots, he said, "I need to ask you something."

She was sitting cross-legged on the end of the bed, rolling up the sleeves of his shirt. "Ask away."

He glanced up at her then looked back down at the boot he was pulling on. "Do you think you might want another threesome?"

The question seemed to catch her completely by surprise. "Why do you ask, Jake?"

He looked up at her again. "Justin and Luke wanted to know. You seemed to have fun."

"Why didn't *they* ask me? Why have *you* do it?"

"I think because they know I want you. And they know we weren't just watching it rain and hail at the cabin. Maybe they figured they needed my approval or something."

She studied him for a moment, her dark eyes flashing. "Why in hell would Justin and Luke need your permission? I'm not your ho. You 'want me.' What does that mean? Is this just about sex? Or are we getting emotionally involved, even though we said we wouldn't? Maybe last night, sleeping together without fucking our brains out, was a mistake. You know this has all been about the sex, Nothing more." Her voice broke a little. "I can't handle this being anything more."

He looked up from adjusting a spur, surprised by the sharp edge in her voice. "Well, hell, they don't need my permission. And yes, I want you. That's pretty obvious. But I don't have my brand on you. And you're done here..." He paused, slightly flustered. This wasn't going the way he'd thought it would. He had begun to have feelings for her beyond the outrageously great sex. But he hadn't expected the same from her. If they would never see each other again, why not let her enjoy one more threesome? On the other hand, maybe he was hoping she would say she didn't want another go-round with Luke and Justin.

"You mean once my work is done," she said, "we probably won't see each other again. Is that right?" The edge in her voice grew sharper.

"Yes. That's partly..."

"And you've enjoyed fucking me and you know I enjoyed the night with Justin and Luke."

"I know you enjoyed it." *Dammit,* he thought. *I should have kept my damn mouth shut.*

"But you also know how much I enjoyed making love to you. How special that has been. Like yesterday at the cabin. And this morning."

"Yes. But I don't have my brand on..."

"Goddammit," she yelled. "Stop saying that! I'm not one of your fucking cows." Amanda was now pacing back and forth, obviously pissed.

"I know you don't want to stand in the way of my sexual pleasure, but why would you *pimp* me out to other men?"

"No. That's not what I..."

"To be honest, Jake, I know that this isn't forever. God, I live in New York. And I'm extremely attracted to you to. Sex with you has been the best I've ever had. But the rest is true too. I did enjoy that night with Justin and Luke and wouldn't be opposed to another threesome under the right circumstances. But I never imagined doing it without you. It was always about you."

Jake stared at her. Had he been so wrapped up in helping her explore her sexual boundaries that he'd misread her feelings for him? He stepped toward her. "Amanda..."

She held up a hand, stopping him. "Let me finish, Jake. I realize my time here is short, but you've helped me in ways I can't even describe. My only regret is that you weren't a part of my fantasy, that you stood aside that night. The same with Luke in the barn. It was so erotic with you watching, but it would've been so much hotter if you had fucked me, too." She stopped abruptly with her hands on her hips, facing him.

He stared at her, his second boot half on, unable to collect his thoughts or say what he felt at her admission. Mimicking the move he'd made in the barn, Amanda reached out and grabbed the back of his neck, pulling his lips to hers for a passionate kiss. Just as he started to reach for her, she ended the kiss and turned toward the balcony door. Then she stopped and looked over her shoulder. "And I'm keeping this shirt."

Jake sat dumfounded, watching her leave. He finished putting on his boots and spurs and stood up, reaching for his chaps. He needed to get on a horse and ride away. Far away. What the hell was going on around here?

****

Back in her room, Amanda felt surprisingly elated. Her mostly one-sided conversation with Jake had cleared the air a bit, allowing her say some of the things she had been thinking. She also had a good feeling about the Indian blanket still spread out on her bed. If Chi Long was willing to fly from New Mexico to Texas, just on the strength of the photos she'd sent, the blanket must have some value. And unlike the fake Randell painting, it had to be real and valuable. The question would be just *how* valuable. Hopefully Chi Long could answer that.

There was a knock at the door and she opened it to find Julie standing in the hallway. The petite blonde was dressed in ordinary ranch work clothes.

"How you doing, Mandy?" she asked, stepping into the room. "After our night at the Rusty Buckle? You okay?"

"I'm fine, Julie. Except for a few lousy minutes in the parking lot, I had a really good time."

"Buck's in the hospital in San Angelo. Thanks to Jake, his abusive ways are over. By the way, I like your shirt."

Amanda smiled. "I like it too. I stole it from Jake."

"I'm sure he won't mind. He likes you a lot."

"I like him, too. But I'm heading back to New York. Probably tomorrow." She looked at Julie. "I know I have no right to ask this, but I was just wondering if you and Jake...If you and he...ever..."

"Ever had sex?" Julie finished with a grin.

Amanda blushed, embarrassed that she even wanted to know.

"Jake and I have had sex," Julie said. "But never alone. Luke or Justin were there the few times it happened. He never seemed interested in just me, though." Julie grinned. "The times with Luke and Justin were outrageously good though. Those cowboys do know how to please a lady."

"Then Jake's not really against sharing a woman?"

"Not as far as I know. He seemed to enjoy it." She looked quickly at her watch. "It's almost eight. You should have some breakfast. I've got a few chores to do, but we need to leave at eleven to get to the Walker place by noon." She was gone before Amanda could respond.

****

Jake got a sharp reprimand in Spanish when he hurried through the kitchen without stopping for Rosita's breakfast. *Why the hell did I have to go and open my damn mouth?* Grabbing a cup of coffee, he headed out the back door toward the stables. When he arrived, Justin was tightening the cinch on Cricket's saddle. "You're running a bit later than usual."

Jake scowled at his brother. "Well I'm not punching a goddamn time clock." He grabbed his saddle and threw it up on Ginger's back.

"Whoa, bro. Who put a burr under your saddle?"

Without responding, Jake finished saddling Ginger and led her out of the stable. As he swung up in to the saddle, he growled, "Let's just go move those damn cows."

Justin mounted Cricket and the two brothers rode side by side across the creek. "I heard you knocked Buck McCoy on his ass last night."

"He deserved it."

"So I heard. How's Amanda?"

"Physically, she's fine. Otherwise, I'll be damned if I know."

They rode in silence for a while, then Justin said, "Did you ask her about doing another threesome with me and Luke?"

"Yes, and she damned near bit my head off. Said if you two cowboys wanted to fuck her you should ask her yourselves. Not have me pimp her out." Jake cursed, wondering how the situation must have appeared to Amanda.

Justin reined to a halt. "Pimp her out? What the hell..."

"I don't know what the hell," Jake said. "About women and about Amanda Sloane in particular. And it doesn't make a damn bit of difference anyway because tomorrow she'll be out of here and on her way back to New York." Despite his intention to keep his feelings corralled, her impending departure gave him a pain in his chest.

Justin looked over at his brother. He studied him for a moment, then smiled. "Damn, Jake. I think you're smitten. Did Amanda sleep with you last night?"

"Yes, and all we did was sleep." The hour they spent making love after they woke up was none of his brother's business.

"That's dangerous, Jake. Sleeping with a woman without fucking her is serious. No telling where cuddling will lead."

"Oh, shut up and help me round up those cows."

****

Everyone else had eaten breakfast and left for chores by the time Amanda came down to the kitchen. She had dressed in jeans and a tank top and felt refreshed after a couple of hours sleep and making love to Jake.

Rosita urged her to sit down and put a plate filled with pancakes, eggs, and bacon in front of her. "*Señorita* Sloane," she said, concern in her eyes. "I'm so sorry about what happened to you last night."

The statement startled her. "Rosita, how do you know about that?"

"Cell phones and social networks, Miss Sloane. Ranchers stick together and stay connected. My Manuel says many people are happy Buck was punished. He is a very bad man."

And he got a beating from a very good man, she thought. Amanda wolfed down her breakfast and decided to walk down to see the new foal.

The foal had grown remarkably in twenty-four hours and was much less wobbly on her spindly legs. Amanda stood at the railing watching the new filly nudge its mother's teat for breakfast, amazed at how much bigger she was.

The barn door opened and she turned to see Luke entering with a bucket of oats for the mare. He nodded and smiled. "Howdy, Miss Sloane. How are you?" Then his smile faded. "I'm sorry about what happened last night. I should've—"

"I'm fine, Luke," she interrupted. "How about you? How did things go with the cute redhead you were dancing with?"

Luke grinned. "A gentleman doesn't tell, does he?" He poured the oats into the mare's feed bucket and turned to face her. "Everything okay with you and Jake?"

"Everything is fine, I think." She studied him for a minute. "He did mention last night that you and Justin were interested in being with me again."

Luke's complexion turned from tanned brown to beet red, spreading from his neck to his forehead. She watched the tall, self-assured cowboy squirm, obviously trying to think of something to say.

"Well...um...that cuts right to the chase. Could I ask what your answer was?" His voice had risen half an octave and he still had a russet glow.

"The one night we had was lovely, but since I'm probably leaving tomorrow..."

She left his question unanswered and walked out of the foal barn, leaving Luke still rosy from embarrassment. She hadn't wanted to make him quite that uncomfortable, but she knew it wouldn't permanently damage his ego. Besides, if the two of them wanted to have sex with her again, they should ask her themselves.

****

Amanda and Julie made good time getting to the Circle W, arriving at a quarter to twelve. Julie was obviously curious about the Chinese man they were going to pick up, but she didn't pressure Amanda for information.

The Circle W's airstrip wasn't much more than a long swath of beaten-down grass bordered by rusted airplane parts. A yellow single-engine plane sat at one end of the strip, tied down with cables and stakes so it wouldn't blow away in the Texas wind.

Julie and Buddy Walker began discussing the foal, while Amanda walked out onto the grass strip and waited, scouring the sky for an airplane. It arrived at twelve fifteen, flown by Chi Long himself. As he climbed out of the cockpit, he gave Amanda a friendly hug, telling her how glad he was to see her again. At only five three, he had to reach up to hug her.

After meeting Julie and Walker, Chi introduced his passenger. "This is Dr. Dennis Underwood," he said. "From the University of New Mexico. Dr. Underwood is a world-renowned expert in Native American art and artifacts. We are both excited to see what you discovered."

Given their excitement, Amanda quickly herded everyone to the waiting car. On the way back to the Morgan Ranch, she told the two men about the cabin that had been on the ranch one hundred years or more, and the blankets and pots still on the beds and shelves.

At the ranch, Julie left to do more chores, telling Amanda she would be back for supper. Jake and

Justin were both working on horseback, moving cattle up to higher spring pastures. Amanda brought the blanket and pot down to the main room, where the two visitors could examine them carefully. Underwood took two pairs of white cotton gloves out of his jacket pocket and handed one pair to Chi. They put the gloves on then carefully began to examine the pot and blanket.

Her pulse was racing, but she forced herself to remain outwardly calm, waiting for the collector and artifacts expert to give their appraisals. The men conferred quietly, murmuring to each other.

Finally, they turned to her and smiled. With her heart in her throat, she hoped and prayed for a good appraisal.

The expert, Underwood, spoke first. "This is definitely a first phase Navaho chief's blanket, probably woven in the late 18th century. Notice how tightly woven it is. It's almost waterproof. It's also very warm and very light, lighter than a buffalo robe. These blankets were very highly prized by the tribes."

She continued to constrain her excitement behind a façade of professionalism. *Be calm,* she told herself. *No squealing for joy.* "And the estimated value?" she asked casually.

Underwood looked at Chi, then turned back to her. "There are about fifteen known blankets like this in the world. Mr. Long purchased one at auction in Taos three years ago. Regrettably, each new find diminishes the value of the others...but only slightly. I would estimate this blanket could sell at auction for between two hundred and two hundred fifty thousand dollars."

Chi clapped his hands excitedly. "I knew it, Amanda! As soon as I saw the photo you sent, I knew what you had found!"

She was bursting with relief, joy, excitement—

all the emotions eaten up by the disappointment over the fake Randell.

"And the pot? It's a beautiful design, and it looks old. But does it have any real value?"

Underwood took a deep breath. "I'm almost certain this is a Hopi pot made by an artisan named Onapi. If it is, it was made sometime in the 1880s or 90s. I would need to check to make sure the clay is right, and check the size against other pots Onapi made. But I'm ninety nine percent certain."

"And if it is what you think it is?" Amanda clenched her hands in anticipation.

"I would give it an auction appraisal of twenty five thousand dollars. For insurance purposes, thirty thousand."

Her heart took another leap for joy. There were at least five more similar pots in the cabin.

Chi Long had given up on his reserved demeanor and grinned with glee. "Amanda," he said excitedly. "You mentioned there are more pots and blankets in the cabin. Can we see them?"

"Yes, I'm sure we can," she said. "But it's too far to walk. We'll need to wait for someone from the ranch to get back. We may be able to drive up. I've only been there once and that was on horseback."

"All right," Chi said. "Then we'll wait."

Chapter Seventeen

While they were waiting, Rosita served a lunch of tacos and cold beer. As usual, the lunch was delicious, but Amanda was bubbling over with excitement and could barely take a bite. In her enthusiasm, she told Chi and Underwood the story of the forged Randell painting, and how the Morgans' cousin, Winslow, eventually destroyed it.

"What a bastard." Chi shook his head in disbelief. "To destroy something just because you are jealous and can't have it."

"Indeed," Underwood said. "Jealousy and greed are dangerous emotions."

"How insane," Amanda said, thinking about how the people on the Morgan ranch made relationships fun without any jealousy.

****

Jake and Justin arrived back at the lodge just after lunch.

As Justin lifted Cricket's saddle off, he said, "Any idea who this fella is that flew down to see Amanda?"

"Not really. I haven't asked and she hasn't said. I think he's a collector of some kind. I guess we'll find out soon enough."

"After I shower and get something to eat," Justin said. "I'm filthy and famished."

In the lodge's main room, Jake was surprised to find Amanda with two men, one oriental and obviously the collector she had mentioned, and the other a tall scholarly looking man wearing a tweed jacket with elbow patches.

Amanda and the two men stood up when Jake and Justin entered, but Jake said, "Give us a few minutes to clean up and then we can do introductions."

After his shower, Jake met Justin on the stairway landing and they walked down the stairs together. Jake studied Amanda's expression to see if there was a hint of the anger she had displayed that morning, but found none. If anything, she was glowing happily.

Once introductions were made, Jake and Justin sat down at the big round wooden table with a tray of sandwiches Rosita had provided. Amanda explained that Chi and Underwood had flown down to the ranch to evaluate the Indian blanket and pot, which now sat on a side table. Jake could hardly believe a blanket and pot that had been in their great granddaddy's cabin could be worth a plane trip from Santa Fe, but he had to give Amanda and her appraisers the benefit of the doubt.

Amanda turned to Underwood first, asking him to explain what he knew about the blanket.

Underwood began a long explanation of the art of Navajo blanket weaving. After a few minutes, she interrupted. "Maybe we should just tell them the value that you would place on this blanket." The blanket was folded, lying on a side table. She picked it up and laid it in Jake's lap. The last time he had been this close to the blanket, he had been making passionate love to Amanda.

"Well," Underwood said. "This is a first phase blanket that I would appraise at between two hundred and two hundred fifty thousand dollars. At auction, of course."

"Bullshit!" Justin looked at the blanket, then back at Underwood.

The artifacts expert blinked owlishly, startled by the reaction. "I beg your pardon?"

"Bullshit." he repeated. "How can a blanket be worth that much?"

Jake was holding the blanket in his lap, stroking the soft wool.

"Oh, I assure you, it is worth that much. Maybe more under the right conditions," Underwood said.

Chi Long stepped toward Jake, his gaze glued to the blanket in Jake's lap. "That is an auction estimate of course," he said. "And you will certainly want to put the blanket up for sale with a reputable auction house. There is an auction of Native American artifacts at Delaroche's Taos gallery in five months. Or, if you want more immediate cash, I'll give you two hundred twenty thousand for it now."

"Now?" Jake looked at Justin, then back at Chi.

"Today," Chi said. "By wire transfer to your bank, of course."

"Holy shit," Justin whispered, staring at the blanket in his brother's lap.

"And of course, I will cover Amanda's firm's normal twenty percent brokerage fee."

Jake took a breath and looked at Amanda. She was grinning from ear to ear.

"Well," he said looking at his brother. "The offer is very tempting. But Justin and I need to discuss it first."

"Of course," Chi said. "I would expect nothing less."

Amanda seemed to be having a hard time keeping her jubilance in check. She wrapped the towel around the pot again and handed it to Justin. "Please, Dr. Underwood, tell them about the pot."

Underwood launched into another long explanation of Hopi pottery and the artesian, Onapi, who made pots in the 1880s. After a minute or two, he stopped himself and smiled. "Let me sum up," he said. "I think this pot is a genuine Onapi. But I need to examine it more thoroughly. If it is what I think it is, I would value it at about twenty five thousand dollars at auction. Maybe more."

"And if it proves to be an Onapi," Chi said, "I'll give you twenty thousand cash for it."

Justin now handled the pot very carefully, using the towel to keep from touching it with his fingers. Amanda quickly covered their stunned silence, "I told Mr. Long and Dr. Underwood there are more blankets and pots in the cabin. The blankets aren't like this one, but they may still be valuable. We would like to go back up there and see them."

"Then let's go." Justin handed the pot back to Amanda and stood up quickly. "Let's see what we've got."

Jake was feeling the same urgency to discover what was in the cabin, but he put out a hand, waving Justin down. "Just hold on, little brother. Unless we want to ride horses, we'll have to wait for Manuel to get back with the Jeep. He's fixing the fence that Maurice tore down yesterday." He looked at Amanda and her guests. "So we can ride horses or wait."

"Wait!" The simultaneous response from Amanda, Chi, and Underwood brought a round of laughter from everyone.

Justin began a conversation with Chi and Underwood about the Hopis and their pottery, eager to hear about the pot and why it was so valuable.

Jake took Amanda aside. "You know, you might have just pulled our chestnuts out of the fire. How did you know the blanket was worth that much?"

"I saw Chi buy one just like it at an auction in Taos three years ago. I don't think the other blankets in the cabin are worth nearly as much, but it certainly won't hurt to find out."

"I don't know how to thank you for this," he said. "Maybe you could let me try tonight. If I'm forgiven for that mess with Justin and Luke."

She gave him a sly smile. "I guess you're forgiven. A night alone with you sounds perfect. Especially since I'm probably going to be leaving tomorrow." Her smile turned into a pout.

"Then we definitely have a date."

"I look forward to it." She gave him a seductive glance. "Very much."

Manuel returned with the ranch's Jeep and they piled in; Justin driving and Chi riding shotgun, while Jake, Amanda, and Underwood squeezed into the small backseat. The ride to the cabin took longer than a trip on horseback because they had to skirt around several deep gullies and draws.

When they did arrive, Jake lit the coal oil lamp and they brought all the blankets and pots to be examined out into the daylight. Underwood took his time examining each blanket and pot carefully. Amanda photographed the blankets and pots, then snapped shots of the cabin to give context to the surprising find. Jake and Justin waited patiently as Chi and Underwood talked quietly to each other.

Underwood was finally ready with his evaluation. They had discovered three phase three Navajo blankets that he appraised at forty to fifty thousand each. A bright red, white, and black Sioux blanket he valued at twenty thousand. Underwood believed three of the pots were made by Onapi and would go at auction for thirty to forty thousand each. Two more were of unknown origin and not considered valuable. All in all, the treasures in the cabin could possibly bring them between two hundred thirty and two hundred ninety thousand dollars. With the first phase blanket and Onapi pot, there would be enough to pay off the note at the bank.

"I know you want to discuss this between yourselves," Chi said to Jake and Justin. "And you also have the benefit of Amanda's advice. But if you want to sell what's here outright, I'll give you two hundred fifty thousand for the lot. With the blanket and pot back at the ranch house, that would make a total of four hundred ninety thousand. Plus I'll pay PP&C's commission. That's if Dr. Underwood confirms the pots are, in fact, Onapi."

"We need to think about it," Jake said. "But we will let you know soon."

"Of course," Chi said. "Of course."

Chapter Eighteen

There wasn't room in the Jeep to haul the blankets and pots back to the ranch, so Jake said he would send Manuel back that evening to secure the cabin

For the moment, they stacked the blankets on one of the bunk beds and put the pots on the table where, just the day before, Jake had made Amanda squeal in unrestrained passion.

When they got back to the lodge, Jake and Justin spent some time talking to Chi and Underwood, promising they would let Chi know soon what they wanted to do about the pots and blankets. Justin took the two men back to their plane at the Circle W, while Amanda went to her room. She was just getting ready to call Richard when there was a knock on her door. She opened it, surprised to find Jake in the hallway, smiling brightly, obviously pleased by today's events. She was delighted to see the sparkle return to his eyes.

"Amanda, I can't thank you enough for what you've done for us, for Morgan Ranch." He stepped forward and put his arms around her.

She was enjoying the feeling of his strong arms, of her breasts against his chest. "You're welcome. But our date is for tonight."

"It's getting really late. I think it might be dark out."

Amanda giggled. "You wish. It's not even seven o'clock."

"I always try to get a jump on important projects." Jake's hands slid down to cup her bottom, forcing her pelvis against his erection. His eyes held hers, deep pools she could drown in.

"We haven't had supper yet." Amanda giggled at his determination.

"I'm not hungry. Except for you."

She felt her resolve to wait slipping away. Blinking, she tilted her chin up and kissed Jake quickly on the lips. Her lip still hurt but it was much better. Breaking the kiss, she placed her palms against Jake's chest and pushed, grinning mischievously. "Good things come to he who waits, Jake. So if you want good things from me, you'll have to wait. I'm hungry, and I've got to call my boss. He has no idea what has happened in the past two days. Plus, I've got six text messages and a dozen voice mails."

"Okay." He slowly released his grip on Amanda's ass. "When can I come back and pick up where I was?"

She thought for a moment. "Make it ten thirty and I'll be ready."

"Your room or mine?"

"Here, Jake. Be here at ten thirty."

"On the dot."

As he turned to leave, she said, "Bring condoms."

"How many will I need?" he said with a wolfish grin.

She felt herself blush. "Maybe a few."

When he smiled and turned to leave, she was sure she would be very happy before the night was over.

Closing her door, she picked up her cell to call Richard. She hadn't spoken to him since he had sent her the text confirming her suspicions about the Randell. She dreaded calling him now, doubting she could temper the bad news about the painting with the fact that they had discovered a treasure trove of

Native American blankets and pots. Wonderful though they were, a half million dollars in Indian artifacts hardly made up for a ten million dollar Charles Randell painting.

As she expected, Richard was shocked to hear how Winslow had burned the painting. She thought he would go apoplectic.

"You've got to be kidding, Mandy. How could anyone in his right mind destroy a work of art? Steal, maybe. But destroy?"

"That's the problem, Richard. The man isn't in his right mind. He's barking-at-the-moon loony. He didn't even know it was a fake. He could have easily taken it, but he didn't. He just didn't want his cousins to have it."

"How are the Morgans dealing with the situation? Upset, I'm sure."

"Jake Morgan has been pretty stoic about the painting. I think there's some kind of unwritten code that cowboys can't let their feelings show. I'm sure neither brother is happy that the painting was a fake, or that it was destroyed. Finding the pots and blankets is some consolation. Based on Chi and Underwood's appraisals, the Morgan's will make enough on the sale to cover their note at the bank. At least they won't lose the ranch."

"Do we have a contract to broker the sale?"

"The Morgans have agreed to let PP&C handle the sale whether they sell outright to Chi Long or wait for the Santa Fe auction. Either way, we'll get our commission. We are going back up to the cabin tomorrow to inventory everything and bring it back to the lodge. Our commission should be around one hundred thousand."

"We have you to thank for that, Mandy. What were you doing at the cabin anyway?"

"Another long story. I'll tell you when I get back." *I may not tell you everything,* she thought.

Amanda's phone call lasted through supper so Rosita brought a tray to her room. She ate quickly since it was almost nine. She picked up her supper tray and took it downstairs to the kitchen. At the bottom of the stairs, she saw Justin and Luke in the big cowhide club chairs that filled one corner of the room. As she walked in, both men stood, obviously glad to see her.

"Well, here's the little lady we were just talking about." Luke said.

"Should my ears be burning?" Amanda chuckled softly.

"That's not exactly the area of your anatomy we wanted to heat up." Justin gave her a big grin. "But we could start there and work our way down."

She was still holding the tray from her supper as both men stepped toward her.

"We need to apologize for our lack of proper communication, Miss Sloane," Justin said, moving close.

Amanda made an effort to temper the amusement in her voice. "You mean propositioning me."

"Something like that," Justin said.

"Exactly like that," Luke corrected. He stepped forward and took the tray out of her hands and set it on a side table.

Justin had moved to stand at Amanda's side. "Right. Exactly like that."

Luke moved to Amanda's other side and both men stepped closer, surrounding her with heat. Despite herself, a tingle spread out and upward from between her legs.

"Sorry boys. I already have a date for tonight." A hand cupped her breast and the tingle in her crotch intensified. When she looked down at Luke's hand on her breast, Justin lifted her hair and kissed the back of her neck. Suddenly the memories of how

190

erotic and exciting the sex had been with these two men were spreading through her consciousness, turning her on more and more. It was all she could do to resist. But tonight she wanted Jake. Only Jake.

"Sorry boys. But tonight is important. And I'll be leaving tomorrow."

"All the more reason for you to be with us tonight." Justin inched closer. "Why ride single when you can ride double?" The two men rubbed up against her now, Luke pressed up against her back and Justin against her front. Justin caressed her breast with one hand and slid the other down over her tummy to her crotch.

"Oh Jesus," she muttered, feeling her knees go weak.

Behind her, Luke pressed his erection against her ass.

Amanda thought about Jake and what she had planned for him later. She sucked in her breath and backed away. "No. I really can't." She picked up the tray and hurried to the kitchen. When she came back through the room on her way upstairs, Justin and Luke were still standing as she'd left them.

****

Jake knocked on Amanda's door at exactly ten thirty.

"It's open," she said. "Come on in."

Jake entered a room lit by a dozen votive candles scattered on various surfaces, casting everything in a soft golden glow.

"Candles are pretty," he said.

"I found them in the liquor cabinet. They're romantic, don't you think?" She queried softly.

An upholstered side chair had been pulled over to the end of the large bed. Next to the chair sat a side table with a full snifter of brandy. Amanda lay in the center of the bed, propped up by several pillows. As his eyes adjusted to the flickering candlelight, he saw that she was wearing a matching bra and panty set in black lace. It was some of the sexiest lingerie he had ever seen.

"Sit in the chair." Amanda's voice was seductive, commanding. "I'm going to entertain you."

Jake smiled as he reluctantly sat down. "I wanted this to be about you tonight."

"You'll get your turn. But first, I want to thank you for helping me shed some inhibitions. A *lot* of inhibitions. So sit down and enjoy."

Jake grinned and sat down. He looked more closely at her bra and panties.

The black bra was trimmed with tiny black beads that sparkled in the candlelight. The cups fit her breasts perfectly, but left bead-trimmed openings in the tips large enough for her nipples and areola to poke through. Not the typical underthings Jake had seen on the cowgirls he had been intimate with, and his cock certainly approved.

She stretched lazily, spreading her arms out to each side of the stacked pillows. Gazing at Jake with sultry, half-lidded eyes, she slowly spread her legs, letting him see the panties that matched the bra. The thong was designed as a V of black lace that covered her pubic area. Except the black lace was open at the crotch, leaving her smoothly shaved pussy lips revealed. As she spread her legs wide, Jake could see her arousal, her pussy lips rosy and engorged, so much so that they had extended through the opening in the lace.

The sight of her pink cunt glistening with her nectar made his cock grow even larger. "Damn, Amanda," he whispered hoarsely, staring at her lingerie. "That outfit is smokin' hot."

She giggled. "Do you think? Take off a girl's jeans and top and there's no telling what naughty surprises you'll find underneath. Sort of like stripping away a girl's inhibitions."

He shifted uncomfortably in the chair, trying to adjust his erection inside his tight jeans. At this rate, his zipper may be permanently imprinted against his needy flesh.

"I'd love to see your cock?" she said. "Stroke it while I entertain you. You did bring condoms, didn't you?"

He smiled and took a handful out of his pocket, laying them on the small table. Jake unbuttoned his jeans eagerly. He had gone commando and, as soon as his fly was open, his engorged cock swung up from his groin, pre-cum seeping from the head. As he relaxed back into the chair, she grinned appreciatively and ran her tongue seductively over her lips.

With her eyes locked on his, she used her hands to pleasure herself. Taking it slow and easy, she squeezed her lace encased breasts, lifting them, pinching her bare nipples, and leaning down to lick her nipple with the tip of her tongue. She slid her other hand slowly down over her waist and abdomen to her crotch.

Watching Amanda touch herself for his pleasure was one of the most erotic things he had ever witnessed. He stroked his cock, sliding his hand from the base up to the ultra-sensitive flesh below the corona. With his other hand he lifted his testicles out of his fly, massaging and rolling the hard nuts through his fingers. His breathing had become slow and shallow but his pulse was racing. He was normally always in control, but not tonight, not watching Amanda's sensual display.

Once again, she teased, running her fingers all around her pussy without actually touching it. Turning over on her tummy, she pushed her face against the coverlet and tilted her thong-clad ass toward him. She spread her legs wide, revealing her eager and needy pussy. Reaching back, she grasped her buttocks and spread them apart, revealing the thin black vertical string of her lace thong, so thin it did nothing to hide the puckered rosebud of her anus.

"You like this, don't you, Amanda? Teasing me? I think you have the heart of an exhibitionist."

"Yes. I like it. But exhibitionism requires a voyeur. You do like to watch, don't you?"

She turned back over, smiling at him. The raging hard-on he held in his fist answered her question.

"Yum, yum, yum," she whispered, licking her lips. "I'm going to eat you up." He started to rise but she quickly said, "Sit. I'm not through with you just yet."

Groaning harshly, he sat back down, fascinated, wondering what she would do next. No woman had ever turned him on like she was doing. His cock ached for her sweet body.

She reached underneath the pillows and brought out a vibrator. Turning the dildo on, she slid it slowly up and down the edges of her cunt, and then pushed just the tip into the weeping folds at the entrance to her slick passage.

After several teasing strokes, Amanda slid the plastic shaft into her pussy, pushing it slowly, almost imperceptibly, deeper and deeper. Her sighs of pleasure barely reached his ears. But he could see the flush of her desire rising across her chest. He felt heat spread across his groin, felt his cock so rigid and hard it could burst.

"You know what I want cowboy?" She looked at him with a sexy smile. "I want your big cock in my ass, fucking me until I scream in orgasm. Can you handle that for me? Fucking my tight little ass?" Introducing her to anal sex at the cabin had apparently been a wise move.

Jake swallowed hard and tried to answer but he had to clear his throat. Finally he groaned his answer, his voice a raspy whisper. "Yes. Oh God yes, Amanda. I need to fuck your ass so bad."

She grinned, seemingly delighted by his response to her teasing. "You'll get to. But first I want to see just how aroused you are."

Damn the little minx, he thought. *I'm going to fuck her senseless.*

Sliding off the bed, she walked to his chair and knelt down in front of him. She pushed his hand away from his dick, taking his erection by the base and stroking him up and down. After a few minutes of teasing, she reached over and took the brandy snifter from the table. He had taken barely a sip of the fiery drink but she tipped the glass up and drank it all. Then she leaned forward and took his cock deep in her mouth, her sultry gaze locked on his eyes.

She had yet to swallow the length of his flesh, and he wanted to feel the tip nudging the back of her throat. Reflexively, his hips pumped and the head of his cock slipped completely into her throat. With her eyes still locked on his and cheeks sucked tightly against his flesh, she made swallowing motions, slowly massaging his erection.

"Oh fuck," he muttered. "That's incredible." She kept him deep in her throat for several seconds then pulled back, only to surge quickly back over the sensitive tip.

Urging him up from the chair, she had him lay down on the bed. Kneeling between his thighs, she sucked his cock, repeating her deep throat maneuver. In minutes, she had him at the edge of orgasm. As he tensed up, ready to climax, she lifted her head and began to jack him off, using both hands to stroke up and down the wet shaft. His cock jerked and he ejaculated, semen squirting up and out and running down over the head of his cock and her hands. As he came, he groaned loudly, lost in the pleasure of his orgasm.

She held him in her hands until his cock softened, then slipped into the bathroom for a warm wet washcloth. She wiped the cum from her hands and his cock, then said, "Stand up. I want to undress you."

He stood and started unbuttoning his shirt, but she pushed his hand away. "No, Jake. I want to do this."

He was barefoot, wearing only jeans and a shirt, and she had him naked in seconds. He lay back on the bed watching her. Gazing at him through sultry eyes, she, took off her bra but left her panties on, the black lace creating an erotic background for her glistening, distended pussy lips. Standing at the foot of the bed she lifted and caressed her breasts, pinching her nipples and pulling them outward, making them even bigger. Lifting one breast up, she lowered her chin and extended her tongue, stretching until she could reach her nipple with the tip of her tongue.

She licked her nipple and then smiled down at him. He was already hard again. She quickly rolled a condom over the head of his cock, then leaned down and used her lips to roll it the rest of the way down as she had done that morning.

"You are really good at that," he said.

She smiled at his reaction. "You inspire me. And right now, I'm inspired to fuck you."

Rising to stand over him on the bed, she placed her feet by his hips. Smiling down at him, she slowly lowered herself, squatting until she could slide her wet, lace-framed pussy down over his cock.

"Ahhh, God," he groaned as his cock slid into her heat. "Your sweet pussy is so tight. So wet. It's incredible."

She pressed her hands down on his shoulders, slowly working her pussy back and forth over his cock. As she fucked him, he looked up and saw her eyes close, her head tilt back. Now her breath was coming in quick pants that matched the rhythm of her thrusting hips. Reaching up, he grasped her neck and pulled her head down, guiding her mouth to his for a passionate, tongue-probing kiss. For several minutes they continued to kiss while she fucked him, grinding her cunt down over his rock-hard cock. Finally, she broke the kiss and raised up.

"Wait," she groaned breathlessly. "Don't make me come yet."

Lifting herself off his cock, she leaned toward the night stand and retrieved a bottle of oil. As she dribbled oil on his cock, she glanced at him and he grinned. "You're well prepared, aren't you?" In the glow of the candlelight, he saw her cheeks turn a shade pinker.

She quickly slipped out of her panties, then turned around and straddled him, facing his feet. She lowered herself, lifting his erection as she squatted down, holding it upright as the smooth head touched her anus.

It was all he could do to keep from thrusting his hips up and shoving into her tight opening, but he lay still, letting her set the pace for his penetration.

Amanda pushed herself down over the head of his cock, gasping loudly as the thick corona stretched her tight ring. "Ohhh, God. It's...so...tight. Ohhh...Jesus." She pushed down hard again and Jake could feel the oil lubricating his shaft, easing his penetration. She pushed again and squealed as his full length and thickness shoved into her ass.

Looking down, he could see his cock buried balls deep between the smooth round globes of her ass. He started to lift his hips but she stopped him. When he had fucked her ass in the cabin she had surrendered to his wishes but this time she was in control. "Let me do it," she urged. "Just lay still."

She leaned back, pushing her feet forward toward his and holding herself up with stiffened arms against his chest. From this position, she could slide her ass up and down the length of his cock, fucking him at her own pace. As she fucked him, he groaned in pleasure and reached around to cup and caress her breasts, squeezing and pinching her large nipples.

"Do you like it Amanda? Having my cock buried in your tight, sweet ass? Does it feel good?" Jake groaned and lifted his hips, pushing into her as deeply as he could.

Her answer came in a hissing whisper. "Yesss. Oh God, yes. It feels so fucking good." She reached to one side and picked up the vibrator, then spread her legs wide. Jake couldn't see but could feel the plastic shaft being shoved into her pussy, could feel it sliding in and out next to his cock. She hadn't turned the vibrator on yet, but just the feel of the shaft alongside his cock increased his arousal.

"Is that good baby? Having your ass and pussy full at the same time?"

"Yes. It feels good. Really good."

Jake hesitated before he spoke again. Amanda was now bucking up and down on his cock with wild abandon, shoving the dildo in and out faster and faster. He pulled her back against his chest, her head against his shoulder. "Would you like to have a real cock in your pussy, while I fuck your ass? Have two cocks fucking you at the same time?"

Amanda didn't hesitate when she answered him. "Yes! I'd like that. I'd love it."

Jake felt her reach down and suddenly the plastic shaft hummed to life in a shattering current of vibration. He felt the rapid tremor along the full length of his dick, felt it spreading in waves from the nexus of his cock and her ass.

"Ahhh fuck! Oh God!" Gripping Amanda's waist, he groaned and climaxed, unable to hold back the wave of pleasure that surged through his body.

Above him, Amanda jerked in shuddering spasms. "Oh God, Jake. Oh...oh...oh God! I'm coming!" As her orgasm wracked her body, she screamed and bucked, her ass sliding wildly up and down on his cock. She jerked the buzzing vibrator out of her pussy and tossed it aside, her body quivering as her climax crested and began to fade.

Jake rolled to one side, still holding Amanda close, his cock still in her ass. He was breathing deeply, trying to recover from the intense pleasure of his orgasm. Releasing his grip on her waist, he raised one hand and gently caressed her breast. After a moment, he felt her shudder and sigh contentedly. Snuggling close, he whispered, "Amanda Sloane, you are an amazing woman." Somewhere among the tangled bed covers her vibrator was still buzzing.

****

Amanda felt dazed, as if she had lost consciousness for a moment. She was lying on her side with Jake behind her, nestled like two spoons. He'd found the vibrator and turned it off, and now had one arm around her holding her breast. She had woken up the same way that morning, but then Jake's cock hadn't been buried in her ass as it was now. She felt sweaty and exhausted and sated. Deliriously sated.

She felt Jake stir, his chin against the top of her head. He moved his hand from her breast to brush a lock of hair off her shoulder. He leaned down and kissed her neck.

"You okay?" He whispered.

"Oh yeah. I'm much better than okay. How about you?"

"Wonderful," he said.

She felt his cock growing smaller until it slid out of her ass. "Saying goodbye so soon?"

He chuckled and left the bed to dispose of the condom. He crawled back in bed and wrapped his arms around her again. "Don't worry. I brought plenty of replacements."

"That was so erotic. Being filled so full in both my ass and my pussy."

After a long pause, Jake said, "You know you could have a real double penetration if you wanted."

Amanda was quiet for a moment. "I know. Justin and Luke propositioned me earlier." With her head turned away, she couldn't see his expression.

"What did you tell them?" He asked slowly.

"That I already had a date."

He was silent, but just for a moment, as if weighing his words carefully. "Don't take this wrong. I'm not trying to 'pimp you out.' But I'm just wondering if you *would* like to."

"To have another threesome with Justin and Luke?"

"Yes."

"Maybe. Would you like to watch again? Or would you join in?"

Jake didn't answer for a moment.

"It doesn't matter," she said quickly. "It's a moot point. I'm leaving tomorrow and I don't see any chance of coming back. And I sure don't imagine I'll see those two cowboys in New York City."

"I'm going to be sorry to see you leave. We've been on a hell of a ride."

"I'm sorry I have to leave." She stuck her lip out in a pout. Then she brightened. "But I'm grateful that I'm going back a much less inhibited woman. I think my friend Sarah is going to be very surprised."

The votives had burned down until all but a couple had flickered out. "We should probably get some sleep," Jake said. "You've got a long drive and I've got a lot to do, bringing all of those blankets and pots down from the cabin. Would you consider delaying your drive to help bring everything down to the lodge? Maybe take some photos? You could still leave by noon."

"Of course. I'll be happy to help," she murmured. She drifted to sleep thinking how grateful she was to have met these cowboys, and how hard it would be to leave and never see them again. Especially Jake. In spite of her determination not to get romantically involved, she had to admit she cared for him. A lot more than she should.

Chapter Nineteen

The next morning, Amanda, surprisingly, woke before Jake. It was just dawn and she lay quietly watching the coming light give definition to his face and torso. Even with his beautiful eyes closed, his face was handsome. He was naked, covered only with the sheet at his waist. His muscular physique reminded her of the elegant proportions of a Greek sculpture. She resisted the urge to reach out and stroke his shoulder and chest, but couldn't resist one last look at his cock. Slowly lifting the sheet, she uncovered his waist and groin.

He was hard, his erection a thick rod of flesh rising out of his pubic hair. As the room grew lighter, she could make out the velvet smooth, plum shaped head and the thick gnarled veins that encircled the shaft. His hard-on was probably more about "morning wood" than sexual arousal, but just looking at it turned her on.

"See something you like?" Jake's husky voice interrupted softly.

Startled, she dropped the sheet and looked quickly up at his face. She felt her cheeks go pink. "Sorry," she said. "I didn't mean to wake you." She lifted the sheet again and smiled. "But I'm glad I did. It would be such a waste to ignore an erection like that."

He flipped the sheet off. "You interested in one last ride before you have to say goodbye?"

"I'm very interested cowboy. But we'll have to hurry if we want to get up to the cabin."

"The cabin can wait," he said. "Right now the

treasure I want is your sweet pussy." She retrieved a condom from the pile on the side table and rolled it on his cock, then swung one leg over his waist and wiggled herself into position over his groin. Jake reached down and slid one finger through the folds of her labia. As his fingertip came to rest on her clitoris, her hips jerked in an involuntary spasm. "Oh! Jesus," she gasped. "My clit is so sensitive."

He grinned and circled the swollen bud with his fingertip, causing her hips to buck again. "Maybe we should wait. Give it a rest."

"Fat chance cowboy. Get ready for one hard ride."

She reached down and held his cock upright, guiding it in between the folds of her labia. She was very wet and his cock slid in easily. As his erection went deep, she clutched his shoulders and ground her pelvis down over his groin. Soon she was panting, staring down into his eyes as she fucked him. Leaning down, she kissed him, her tongue slipping deep into his mouth. She pulled back, restless.

"Oh God, I love this. I love fucking you, Jake. I'm going to miss you so much."

"I'm going to miss you, too, Amanda," he said, gripping her hips as she fucked him.

After several minutes, he lifted her from his cock and rolled her over onto her back.

She smiled and lay back, entwining her arms above her head and spreading her legs, her body open, inviting him in. He knelt between her thighs, staring down at her, his gaze hot with arousal. For a long moment, he didn't move and she remembered their first time together, when he had just looked at her so long she'd wondered if he wanted her. As she smiled up at him, she had no such doubts now.

****

Jake looked down at Amanda, knowing this

would surely be their last time to make love. God, she's beautiful, he thought. And so fucking sexy. If this has to be our last time together, I'm going to make damn sure she enjoys it. He leaned down and kissed the inside of her left thigh, starting at her knee and kissing his way wetly up to her pussy. He gave her slit a quick lick that caused her to gasp, then repeated his kisses up the inside of her right thigh. Once again, he licked up through the smoothly shaved folds of her pussy, but this time his tongue lingered, probing the weeping, swollen flesh, licking the sweet nectar of her arousal. In seconds, she was whimpering and writhing under his lips and tongue, lifting her hips from the bed to show him her need. His tongue probed deep then slid up to flick rapidly over her clit.

"OhmyGod! Oh...oh...oh Jesus." She reached down and grabbed his head, tangling her fingers in his hair as she pulled him tight against her core. Jake lifted his head, pulling away from her hands.

"No, don't," he said. "Put your arms back above your head and leave them there."

She looked at him for a moment, studying his expression. Then she smiled, closed her eyes, and raised her arms back above her head. Jake leaned back down and kissed her again, moving from her pussy to her tummy and waist. He spent a moment dipping his tongue into the dimple of her belly button, then moved up to her breasts. He lathed each firm, full globe completely, saving her areolas and nipples for last. Amanda continued to writhe and twist under his touch, moaning her pleasure at what he was doing.

As he sucked her nipples, pressing the large, pebble-hard buds between his lips, her moans and whimpers became more insistent. "Oh God, Jake...please..."

He kissed up her neck to the hollow beneath her

ear. "Please what, Amanda? What do you want? What do you need?"

She looked at him through half-lidded eyes. "You. Your cock. Oh God, Jake. My pussy's on fire. I need you to fuck me. Fuck me now."

Jake held himself above her on one arm. With his free hand he gently stroked her face. *Goddamn, she's beautiful,* he thought. How can a woman so sexually erotic be so fucking beautiful?

Holding her chin and cheek in his hand he tilted her mouth toward his. Just as he slid his tongue deep into her mouth, his cock nudged the entrance to her pussy. With one thrust of his hips, he shoved his dick into the depths of her core. Taken by surprise, she clawed at his back, her loud moan muffled by his passionate kiss. Pushing her arms back above her head, he secured both of her wrists in one hand, pinning her to the mattress. He broke the kiss and lifted his head, looking down at her. She stared up at him through lust-glazed eyes, her mouth open, her breath shallow. He could feel her vaginal muscles clutching at his cock, squeezing him in rhythmic spasms.

"Amanda Sloane, I'm going to fuck you senseless." He began to fuck her, his hips and cock a ramrod plunging over and over into her wet flesh.

"Yes Jake! Yesss! Fuck me. Fuck me...fuck me...fuck me..."

Amanda came with a scream, her head back, her eyes shut tight, her hips thrusting her pussy up to meet his plunging strokes. Jake felt his own climax ignite, a burst of white-hot flame that started in his cock and spread like a wildfire to every cell in his body. He groaned and shoved his cock deep, surrendering to the surge of pleasure that roiled his consciousness.

Finally the waves of ecstasy subsided and he collapsed, his body immobile on top of Amanda.

"You can let go of my wrists now. I'm not going to scratch you again."

Jake unclamped his hand and rolled to one side with a deep sigh. He put an arm around her. "My God, that was..."

"Bliss," Amanda said. "Pure bliss." They lay quietly for a moment and then Amanda said, "I guess you know you've ruined me. For sex."

Jake lifted to one elbow and looked at her curiously. She looked back at him and grinned. "Where am I ever going to find another man who can fuck me like that? My toes are still curled."

"New York is a big city. Got to be a lot of men there."

"You'd be surprised," she said, sliding out of his embrace. "Come on cowboy. I've got a plane to catch."

****

As soon as Jake had his jeans and shirt on, Amanda gave him a quick kiss and pushed him out the door. It took her ten minutes to pack and dress for the trip to the cabin and then back to New York. She found Jake in the kitchen, where Rosita had prepared breakfast burritos they could eat on the way. Amanda had brought her camera to take pictures. The cabin was an interesting historical facet of the provenance of the Indian artifacts. Jake tossed some empty boxes and packing material in the back of the open top Jeep, and they set off across the creek and up the rolling hills.

When they were within half a mile of the cabin, Jake said, "What the hell," and sped up, the Jeep jostling from side to side as it bounced over the rough terrain.

As they got closer, Amanda could see that the cabin door, which Manuel had been sent to padlock the evening before, stood wide open. A wisp of dark smoke curled up from the cabin's chimney. "What the fuck," Jake muttered as the Jeep dropped into a shallow draw and rose back up, the front wheels catching air as it soared over the opposite side. He punched the accelerator, guiding the vehicle around boulders and through patches of cactus and thickets of mesquite.

As they reached the cabin, Jake stomped on the break, sliding up next to the open door. He and Amanda both leaped out of the Jeep and rushed to the open door. The new padlock dangled uselessly, hanging on a hasp that had been ripped out of the doorframe.

Amanda stepped inside, a hard knot forming in her tummy. She felt something crunch under the sole of her boot. "No!" She cried. "Oh my God, no!"

The floor was littered with shards of broken pottery. Broken chunks were also scattered on the table and bunk beds. As she looked around in the dim light, she saw that every pot had been shattered. The Native American blankets had been sliced to shreds and burned in the pot-bellied stove where they still smoldered.

The chests at the ends of the beds were open, their contents scattered. She couldn't believe the destruction. Why in God's name would the man do this? The only answer was that he was truly insane. She looked around, her eyes filling with tears. Based on what Chi and Underwood had estimated, she was looking at a quarter of a million dollars' worth of destruction. Native American artifacts destroyed before they could be appreciated.

"That goddamn cock-sucking son of a bitch!" Jake was livid with anger.

"Do you think your cousin...?"

"Hell yes! Who else would do it? I'm going to kill the son of a bitch for this."

"Jake, you can't..."

"Yes, I can. Watch me. When a rattlesnake is

207

that dangerous, you have to kill it. Get in the Jeep. We're going back to the lodge."

As they got in the Jeep, Amanda said, "How did he find out about the pottery and blankets? How would he even know what was in the cabin?"

"Hell, Amanda, half a dozen hands knew we took Chi and Underwood to the cabin. And I sent Manuel up here with a goddamned fifty cent lock!"

On the trip back to the lodge, Jake was silent, but she sensed she was sitting next to a seething volcano. She wanted to comfort him, but didn't know what to say. What could she say? This man she was beginning to care about was plagued by a man—a monster. "Jake, I'm so sorry..."

He said nothing. But when he looked at her, his eyes were as hard and dark as flint. When the Jeep pulled up next to the lodge, Justin was standing on the porch, waiting for them. He looked at Amanda, and then at Jake. "What's the matter? What's wrong?"

"The pottery and blankets in the cabin were destroyed." Jake said. The fire in his eyes was now at a slow burn. "The son of a bitch smashed every pot, burned every blanket. A quarter of a million burned and smashed to smithereens."

Justin's face went pale and he glanced at Amanda. She nodded her confirmation of Jake's unbelievable statement. Justin turned livid. "The goddamn fucking son of a bitch. You should've let me shoot him."

"I should have. But then I'd have to run the ranch all by myself once your ass was in prison down at Huntsville."

"If we don't come up with another quarter million dollars soon, we may not have a ranch to run. Unfortunately, I know why the son of a bitch is doing it."

"Because he's an insane asshole."

"He is that," Justin said. "But he's also a sneaky fucking sidewinder."

Amanda watched Jake and Justin, waiting.

"He's got Daddy's note. He bought it from the bank." Justin seemed broken.

"How the fuck do you know that?" Jake looked at his younger brother in disbelief.

"I called Lloyd Masters at the bank this morning. Told him we would have half the money this week when we sell the blanket and pot to Chi Long. I said we would have the other half once we sold everything still in the cabin at auction. Told him we would need a month's extension until the Santa Fe auction in June. Masters said if it was up to him that would be no problem. But it wasn't up to him. It was up to the man who held our note. And that man is…"

"Winslow," Jake said, his voice barely a whisper. "That sneaky son of a bitch. He didn't want the painting. Or the pots and blankets. He wants the goddamn ranch!"

"And he may get it, too, now that he's destroyed our chance to sell the pots and blankets."

"That fucking piece of cow shit," Jake snarled, his voice laced with venom.

"He needs to be shot." Justin's body seemed to seethe with rage.

"Yes," Jake agreed. "But we won't be the ones to do it. You were right when you stopped me before. Now take your own advice and back off."

Amanda was relieved to see Jake take a deep breath and begin to calm down. Nothing good could come out of a confrontation between Winslow and Jake or Justin.

"The question," Justin said, "is what do we do now?"

Jake had gained control of his anger and now seemed to be thinking rationally. "First," he said, "I think we should sell the first phase blanket and Onapi pot to Chi Long. He said he would fly back down to pick them up if we wanted to sell. At least then, we will have half the money in the bank."

"I agree," Justin said. "I'll call him today. And the pots and blankets in the cabin? Was there anything salvageable?"

Jake shook his head, looking at Amanda.

"No," she said. "It was all destroyed."

"We need to go back and clean it up." Jake said. "Manuel could go, but I think I'd rather do it myself. I'll get a broom and some plastic bags from Rosita."

"I'll come." Justin said. "I want to see just what the bastard has done."

Jake looked at Amanda. "I guess you'll still be leaving this afternoon."

"No," she said. "If you don't mind, I'd like to go back to the cabin with you and clean up. Tomorrow is Saturday. I can leave then. If I can rearrange my flights, I'll still be able to stop in Austin and see a friend from college."

"You're welcome to stay another night," Jake said. "But you don't have to help us clean up the cabin. I'm afraid that's going to be a depressing chore."

"I know," she said. "But I want to help."

A dark cloud of discouragement hung over the Jeep as Justin, Jake, and Amanda drove back up the winding path to the cabin. It was hard for her to believe anyone could be as evil as the Morgans' cousin. But the evidence was on the cabin floor and in the pot-bellied stove. She certainly couldn't forget the burned painting that had brought her to Texas in the first place.

Chapter Twenty

At the cabin they opened the door and windows to let in light, and Jake lit the lamp sitting on the table. The image of Amanda sitting on the table with her legs wrapped around his neck, screaming in orgasm, seemed a lifetime away.

Any hopes they might have harbored that the pots could be glued back together vanished when they saw the destruction on the cabin floor. Every pot was smashed to bits, leaving no piece bigger than a silver dollar.

While Jake began to sweep up the shards of pottery, Justin and Amanda pulled what was left of the blankets out of the pot-bellied stove and stuffed the charred remains in large plastic bags.

"Jesus," Amanda muttered, holding up a two foot square corner of a beautifully woven blanket. "There's not even enough left to make a shawl."

"That bastard," Justin raged. "That limp-dicked fucker. You should have let me kill him the other day when he burned the Randell painting."

"The fake Randell, you mean," Jake corrected.

"Let's finish up and get out of here," Justin said. He kicked a shard of pottery across the floor. "I'm tired of looking at our last hope of paying off Daddy's note scattered all over the goddamn floor."

They finished cleaning up the cabin and loaded the bags of trash in the Jeep. As Justin cupped his hands around the lamp chimney to blow it out, Jake had the disheartening thought that blowing out the lantern was akin to extinguishing their future. Try as he might, he couldn't see a flicker of light at the end of this dark tunnel.

****

"Wait," Amanda cried, a moment before Justin blew out the lantern. "Wait. What's that?" She was pointing to an object tucked in a corner above the cabin's central rafter.

"I don't know," Jake said. "It's not big enough to be another blanket."

The object was just out of Jake's reach so he pulled one of the chairs over to stand on. The object was stuffed tight between the rafter and roof and it took a minute to work it free. "It's a bedroll." Jake stepped down from the chair and held it out. "A really old bedroll."

The canvas bedroll was weathered to a dark grey. It was about three feet wide and six inches in diameter, tied in a roll with two strips of rawhide. "It looks like it was stuffed in there to stop a leak in the roof," Amanda said. She could see daylight coming through a hole in the roof and the bedroll had a large water stain on one side. She moved closer to see what Jake was holding.

"Let's take it outside," Justin said. "So we can see it better."

Jake took the bedroll out and laid it on the hood of the Jeep. He tried to untie the rawhide strips that held it together.

"Wait," Amanda said. "It's filthy." she took a broom and dusted off the outside, brushing off a thick layer of dirt. One again Jake tried to untie the rawhide strips. The leather was so old and brittle, there was no way to get them undone.

Justin stepped up next to Jake. "Here." He handed his brother a pocketknife. "Cut the damn things."

Jake took the knife and cut the binding strips, then slowly unrolled the stiff fabric. Amanda could see that the water stain on the outside of the canvas

212

had not seeped into the interior and, while the bedroll looked old, the inside seemed to be fairly clean and in remarkably good condition.

"I'll bet this has been tied behind a lot of saddles," Jake said. "And slept on under a lot of starry nights. It looks like it's at least a hundred years old." As he unrolled the bedroll, they saw that it was two layers of canvas sewn together with a thin pad between them. "The pad is probably horsehair," Jake said. "They used that a lot back in the 1800s. And it looks like one side has been coated with something, probably buffalo fat, to make it waterproof."

Halfway down the length of the bedroll, another piece of canvas appeared—white and small, about twelve inches wide by eighteen inches high.

"Careful Jake. Go easy." Justin cautioned.

Jake gave his brother a look and then continued to slowly unroll the bedroll, revealing more of the smaller canvas.

"It's got writing on it," Amanda said. She felt her pulse suddenly speed up. The three of them moved closer, crowding in to read the message on the small canvas. The writing had been done with paint and a small brush.

Amanda read slowly, "To gunslinger Odel Morgan—thanks for posing for me. *Rawhide Outlaws* has returned my illustration, which I'm giving to you. Your picture will be in the June issue if you have a chance to find a copy. "Hot Lead for Horse Thieves" is a good yarn. I think you will like it. Thanks again for the canvas you gave me. I hope Mr. Goodnight wasn't too upset about you cutting up his chuck wagon. Good luck with your ranch. I know you'll do fine. Your friend. It's signed, CMR." Amanda said. Beneath the initials was an outline of a buffalo scull.

Amanda's heart was pounding, racing so fast

she thought it might explode from her chest. Reaching out, she gently picked up the small canvas and carefully flipped it over on the bedroll.

"I'll be damned," Justin said. Jake echoed his comment.

Amanda whispered, "Oh my God."

In the center of the small canvas an elegant illustration had been drawn of a young cowboy dressed in chaps and boots and hat with a pearl-handled six-shooter in a holster at his side. The gunslinger was wearing a blue shirt with a bright red bandanna knotted loosely around his neck. The colors seemed as bright and vibrant as the day it must have been painted. The cowboy was the central figure of the illustration, with only a few strokes of paint indicating a corral and Western saloon in the background. Otherwise, the cowboy was surrounded by plain canvas. The canvas had yellowed slightly, but the painting looked as if it could have been painted yesterday.

Across the bottom of the painting was the notation: *R.O. 04 / 89—Hot Lead for Horse Thieves.*

Amanda turned toward Jake. She had been holding her breath and had to exhale before she could speak. "You know what I think this is?" Her excitement was barely contained.

Jake looked at her, waiting.

"I think this is an original Charles Marion Randell illustration for a story in the Western periodical *Rawhide Outlaws.* I'm sure I saw a copy of this very illustration while I was researching the painting you own."

"You mean the fake, burned Randell we own." Jake said. "What makes you think this one is real?"

Amanda glanced up at him, sensing his hesitation. "Mostly a gut feeling. We need to get back to the lodge so I can compare it to the examples on my computer. *Rawhide Outlaws* used several

Randell paintings to illustrate their stories about the West. Time-wise, the stories were published about the time Randell was painting in Judith Basin, Montana."

Justin leaned in over her shoulder. "What about the signature? Does it look real?"

"There is no signature. Just the line with the April '89 date and title. But that's better than a signature. That ties this illustration to *Rawhide Outlaws*, which is a well-documented publication. If the magazine actually used the illustration, and I'm almost certain I've seen it, we'll be able to find it."

She turned to Jake. "Do you notice anything in particular about the date?"

Jake examined it a moment then looked her with a sly smile. "Well, the tail on the nine is straight."

"As an arrow," she added.

They studied the painting for several minutes. Finally Justin said, "So if this is the real deal, actually painted by Randell, it could be worth a lot of money, right?"

She smiled. "It could be," she said. "Maybe not as much as a large oil. But yes, it would be worth a lot."

"Millions?"

"Oh yeah," she said. "Millions."

Justin turned the painting over again and reread the note. "So this may be a note Randell wrote to our great grandfather Odel. In the letter Great Granddad Odel wrote to his mother, he said an artist named Kid Randell gussied him up like a gunslinger. And he said he gave the artist some blank canvas from the chuck wagon. This note on the back of the illustration confirms what Great Granddad Odel wrote doesn't it? It *must* be a real Randell."

It looks real to me," Amanda said. "But let's not

get our hopes up too high just yet. We got shot down with the painting at the lodge. I need some time to really study this and compare it to the printed illustrations in *Rawhide Outlaws*."

"Then let's get back so you can get busy." Justin said. "Our future is in your hands."

"No. Your future may be wrapped up in this bedroll." She cautioned.

"If it gets authenticated," Jake said.

Amanda could see that the roller coaster of good news, bad news he had been riding had made him cautious. She couldn't blame him or Justin for having doubts. "It will be Jake. I'm almost certain of it. But I need some time with the illustration and my computer."

Jake had rolled the painting up in the bedroll again and handed it to her.

She took the bedroll, handling it carefully. "Do you trust me with this?"

"Totally," he said.

Jake took it much slower on the drive back to the lodge. So much so that she had to bite her tongue to keep from telling him to speed things up. She was certain she had seen the gunslinger illustration before. And she remembered a reference to the *Hot Lead for Horse Thieves* title. She could hardly wait to get back to her research.

In her room, she opened the bedroll and laid the painting on the bed. She flipped open her laptop and began the search. It took her less than ten minutes to find what she was looking for. She also found some related information that made her heart race.

A knock on the door startled her. When she opened it, she was surprised to see Jake standing in the hallway. Outwardly he was his calm, taciturn self. But she knew that inside he must be churning with excitement and anticipation.

"Find anything yet?" he asked.

"Look." She grabbed his arm and pulled him into the room, then turned the computer to face him. "Fortunately, the folks at *Rawhide Outlaws* were meticulous about keeping records of their publication."

The screen of her laptop was filled with an illustration that looked identical to the original canvas lying on the bed. The only difference was that the handwritten note on the original had been replaced with a printed caption in italic that read, "Fast as Lightning."

"And look at this." She scrolled down below the picture to a block of text that read: *"Gunslinger illustration by CM Randell. Purchased April 1889. Price $85. Printed June 1889. Original returned to artist."*

"Jake, we're building a chain of evidence that will be hard to refute. I've got to spend more time with this, but right now I'm betting my reputation on it being real.

"I do have to tell you that illustrations are fairly easy for a forger to copy because they have the printed work to go by. But the artist has to be really good because even minor mistakes or discrepancies will show up in a comparison. If this painting is a forgery, and I don't think it is, it's better than the painting that got destroyed."

She looked at him, her face still beaming with excitement. Her enthusiasm was contagious and he returned her smile, his eyes twinkling. He reached for her with both hands and held her waist, pulling her toward him. She let her body mold into his, happy to see the sparkle returning to his expression.

"I'm really glad you saw the bedroll in the rafters," he said.

"It was sheer luck."

He pulled her close and leaned down to kiss her. "You are an amazing woman."

She gave him a quick kiss and then pushed away. "Later. I've got to get back to my computer. And I need to call my boss."

"All right," he said, moving through the door. "Until later."

She spent the rest of the afternoon researching *Rawhide Outlaw Publishing* and the gunslinger art.

At seven-thirty she called Richard. Her last conversation had been about the destruction of the pots and blankets in the cabin. This time she had good news. Very good news.

"Oh my God!" He cried, when she told him about the painting and how it was discovered. "Do you really think it's genuine, Mandy?"

"I do. Right now, I would stake my reputation on it. There's overwhelming evidence that points to it being the real thing. It's been tucked away in the rafters of the cabin for a hundred years or more. I've studied it all afternoon, comparing it to illustrations printed by *Rawhide Outlaws*. We've got the printed illustration to compare it to and the written notes and letters that tie it all together. I swear it looks authentic, Richard. I want to bring it with me when I come back to New York."

"And not send it to Montana?"

"No. Under normal circumstances I would. But you know those academics. They might take weeks or months to come to a decision. The Morgans don't have that much time. Chi Long is making a cash buy for the first phase blanket and Onapi pot, but they still need another quarter million by the end of the month. We might speed things up, but I need the painting in New York."

Richard was hesitant, but finally said, "All right, Mandy. But I don't want you to leave without it being insured. Send me photos of it and I'll get it insured for say, four million, on the strength of your analysis. PP&C will cover the cost of the premium.

Then we need to revise the contract with the Morgans. It can be basically the same as before, just substitute the new painting for the old."

"I'm sure the Morgans will be fine with that. Now, let me tell you what I have in mind."

It took her half an hour to tell Richard what she wanted to do. When she finished, he said it might be a long shot but it was worth a try. She e-mailed him several pictures of the illustration, both the front with the gunslinger art and the back with the note to Odel Morgan. When she finished, she realized she was starving.

She rolled up the small canvas and took it downstairs. Jake and Justin were in their office. They were both in far better spirits than they had been on the trip up to the cabin that morning.

She smiled at their change of mood. Unrolling the canvas, she laid it on the desk. "PP&C is e-mailing a revised contract," she said. "Essentially the same as before, with the gunslinger illustration substituted for the original art. And Richard is insuring the illustration for four million. That's not to say it will bring that much when we sell it. We just want to make sure if something happens, we are well covered.

"One more thing," she added. "I'd like to take the painting with me to New York."

"Not send it to the museum in Montana?" Justin asked.

"No. I have a plan I think will speed up authentication. But I need the painting in New York. If you have a mailing tube, I can tuck it in my carry-on. I'll have it with me the whole trip."

"No problem," Justin said. He opened a cabinet door and took out a plastic tube just large enough to hold the roll of canvas.

"You are still planning on leaving tomorrow?" Jake asked.

"Yes. I am." She wasn't sure if the hint of sadness she suddenly felt was from his question or her own heart.

"So tonight will be your last night here?" Justin said.

"I'm afraid so. We need to get the painting looked at as quickly as possible. And I need to get back to work."

Rosita called everyone for supper. Julie and Luke were there and, as they went to the dining room, Jake quietly said, "Let's not say anything about the illustration, okay?"

"Sure," she said. "I think that's wise."

After supper, Luke and Julie invited Amanda to join them for another night at the Rusty Buckle.

"I'll make sure no asshole tries to lasso you," Luke said.

"Thanks, but I think I'll pass. I need a night to rest up. It's probably best if I avoid that much entertainment." She looked from Luke and Julie to Justin and Jake when she demurred, silently letting them know she wanted to spend the night alone. She sensed both Luke and Justin were disappointed. But she had already indulged in more sex in the past five days than she'd had in five months in New York. And not just sex. She'd had *great* sex.

After supper, she watched Jake and Justin walk through the main room to their shared office, their tight asses almost begging to be caressed. For a moment, she thought spending her last night at the ranch with Jake and one of the other cowboys might not be such a bad idea. But then they closed their office door, and she decided to stick with her decision to spend the night alone.

Chapter Twenty-One

Amanda took another long hot bubble bath in the claw-foot tub. At home she usually showered, her tub being much smaller and not nearly as luxurious. As she soaked in bubbles up to her neck, she thought about the roller coaster ride they'd been on. It seemed every high point had been followed by disaster. But, she felt certain that, unless she got blown away in a tornado, finding the gunslinger art was not going to be shattered by bad news. It was, however, critical to get the painting appraised and sold by the time the Morgan's note was due at the bank. There was no guarantee she could pull it off, but it was their best shot.

She got out of the tub and dried off, then slipped on her sleeping tee. She turned off her bedside lamp and opened the drapes. The stars were once again brilliant, a vast, deep bowl filled with diamond points of light.

Just as she turned away to get in bed, she saw a movement on the balcony. She stepped to her doorway and looked more closely. It was Jake, outside his room, leaning against the balcony railing and looking up at the same night sky. He was barefoot and shirtless, wearing only a pair of jeans. She reached for her door handle, then hesitated. If she went out onto that balcony, it would be a while before she got to sleep. Then she remembered how wonderful it had been making love with Jake. This might be her last opportunity for a long time. Maybe forever.

She opened her balcony door and stepped

outside into the warm Texas night.

Jake turned his head when he heard her door click open. In the starlight, she could see him smile. She walked up next to him and turned to lean against the railing.

"Trouble sleeping?" he asked.

"A little. How about you?"

"Well, it has been one hell of a day." She could see his grin even in the dim light.

"Yes. It has." She turned toward him. "I'm so sorry about the pots and blankets, Jake. I really am. But you do have the painting."

He turned to face her. "Thanks to you." His muscles rippled in the starlight.

She reached out and put one hand on his chest. He moved a breath closer and put his hands on her waist, pulling her close. She tilted her chin up to meet his lips, their tongues probing, searching each other's mouths. Her pussy moistened and her nipples stiffened against his chest. She reached down, cupping his cock with her palm. He was hard, rigidly erect. They continued to kiss and she stroked his erection, their passion growing.

Suddenly, she felt another presence. A warm breath on the back of her neck and pressure against her ass. She started to pull away but Jake held her close, continuing the kiss.

****

"Is there room for one more?" Justin slid his hands around to angle her slightly away from Jake's chest. Jake could feel his brother's hands as Justin cupped her breasts, fondling her nipples through her T-shirt.

She broke the kiss and looked up at Jake, her dark eyes wide. He looked at her, waiting for her reaction. "That's entirely up to Amanda," he said.

"Oh God," she whispered, her breath shallow, her voice husky.

Justin was holding her waist, nuzzling her neck with his lips and tongue. He leaned in close, whispering in her ear. "Amanda?"

She sighed deeply. Jake felt her slide one hand around behind her to palm Justin's cock. She turned her head, whispering over her shoulder. "Yes, Justin. There is room for you."

"Give me a minute," he said. "I'll get some condoms."

As Justin went to his room, she looked up at Jake, her eyes imploring. "Are you okay with this? Having Justin..."

Jake looked at her for a long moment, his gaze earnest. Then he slowly smiled. "I know you want this. You were so turned on when we talked about it. I think it's an experience you need. An experience I'm pleased to help make happen." She gave him a slight smile. "I care about you, Amanda, deeply. Enough to help you discover all the sexual pleasure you deserve." He studied her expression. "You do want this, don't you?"

She closed her eyes and took a breath. "Yes," she whispered. "Oh God, yes I do, as long as you're with me."

Jake gripped the tail of her T-shirt and pulled it up. She helped, lifting her arms as he stripped it up and off. He stripped his jeans off, shoving them aside with his foot. Justin was back in a moment, handing him a condom. As Jake rolled it on, Justin quickly shucked off his jeans. Amanda melted into Jake's arms for a kiss. After a moment, he turned her around for a, deep open-mouthed kiss from Justin. Even from his perspective, their bodies shown luminously in the starlight.

Amanda faced Justin, her back pressed tight against Jake's chest. She reached back, her hand searching for his cock. He reached down, stroking her pussy with his fingers, sliding through the creamy moisture of her arousal. "God your pussy is wet. You really want this, don't you Amanda? Feel how hard my cock is? I want it, too. We're going to give you exactly what you want. Exactly what you need. Right, Justin?"

"And then some," Justin said. He reached down and grasped her ass, lifting her until her bare feet were off the balcony deck. As she spread her legs Jake could see Justin's cock probing the wet folds at the entrance to her pussy. Then he was inside her, his cock sliding deep.

"Oh God," she whispered. "Yes! Fuck me!"

She shifted against Jake's chest as Justin lifted her ass up and down, sliding his dick faster and faster in and out of her pussy. Jake held her back and shoulders, supporting her as his brother fucked her with deep steady strokes. Amanda, off her feet and unable to control her movements, had surrendered completely to the two men. Her neck was arched, her head back against Jake's chest. She looked up, her breath shallow, her eyes glazing with pleasure. Jake smiled as he held her for Justin's penetration.

"Squeeze your breasts, Amanda," Jake said. "Pinch those pretty nipples."

She complied, lifting her hands to her breasts, pinching the large pebbles between her thumbs and forefingers. She reacted immediately to the added stimulation, her hips bucking against Justin's driving cock.

"Oh God," she whispered. "Oh God! Oh God!" she repeated, her voice rising. "I'm going to come. Fuck me, Justin. Don't stop."

Justin fucked her faster, plunging deep as he gripped her hips tightly. Her body twisted in Jake's arms and he held her tighter. She slid one hand down from her breast to her clit, rapidly stroking the engorged bud and propelling herself into climax.

Jake clutched her closer as her orgasm wracked her body, her heat threatening to ignite his own and spark a spontaneous orgasm. As she jerked and twisted in his arms, her pussy filled with Justin's cock, a wail of ecstasy echoed through the night. Jake had to hold on tight to keep from dropping her writhing, thrusting body.

Watching Amanda being fucked to orgasm by Justin stimulated all of Jake's voyeuristic impulses and his arousal level rose to red line. His turn to pleasure her couldn't come soon enough to ease the ache in his rock hard erection.

****

With a final shudder, Amanda's orgasm subsided and she was still, gradually trying to absorb the amazing pleasure. Justin gently lowered her hips and let her legs slip slowly to the deck. Jake helped her find her balance, lifting her upright but holding on, letting her get used to standing on trembling legs.

"Oh my God," she whispered. "That was amazing." She paused quietly for moment, regaining body consciousness, then asked shyly, "Did I scream?"

Jake chuckled. "Just a little."

"The ranch hands probably thought it was a coyote," Justin added.

She felt her cheeks grow warm. The lack of inhibition that allowed her to enjoy incredible orgasms came with unintended side effects— Amanda was extremely vocal in her pleasure. She sighed. "How many coyotes do you have around here that scream, 'Fuck me Justin!' "

She finally gained control of her quivering legs and turned toward Jake. He pulled her close and kissed her, then said "Now it's my turn. Turn around." She grinned up at him then turned her back to his chest. "Spread your legs," he said. "And put your hands on your knees."

Amanda followed his directions quickly, anticipating the pleasure she knew he was capable of stirring in her body. She tilted her bottom up, her pussy at the perfect height for Jake's cock. Justin discarded his condom and stepped in front of her. The men had placed her perfectly; she could suck Justin's cock while Jake fucked her from behind.

As soon as Jake's cock slid into her, she moaned, reveling in the exquisite pleasure of his hard flesh stroking her pussy, plunging deep into her core. She leaned forward and opened her mouth wide, taking Justin's cock deep in her throat.

The two men began to fuck her mouth and pussy in a practiced, steady rhythm, filling her with cock and then pulling away. At first they fucked her slowly, steadily, letting her feel every sensation of their penetration. Jake held her hips firmly, keeping her in position as his thick cock slid in and out of her pussy. She knew he was watching her suck Justin's cock and knew the sight must be turning him on. She could feel his growing arousal in the tightening grip of his hands on her hips. She sucked Justin's cock with salacious abandon, performing for Jake as much as pleasuring his brother. Justin tangled his fingers in her hair, not gripping her head tightly but keeping her in position as his cock thrust in and out of her mouth.

She lifted her hands from her knees and reached forward to grab Justin's hips, pulling him closer and taking his cock deeper into her throat. Her own arousal was spreading sizzling heat throughout her body, and she slammed herself back against Jake's cock as she sucked Justin deeper into her throat.

After several minutes of fucking her mouth and pussy at the same time, the men stopped, pulling away simultaneously and leaving her whimpering for their cocks.

"Just hold on sugar," Justin said, rolling on another condom. "We aren't through yet."

"Come here, baby," Jake said, turning her to face him. Reaching down, he grasped the firm globes of her bottom and lifted her up. When her pussy was just above his cock, he lowered her hips to slowly envelop his erection. Once fully impaled on his rigid cock, she leaned back, expecting Justin to hold her as Jake had done.

"No," Jake said. "Lean forward. Lock your legs around my waist and your arms around my neck."

As she readjusted her position, Justin stepped up behind her. "I brought some lube," he said, picking up the tube from the balcony railing. She trembled as Justin squeezed some lubricant onto his finger and reached for her ass. Her hips jerked in surprise when the cool lube was pushed into her anus. "Don't worry," he whispered in her ear. "We'll take it slow and easy."

Jake lifted her a few inches and she felt the head of Justin's cock nudging her tight opening.

"Oh God," she whispered. "Oh God, yes."

Jake lowered her as Justin tilted his pelvis forward to get himself in position. She felt a brief pinch of pain as his cockhead pushed through the ring of her anus, quickly replaced by intense pleasure as he slid fully into her. She could feel nothing but the fullness of both cocks deep inside her, two thick, hard shafts separated only by a thin membrane of flesh. Sandwiched between the two strong men, she felt helpless, totally in their power, but protected in a complete physical caress.

Jake held her ass while Justin gripped her waist. Working in sync, the brothers lifted and lowered Amanda, using their strength to fuck her simultaneously on their engorged cocks.

"Oh God. It's so good," she cried. "It's so good!" Having both cocks in her at the same time gave her a sensation of intense erotic pleasure. The lubricant made it so much easier to enjoy the cock sliding in and out of her ass, and she moaned with continuous sighs of pleasure.

"It is good, isn't it?" Jake asked. "Having your tight ass and sweet pussy filled with both of our cocks. My cock aches with pleasure. I could fuck you forever. Justin, do you like fucking Amanda's tight ass?"

"Fuck yes," Justin moaned. "It's incredible. Do you like my cock in your ass, Amanda?"

"Yes! Oh, fuck me!" She pulled Jake's head down for a voracious kiss. He returned the kiss eagerly, his mouth and lips and tongue ravenous, as if he needed to devour her. At her back, Justin kissed her neck and shoulders, nipping at her flesh with gentle teeth. The men moved faster, the double penetration bringing all of them closer and closer to climax. Jake pulled away from their frantic kiss and looked over her shoulder at Justin.

"Now, Justin," Jake gritted out. "I can't wait any longer."

"Yes," Justin answered hoarsely. "I'm ready."

She realized her two lovers were at the brink of orgasm, each ready to fill her with cum. "Yes!" she cried. "Now. Come in me now."

At some imperceptible signal, the two men stopped dead still. Their cocks twitched and spasmed, erupting into Amanda's ass and pussy with frightening force. They both groaned loudly, their fierce roar and thrusting cocks igniting her own orgasm. Rocked by waves of pleasure flooding through her body she screamed in ecstasy, her inner muscles clenched from the involuntary contractions of her climax. Jake and Justin held her firmly in place, keeping her sandwiched tightly between their muscular bodies, their cocks buried deep in her pussy and ass.

When her shuddering spasms finally faded and her muscles quit jerking, they gently lifted her off their cocks. Her body was still tingling from currents of electricity skittering up and down her spine.

Amanda was amazed she could actually stay upright on her trembling legs. She turned to each man, kissing them in turn. "I can't tell you how amazing that felt."

Both men were grinning at her. "I think we have a pretty good idea," Jake said.

She turned toward her room but her legs were still trembling and she had to grab the balcony railing to keep from stumbling. Jake reached down and picked her up, cradling her in his arms. As he started toward her room, Justin stopped him.

He leaned down and gave her a gentle kiss. "Goodnight, Amanda. It's been amazing getting to know you."

She sighed and kissed him back. "You too, Justin. It has been amazing."

Jake carried her to her room, where he tucked her in bed, then gave her a soft kiss and said goodnight. As he rose up, she reached out and clasped his hand, stopping him. "Jake..."

"Yes?"

She hesitated, then said, "Thank you. It was...it was just what I imagined. An experience I'll never forget. Thank you, and Justin, for...for sharing."

Jake grinned and squeezed her hand. "No Amanda. We thank *you* for sharing."

As he left, she remembered that her nightshirt was still on the balcony. It didn't really matter. She would sleep naked. Naked and well satisfied. Moments later, Amanda drifted off to a sound asleep.

Chapter Twenty-Two

The next morning, Amanda said goodbye to Jake in his room, their arms around each other as they kissed a final time. "I'm going to miss you, Amanda," he said.

She stared up into his deep green eyes, trying to keep her own eyes from tearing up. "I'm going to miss you, too, Jake. More than you know. I don't know how it might happen, but I hope we can see each other again. I've loved our time together." Her brave face began to crumble and her tears welled up.

"It has been special."

They kissed again, more quickly, then broke apart. She stepped toward the door, not wanting him to see the tears that filled her eyes. It was hard to understand why she was so emotional about leaving. She had known this man—these men—for only a few days. Okay, she and Jake both said they loved the sex. But that wasn't the same as saying they loved each other. Loving a man, even one as hot as Jake, is not what Amanda wanted right now. *And it's not what Jake wants. Is it?* She studied the man in his chaps and boots and spurs, his black cowboy hat shading his face. He was so different from New York City's metrosexuals in their pinstriped suits.

As she opened the door, he said, "Wait. I want to give you something." She turned around as Jake sat down and quickly took off his spurs. "Here," he said. "I want you to have these."

She took the spurs, surprised at the gesture. "Jake, I can't take these. They are beautiful, but I know how much they mean to you."

"That's why I want you to have them. Because they do mean a lot to me."

She looked at the hand-worked silver spurs. Even after a hundred years, they were still beautiful. Once again, she fought back tears, determined that this was not going to be a day of weepy goodbyes.

"Thank you, Jake. They're beautiful." She rose on tiptoe and kissed him, then hurried out of the room and down the stairs, knowing he would follow her out.

Amanda and Jake walked out onto the porch to find Rosita, Justin, and Luke waiting at the bottom of the steps. The two men were dressed in chaps like Jake, ready to ride. Luke and Justin saw the pair of spurs she was carrying and looked at each other with raised eyebrows.

Luke chuckled. "Those ought to keep those city dudes in line. A couple of pokes in the flank will have those boys bucking like broncs."

She blushed and laid the spurs on the passenger seat with her purse. When she turned back, Rosita was waiting with open arms.

As Amanda hugged her, the housekeeper said, "Miss Julie told me to tell you goodbye. She is on her way to San Antonio."

"Say goodbye for me, too, Rosita. And thank you for the beautiful dress. And the wonderful meals." She turned toward Luke and Justin. "It's been wonderful getting to know you two cowboys," she said with a mischievous gleam in her eyes. "I had no idea life on a Texas ranch could be so...so damned much fun."

"We've been on a hell of a ride these past few days." Justin said with a wide grin.

Her suitcase and carry-on bag were already in the car. The gunslinger painting was rolled carefully in the mailing tube and tucked in her carry-on along with her hat, her laptop, and the contract Richard had e-mailed for Jake's signature. With a final hug for Rosita, Amanda got into the car and started it. She stuck her arm out the window and waved to everyone as she pulled onto the gravel drive. By the time she rolled under the six-foot-wide set of horns at the gate to the ranch, her vision shimmered behind unchecked tears. She had reached the county road and turned south toward Austen before she could stop their flow.

The weather was beautiful. It was unseasonably warm for early May and the clear skies and gentle breeze seemed a stark contrast to the torrential thunderstorms and hail that had welcomed her six days ago.

Had it been just six days, she thought? It seemed much longer.

What a joyfully uninhibited, delightfully wanton, naughty woman she'd become. She dropped one hand to her crotch, pressing against the denim to stop the tingling in her pussy. The gesture didn't help but the memories would be a wonderful treat to see her through the coming days.

She tried to convince herself that she would soon forget about the sexy cowboy who had done so much to help her shed her inhibitions. She worked even harder to convince herself that the relationship with Jake was based on sex only, a fun, one-time pony ride. Yet sadness lurked just beneath the edges of her emotions the farther she got from the ranch. What she needed to do was get back to New York and immerse herself in her work.

The county road was virtually empty. She had seen only one other vehicle since she'd left the ranch. Then, just as she topped a gentle rise, she saw something in the road ahead. A horse and rider stood on the asphalt pavement, directly in her lane. Amanda slowed, expecting the rider to get out of her way. When the horse didn't move, she pulled into the other side of the road. To her surprise, the rider nudged the horse and moved directly in front of her again.

"What's up with this asshole," she muttered, slowing down even more. Suddenly, her stomach tied in a tight knot. The man on the horse was Winslow Morgan. She stopped the car, not sure what she should do. One thing she didn't want to do was have a confrontation with the crazy bastard.

The only time she'd met him, he stomped on her carry-on and then tried to hit her. She'd been saved when Jake punched the man in the nose, but Jake wasn't here now. It was just her and this insane idiot. She needed to call Jake. Amanda reached for her purse and grabbed her phone. *God, please let there be a signal!* Her heart pounding and pulse racing, she scrolled through the numbers until Jake's came up. She hit dial and looked up. Winslow had started walking his horse closer to her car. Jake's phone rang and rang, then finally she heard his voice. It was barely audible beneath the static.

"Jake," she yelled. "I need your help. I'm on the county road about a mile from the ranch turn off. Winslow is blocking the road. What should I do?"

Through the crackle of static, Jake said something, then broke up into bits of silence. All she could make out of it was, "Justin" and "coming," but the rest was indecipherable. And Winslow was even closer now.

Amanda threw the car in reverse, then changed her mind. Hell, she couldn't back all the way to the ranch. She put the car in drive again and edged forward until she remembered how her horn had spooked the cattle. She accelerated forward quickly and laid on the horn.

Winslow's horse, a spotted Appaloosa, reared up, his front feet chopping air. Winslow seemed surprised at first, losing his hat and almost becoming unseated, but managed to hold on and bring the horse under control. She pulled to the right, her tires off the pavement at the top edge of the sloping ditch. She tried to drive around the horse, but Winslow once again moved in front of the car.

If it had been just Winslow, she thought, she would run over the son of a bitch. But she couldn't hit the horse. Suddenly, Winslow swung down out of his saddle and grabbed something—a gun?—from the back of the saddle and started toward her. He was close enough now that she could see his eyes gleaming crazily.

Amanda quickly locked the doors and shoved the car in reverse. Stomping on the gas, the car lurched a foot backward and died. Winslow stood next to the driver's side window and lifted his arm. What she thought might be a gun was actually a crowbar.

"Oh shit!" She cried, leaning away just as Winslow swung the crowbar at the window.

"Give me the blanket, you fucking bitch!" The crowbar hit the window with a sound like a gunshot. The shatterproof glass cracked into a thousand tiny pieces but held. "Give it to me, you cunt. It's mine. Everything in that cabin is mine." Winslow swung the crowbar again. This time she was splattered with tiny cubes of glass as a six-inch hole appeared in the window.

Christ, he wants the Navajo blanket. He must not know about the gunslinger painting.

"I don't have the blanket. It's at the ranch," Amanda yelled through the broken window.

"Bullshit! I know you have it. You're taking it to an auction. Justin told Lloyd Masters at the bank you were, and Lloyd's got a big mouth." Winslow stuck the hooked end of the crowbar in the hole in the window and jerked, pulling the entire glass out and onto the ground. The man was red faced, livid with anger. Screaming curses, he reached inside the car, trying to grab the keys. They were out of reach so he grabbed Amanda's upper arm, squeezing tightly.

She screamed in pain and tried to pull away, leaning toward the passenger seat and trying to find something to hold on to. He would not get her out of the car! Her right hand hit something sharp and she cried out in pain—Jake's silver spurs. She looked back and saw that Winslow, his head halfway through the window, had managed to unlock her door. Grasping the strap and shank of the spur, she swung hard toward the bastard's face.

The sharp spur struck Winslow in the forehead, then rolled down across one eye and over his cheek. He screamed as the spikes rolled across his face. She'd put as much force as she could behind the blow, and the spur cut as deep as the spikes could penetrate. Blood oozed out of a dozen holes. Grabbing his eye, he staggered away from the car. As soon as he released her arm, Amanda started the car and put it in gear, ready to drive around or over the horse, whichever she had to do to get away from that madman.

Suddenly, Winslow darted away from the car and swung quickly up into his saddle. He was obviously panicked and, when she looked out the passenger window, she saw why. Jake and Justin were riding full out across the pasture, racing toward her. Winslow turned the Appaloosa and spurred him into a run. As Jake and Justin neared the car, Jake reined in, slowing Ginger until she came to a sliding stop next to the damaged car.

Justin continued toward Winslow, gaining on him second by second. Amanda saw the spotted horse jump a barbed wire fence and disappear over a hill with Justin in hot pursuit.

Jake was out of the saddle before Ginger had come to a full stop. Amanda unlocked the car door and opened it, tumbling out into Jake's arms. She was covered with little cubes of glass.

"Are you all right? Did the bastard hurt you?" Jake was breathing harshly.

Amanda was gasping, trying to catch her breath. Her wide eyes were dry, her emotions overwhelmed by the shock of the attack. "I'm okay." She massaged her arm. "He bruised my arm a little, but I'm okay."

Jake's arms came around her as his expression fluctuated between worry and wrath. "That goddamn son of a bitch. What if I hadn't gotten here in time? This time, he's gone too far. If Justin doesn't kill him, I will."

"Jake, he was after the blanket. He kept yelling the blanket was his. He doesn't know about the gunslinger illustration."

Before Jake could respond, they saw Justin cresting a hill in the east pasture. His black stallion jumped the barbed wire fence easily before he turned toward Jake and Amanda.

"What happened, Justin?" Jake continued to hold Amanda, his arms strong, protective. "Did the bastard get away?"

"No." Justin said, still astride his horse. "He tried to jump that sandstone gully and his horse couldn't make the distance. Winslow got dumped and the horse fell on him. I think his back is broken. He's alive and in a hell of a lot of pain, but he can't move."

"Oh my God," Amanda whispered, her hand to her mouth.

Justin looked at her. She had regained some of her composure and had stepped away from Jake. "You okay?" He asked. Amanda nodded her head. "I am now. I'm glad you and Jake were able to get here so quickly."

"Yes," Justin said. "No telling what the insane bastard might have done."

Justin looked at Jake, his gaze steady. For a moment neither man spoke. Finally Jake said, "I reckon we should call 911 for a Medivac helicopter."

Justin shrugged his shoulders. "I reckon. We also need to call the vet. That little Appaloosa broke her foreleg. She'll have to be put down. We could do it but we don't need anyone from Winslow's spread blaming us for shooting his horse or saying he fell *because* we shot his horse."

"Good thinking, Justin. You want to go back up there and tell him we've got someone coming to haul his sorry ass to the hospital?" Jake asked.

"No, not really." He turned, obviously pissed, and started off. "But I guess I will. I'm a damn sight more sorry about the horse than I am about Winslow."

Amanda certainly agreed with the sentiment as she watched Justin ride away.

Jake dialed 911 but it took twenty minutes before he finally got connected to the Medivac service in San Angelo. He gave the pilot directions on how to get to Winslow, then called his vet. Amanda wondered if the vet would use drugs like they did with cats and dogs. He looked at her for a long moment, his gaze steady. He shook his head slowly. "No, sweetheart," he said. "Not out here. A pistol is quick and sure. We'll bury the horse where she lays."

For the first time since she'd seen Winslow blocking the road, she felt tears well up in her eyes. She leaned into Jake, who took her in his arms, holding her while she cried her eyes out.

Twenty minutes later, she had bawled herself into a red-faced, snot-nosed mess. She leaned back from Jake's chest. A wet spot covered one whole shoulder of his vest. She sniffed loudly and he unknotted his blue paisley bandanna and gave it to her to wipe her eyes and nose.

"I'm sorry," she said, sniffing loudly. "I'm such a wimp." She leaned back, looking up at him, his expression filled with concern.

"No you're not. My God, Amanda, you were just attacked by a madman."

"I know," she said, her face scrunching up again. "And I'm not sorry he broke his back. But I am sorry about the horse." She fell back against his chest for one last sob.

The Texas Ranger she'd met at the Rusty Buckle showed up to take her statement. "I can't say I'm surprised, Jake," Skeeter said. "Winslow's wagon always had a couple of wobbly wheels."

This process delayed Amanda another hour. When Skeeter finished, Jake took her in his arms again. "You stay in touch, all right?"

"Yes. I will. At least I don't have to worry about your insane cousin anymore."

His tanned face turned a shade redder and his gaze dropped away. "No, you won't."

"I'm sorry, Jake. I didn't mean that as a reflection on you."

He looked up. "I know, Amanda. I'm just sorry you ever had to meet the bastard. But it looks like karma finally caught up with him."

"Well, I can't say I'm sorry." She started to get in the car, but Jake had her wait until he used a gloved hand to clear the remaining fragments of glass from her smashed window. When he was finished, she turned and stepped close to him, lifting her lips toward his.

They kissed, gently at first, then with increasing passion. When they broke the kiss, she was breathless. "Wow," she said smiling up at him. "Now that was a kiss to remember you by."

He grinned, his eyes twinkling. "You can say

that again."

She got in the car and started it. He leaned down for a quick kiss through the broken window. When he stepped back, she put the car in gear and pulled back onto the asphalt. She stuck her arm out the broken window for a final wave.

Chapter Twenty-Three

As Amanda drove away, she looked in the rear view mirror. Jake, standing at the edge of the road holding Ginger's reins, raised a hand in farewell. The simple gesture and the melancholy look on his face made the tears well up again and she had to fight to hold them back.

"No," she muttered. "No, no, no. I am not in love. I can't be in love when there is no possibility of being together."

She adjusted the mirror so she could see herself and her heart sank. Her eyes were swollen and bloodshot against the black mascara smears under her lower lids. Her face was streaked with tears, her nose rosy red. God, what a mess. Great last impression to leave the man with. She sniffed loudly and wiped her nose with Jake's bandanna. She glanced over toward the passenger seat. His spurs were lying on top of her purse, one with blood on the sharp spikes. Knowing she might have blinded Winslow made her shudder, but she knew she would do it again if she had to.

She got to Austin much later than she had planned. She missed her afternoon flight and had to book another for noon the next day.

After booking her ticket, she called Nikki, who gave her directions to the university. "I need to be in my office for a couple of hours," she said. "Then we can escape and have dinner."

"I'll be there after I take care of this mess with the rental car." Amanda responded before hanging up.

With the hail damage and broken window, it took her a lot longer than she expected to exchange her car for a new vehicle. She blamed the broken window on the hail, figuring it was less complicated than explaining an attack by an insane rancher with a crowbar.

As she retrieved her suitcase and carry-on from the car, she thought how glad Richard would be that she had opted for maximum insurance coverage. Once she had a new car, Amanda cleaned off Jake's spurs and packed them in her suitcase and headed for the university.

In twenty-five minutes, she was knocking on the office door of *Nicole Nelson, Professor of Art History* and *Acting Dean, College of Fine Arts.*

Nikki called out "enter" and she let herself in. She was surprised to see that the pretty blonde with the formidable figure had hardly changed at all. It had been five years since the two coeds had roomed together and Amanda wasn't sure what she'd expected.

Nikki greeted her with a big grin and a Texas hug, which she returned with a smile. She'd tried to repair her makeup, but knew she still looked a mess. Nikki was polite enough not to mention it. While neither woman would consider the other their BFF, they had been close for the semester they'd roomed together. And while she hadn't enjoyed Nikki's uninhibited sexual lifestyle, she could certainly appreciate the benefits of one now.

When Nikki heard that Amanda would have to spend the night in Austin, she insisted that Amanda stay with her. "I've got a decent guestroom and my duplex is just two blocks off campus."

Amanda agreed and they left Nikki's office, stopping at a nearby restaurant for Italian take-out and a couple bottles of wine.

Nikki's duplex was large compared to Amanda's

own New York-sized rooms, but was decorated in a similar fashion, with nice but not expensive furniture and decor. Several nice prints adorned the walls. The extra bedroom was small but cozy and had a separate bathroom.

"This is lovely," Amanda said, admiring the guest room. "Would you mind if I took a quick shower before we eat? I've driven three hours with a broken window, and I feel like I've got a ton of Texas dust on me."

"Of course, Mandy. Take your time. Put on your PJs if you want. We can talk until we're tired and then go straight to bed."

Amanda showered and washed her hair, amazed that there were still little cubes of window glass stuck in her thick tresses. When she was finished, she halfway blow-dried her hair, then put on a tank top and a pair of jeans. Nikki had changed into sweats and had transferred the lasagna from the takeout containers to china plates. The coffee table had been set with silverware and glasses of wine. She had also heated up a loaf of Italian bread spread with garlic butter. They sat on the floor across from each other at the coffee table and chatted about their lives since college.

Amanda told Nikki how much she liked her job working with art. "It looks like the ranchers I was visiting, the Morgan brothers, may have a genuine Randell. If it's what I think it is, they could become rich cowboys very soon."

She considered showing Nikki the gunslinger art, but decided it should stay tucked away in her carry-on.

"By the way," she said. "Congratulations on being named acting dean. That's quite a coup for someone so young, isn't it?"

"It is," Nikki said. "It will be for a couple of years. Dean McAllen is taking time off to do research in Europe. If he decides not to come back, I may be named dean permanently."

"That's great," Amanda said. "I'm really happy for you."

"It is great. Except it's a lot more work for not a lot more money."

The first bottle of wine became two, and then Nikki opened a third bottle from her wine rack. Eventually the conversation turned to men and some of Nikki's wilder exploits, most of which had been witnessed by Amanda.

"Do you remember that night Brad's friend came over to my bed? I knew you were watching." Nikki grinned in remembrance. "That was an extremely erotic evening,"

"It was pretty hot." Amanda admitted.

"I was a total exhibitionist back then."

"And now?"

Nikki smiled. "Not so much. Although if the right opportunity arose..." She let her words trail off, still smiling.

Amanda grinned. "I have to admit, I still remember the night of your threesome. Especially when I'm..." she paused. The third bottle of wine had definitely loosened her tongue.

"When you're horny?" Nikki giggled. "That's when I think about it, too."

"I thought you were so naughty. But I really got turned on watching."

"You were so shy then." Nikki poured more wine. "Are you still so inhibited? Not that I want to pry into your sex life."

Amanda felt herself blush. "Until a week ago, I hardly had a sex life. And yes, I was pretty inhibited." She looked at Nikki, letting her lips slowly curl up in a knowing smile. "Right now, however, I think I'm leaving a lot of those inhibitions on a Texas ranch."

Nikki raised an eyebrow. "Ah," she said. "So can I assume you met a rugged, randy cowboy on this trip to Texas?"

"I may have met one or two." Amanda was sure she wore the quintessential shit-eating-grin.

"One or two? Why you naughty girl. Did you actually have a threesome?"

Amanda was blushing brightly now, from the wine and Nikki's questions. "There are some things a lady doesn't discuss."

"Bullshit. There are no ladies here. Only a couple of horny thirty-year-old women who sometimes fuck their men two at a time. So come clean. Did you enjoy the ménage?"

"Yes. It was out of this world," Amanda admitted ruefully.

Nikki laughed out loud. She raised a hand to high five Amanda. "You *are* a naughty girl. I guess you have broadened your horizons a bit." Nikki opened a fourth bottle of wine. "So share some details, girl. I need some visuals before I go to sleep."

"Let me just say that I've discovered if the men are willing to share and eager to please, the results can be sensational." She finished with a giggle. "And Texas cowboys are very eager to please." She swirled the wine in her glass. "One cowboy in particular. Jake really helped liberate my libido. He showed me how pleasure was meant to be enjoyed."

"I hear a bit of wistful longing in your voice. So maybe there was a little romance in your sexual fun and games?"

She looked at Nikki and then shook her head. "I don't know. Maybe. Probably. We did share something very special. At least it was for me. I think it was for him, too. But under the circumstances, I guess neither one of us wanted to commit to anything even approaching the L word. Unless L is for Lust. There was plenty of that."

"So you think you might be in love with the rancher?"

"I don't know. I've only known him for six days." Amanda wondered if love could happen that quickly.

"I'm not sure time is always a factor when emotions are concerned."

"Has it ever happened for you Nikki? Have you ever been in love?"

Nikki was quiet for a moment. "I don't think so," she said. "I had strong feelings for a man I met when I first moved here. Then I found out he was married. I guess I'm still a little bitter about the whole thing. So I'm definitely not the one to offer advice on love." Nikki took a sip of wine and grinned. "Lust, however, is a different matter. *That* I can give advice on. Speaking of lust, tell me about your threesome. Was Jake involved?"

Amanda felt heat creep up from her neck to her cheeks. "Yes. Not the first time. But the second."

Nikki laughed out loud again. "You naughty, naughty girl. So you had sex with two men besides this fellow Jake? And Jake wasn't jealous?"

"No. I think that's one of the things I love—at least like—about him. He seemed to know that I needed to...I don't know...explore my sexual boundaries. Maybe live out some fantasies."

"Like having a threesome?"

"Yes. That. And a lot more."

"So he was okay with you having sex with another man?" Nikki asked in surprise.

"Not only okay with it. He set it up. At least the first time." Amanda was still amazed at the man's daring.

"Was he a good lover?"

"Sensational," Amanda whispered softly.

"Nice looking?"

Grinning, Amanda couldn't help remembering Jake's sculpted face and defined body. "Gorgeous."

"He sounds like a catch. A handsome, sensational lover who doesn't mind if you have sex with other men."

"He might be a catch," Amanda said with a sigh. "Unfortunately, we live eighteen hundred miles apart."

"Yeah," Nikki said. "I can see where that might be an issue. Do you think Jake has feelings for you, too?"

Amanda took a slow sip of wine. "It's hard to know what these stoic West Texas ranchers might be thinking, but yes, I think it was more than just mind-blowing sex. Although, after what I've experienced this week, I'll take what I can get."

Nikki giggled and poured the last of the wine. "That's my philosophy too. Don't waste opportunities."

"I just wish Jake and I could have spent more time together outside of the bedroom. There was so much going on that we never had a chance to really get to know each other. I mean other than the fact that he is an incredible lover who has turned me into an insatiable nympho."

Nikki smiled and shook her head. "You are on the horns of a dilemma aren't you?"

After the fourth bottle of wine they went to bed, where Amanda had muddled dreams of long-horned cattle and horny cowboys. At some point Winslow intruded, swinging a crowbar, but Jake swept her up on Ginger and they flew across the prairie with the little sorrel's hooves never touching the ground.

Amanda awoke with the early morning light, thoughts of Jake pinging through her mind. She was horny but knew her vibrator just wouldn't do the trick.

With a groan, she crawled out of bed and found Nikki in the kitchen toasting bagels. She had a slight hangover from the wine but, in general, she felt okay.

Nikki served scrambled eggs and orange juice and, as they ate, she said, "I have an idea I want to run by you."

"Sure," Amanda said. "What's up?"

An hour later, they were still discussing Nikki's idea. As exciting as the prospect seemed, Amanda just wasn't sure it would work or that Jake would be interested in seeing it to fruition. Only time would tell.

By the time Amanda finally looked at her watch, she realized how late it was. "I need to go," she said. "But we can talk more by phone. I can't tell you how much fun this has been. No matter what happens, we need to stay in touch."

Amanda made it from Nikki's to the airport just in time to catch her flight. The flight back to New York was uneventful and Amanda was back in her own apartment by nine that night. She'd kept her carry-on with the rolled up gunslinger canvas close at hand for the entire trip. She would be glad to turn it over as soon as she could.

As soon as she arrived home, she called Jake, as she promised she would.

Jake answered after the second ring. "It's good to know you're back safe and sound. I miss you already."

"I miss you, too, Jake."

"Did you have fun with your friend from college?"

"Nikki? Yes. We had a great time."

"Let me know how it goes authenticating the illustration."

"I will, Jake. I'll call as soon as I know anything." Too soon, they said their goodbyes, leaving Amanda lost in thought and wondering if she could really make things happen.

Chapter Twenty-Four

Amanda was able to call Jake sooner than she expected. Richard had followed through on her plan and, when she got to the office Monday morning, everything was on track for a quick resolution. She hustled all week to make sure things were in place.

On Friday, she called Jake.

"I didn't expect to hear from you so soon," Jake said, surprised at her phone call. "I thought it would be a couple weeks at least."

"Things are moving quickly. Can you be here next Tuesday?

"I guess. You think I need to be there?" Jake seemed surprised at the request.

"Yes. It's best if you are here. Let Justin and Luke run things. Just be here Tuesday by ten."

"Okay. I'll try to get there."

"One more thing. I need you to bring the bedroll the illustration was wrapped in."

"No problem." Jake paused. "I really look forward to seeing you again."

"Me too, Jake. Me too."

The next two days were a whirlwind of activity, with Amanda, Sarah, and Richard all working to put Amanda's plan into action. By Monday afternoon, final arrangements had been made and she left the office for a late lunch. As she was leaving, she got a call from Jake.

She glanced around to see if anyone was listening, then lowered her voice. "I'm really, *really* looking forward to seeing you tomorrow."

"I was thinking we might get together today."

"You're in town already?"

"I am," Jake said. "Shall I come by your office?"

She started to say yes, but changed her mind. "Let's meet at your hotel first. I want to welcome you to New York properly."

Jake chuckled. "Sounds like a plan. I'm at the Plaza. A little pricy but nice."

"I'll be there in fifteen minutes. What room are you in?"

"Fifteen twenty one. I haven't even taken my hat off yet."

She lowered her voice again. "I'll bet I can help with that. And anything else you might want taken off." Dropping her cell phone in her purse, she hurried past Sarah. "I'm taking the afternoon off," she said as she rushed to the elevator. "There's a cowboy I need to see."

Amanda arrived at the hotel in less than fifteen minutes. She checked her makeup in the mirrored elevator on the way to Jake's floor. She wished she had worn something sexier. On the other hand, she thought, she looked pretty damn sexy as she was. In the week since her return from Texas, her wardrobe had become noticeably sexier, changes inspired by her less inhibited attitude about sex in general.

The red and yellow flower print spaghetti strap sundress came to mid-thigh, showing plenty of her trim legs. The inverted Vs that formed the bodice of the dress showed off her breasts perfectly, even without a bra. Under the dress, she wore a simple, but skimpy, red lace thong. Her pussy was completely shaved, another fashion she had adopted on her return from the Morgan ranch. Hopefully Jake would appreciate the effect.

****

As soon as Jake opened the door, Amanda flew into his arms, her arms around his neck, standing on tiptoe to kiss him. He couldn't believe how good it felt to hold her.

"Oh God, it's good to see you," she said when she finally stepped back to get her breath. "I've missed you."

"I've missed you, too, Amanda." He held her at arm's length and looked her up and down. "Damn, you look as pretty as a brand new foal. Sexy, too."

A rosy tint covered her cheeks. "Do you think so? You look pretty damn sexy yourself. A lot sexier than all these pale New Yorkers in their suits and ties."

Jake kissed her again. "Are you hungry?"

"For you," she said, reaching out and placing her palm over his cock. He was already hard.

"You New Yorkers get friendly quick, don't you?" He couldn't resist reaching out and cupping her breasts. Her nipples were hard and erect, pressing out against top of her sundress. He swirled his thumbs in circles around each nipple, causing her to quiver.

"Getting friendly quick is a trick I learned in Texas. They don't mess around down there."

Jake backed her slowly toward the king-size bed. When her knees hit the edge of the bed, she sat down and reached for the oval silver buckle of his belt.

"You don't need this on do you?" She unhooked the buckle and unbuttoned his fly. She took her time, letting his anticipation build. She reached for the waistband of his boxers, finally working his underwear down over his erection. Leaning forward, she licked the smooth pink head of his cock, then took him deeply into her mouth.

He remembered how exquisite her mouth felt on his throbbing dick and, in minutes, he was at the brink of orgasm. He couldn't resist watching her as she worked his erection. Her dark eyes were wide, staring up at him. Her lips were stretched around his thick cock, her cheeks hollowing as she sucked him. The sight of her looking up at him and the sensation of her wet mouth and tongue on his cock was too much. A shudder swept through him and he tangled his fingers in her thick curls. She reached around to hold his ass cheeks, pulling him toward her, pulling his cock deeper into her throat. She looked up at him one last time then closed her eyes as the full length of his cock disappeared between her lips. The sensation of his cockhead completely inside her throat was more than he could stand. "Ahhhh, God! Yes! I'm going to come!" He groaned loudly and grasped her head, clutching her close. She looked up at him, her eyes shimmering wetly from controlling her gag reflex, her hands tight on his ass.

When he came, he came so fiercely that it spurted to the back of her throat. As the hot liquid erupted, she kept swallowing, trying to take it all, finally sucking him completely dry.

"Wow," he said, taking a deep breath. He watched her lick her lips, then use a finger to wipe an errant drop of cum from her chin and another from between her breasts. She stuck the finger into her mouth then slowly pulled it out with a mischievous grin.

She stood up and pushed Jake back onto the bed. He loved it when she took control. "Take your shirt off. I'll deal with these." She worked his boots and socks off, then began tugging his jeans and underwear down. In moments, he was naked.

"I've got condoms in my pocket," he said.

She grinned and reached in his pocket, pulling out several foil packets. "I like a man who comes prepared. Now lay back, cowboy, and get ready for a ride." She lifted the hem of her short sundress and stripped it up over her head in one smooth motion.

"That's cute." Jake pointed to a silver ring in her

belly button.

"Julie sent me a rhinestone horseshoe belly dangle. Said she was sorry she didn't get to say goodbye. So, I figured I had to get my belly button pierced. I can switch to the horseshoe in a few weeks."

"Did it hurt? Getting pierced?" Jake asked, softly caressing her tummy.

"Not as much as getting poked by that damn barbed wire." She opened her legs, showing him her thighs. "See, they're all better now. No scars at all." She quickly stripped off her thong.

"That's a new look." Jake stared at her completely shaved pussy. *Christ, could he already be getting hard again?*

"Like it?" She opened her legs wider and he felt himself get harder.

"I like it very much. Come here and let me see how smooth it is."

Stepping toward the bed, she spread her legs. He could see that she was already wet. He reached out and caressed the smooth bare skin of her pussy. "This is really sexy. Does it feel sexy to you?"

He saw her cheeks go a shade rosier. "As a matter of fact, it does. Just knowing I'm bare down there is a bit of a turn-on."

Jake slipped a finger between her pussy lips, sliding it back and forth before dipping into the hot channel beyond. "Ohhh," she gasped, her knees starting to buckle. She reached out and grabbed his shoulder. "Now *that* feels very sexy. Makes me want to show you just how turned on I can be. Since I don't have a horse, how about I ride you instead, cowboy? I'll show you a few tricks I learned down in Texas."

Jake smiled and lay back on the bed, wondering just what she had in mind. Whatever it was he was ready. Just playing with her bare pussy had him hard as a rock again.

Amanda rolled a condom onto his cock, then swung one leg over his waist and straddled him. Jake lay back, his hands above his head as she took the lead.

"Are you ready, cowboy?" she asked.

Jake grinned at her. "Sugar, you call the shots."

Amanda squatted over his pelvis, balancing herself with her hands on his chest. As she lowered herself, her pussy pressed against the length of his shaft, pushing his cock back against his groin. She began to slide her pussy lips up and down the length of his shaft, using the wet, swollen folds of her cunt to massage the underside of his cock. She took her time, letting him enjoy the slippery feel of her pussy gliding back and forth over his erection.

He stared up at her, saw her dark eyes glazing over with arousal. She grinned down at him. "You like that? My wet pussy sliding up and down your big cock?"

"Oh yeah. I like it. And I'll like it even more when my big cock is sliding up inside your sweet, tight pussy."

She reached down and wrapped her hand around his cock, lifting her hips so she could position his cockhead at the entrance to her core. As she engulfed his erection, they both sighed. "Oh God I've been wanting this," Amanda said, rocking her hips over his cock.

"Me too, baby," Jake said, his concentration focused on the friction of her pussy sliding over his dick. With her knees on each side of his waist and her hands gripping his shoulders, she fucked him eagerly, sliding up until just the head of his cock was in her pussy, then plunging down hard, taking the full length of his dick into her cunt.

As her thrusts came quicker and quicker, he huskily whispered encouragement. "Yes! Fuck me baby! Fuck me until you come!" He reached forward and found her clit, flicking his fingers rapidly over the swollen bud. His touch set her off and she fucked him frantically, her pussy slamming down on his cock, her fingers digging tightly into his shoulders. Jake felt his desire smoldering, ready to burst into a raging wildfire as her pussy pulsed and squeezed his cock.

Amanda's panting moans came quicker and quicker until she was crying out in a continuous keening wail. As her hips jerked in uncontrollable spasms, she buried her face in the hollow of his neck and shoulder. Jake wrapped one arm around her upper back and the other around her bottom, pulling her tightly to his chest and pelvis. For a moment he imagined holding her like this forever, never letting her go.

As the spasms of her orgasm faded to quivering shudders, he heard her gasp and felt her struggling against the strength of his embrace. "Jake...I can't...breathe."

Jake eased the pressure of his hug but kept his arms wrapped around her. She sucked in air and then relaxed against his chest, her head on his shoulder. "God, I needed that," she said. "But you didn't come." His cock was still hard and still deep in her pussy.

He chuckled. "That's the very next thing on my agenda. But I have something a little different in mind." Holding her hips to keep the connection of his cock in her pussy, he rolled her over onto her back. He stared down at her, his eyes locked onto hers as he began to slowly ease his cock in and out of her pussy.

****

Amanda studied Jake's face as he fucked her. His expression seemed to be a combination of raw lust and loving adoration. As he thrust into her faster and faster, she could sense the aching need of his arousal driving his body. She spread and lifted her legs, grasping herself behind her knees to open herself completely to him. He held himself up on stiffened arms, his pelvis and cock a piston driving into her faster and faster.

"Fuck me, Jake. Fuck me hard. Come in me." Amanda's body was responding to Jake's pounding cock and she knew that she would be the one coming, unable to hold back the climax that had been building in her core. Through half-lidded eyes, she saw Jake's approaching orgasm—his head back, his eyes scrunched closed, a thin sheen of perspiration coating his forehead and chest.

The piston rhythm of Jake's cock suddenly stopped and she felt him press deep and hold still. Then his cock was jerking inside her and he roared his release. "Ahhh God! Yes! Yes!"

His climax spurred her orgasm and her hips jerked and bucked as electric currents pulsed through her body, propelling her into ecstasy. Her cries of pleasure rose to blend with Jake's masculine growl, fading only as their orgasms ebbed away.

Jake discarded his condom and crawled back into bed to snuggle with Amanda. In the afterglow of their climaxes, she lay cradled in his arms, sighing contentedly. "You know, we almost came at the exact same time," she said. "And we haven't even been practicing."

"We'll have to make up for that over the next few days." Jake grinned with sated pleasure.

She stuck her lower lip out. "Few days? How few?"

"A couple maybe. I need to get back to the ranch. It's calving season."

"If tomorrow turns out the way I hope it will, you could hire somebody to take care of your calves. Spend some time getting to know what city life is like." She glanced up to see his brow furrow, felt his arms grow slack. She winced and raised herself on one elbow.

"I'm sorry, Jake. I shouldn't have said that. I know you can't leave the ranch. It's just that meeting you, making love to you, has been one of the best things that has ever happened to me. You've helped me get past hang-ups and inhibitions in ways you can't imagine. It's hard for me to imagine that we won't be able to see each other whenever we want." She lay back down with her head on his chest, snuggling close.

Jake pulled her closer and kissed the top of her head. She sighed contentedly, relieved that he wasn't upset. "Meeting you," he said, "making love to you, has meant a lot to me, too, Amanda. Finding someone who embraces the kind of loving we share on the ranch doesn't happen often. But you're right. I can't leave the ranch. And I know you can't leave New York."

"Actually, Jake..." She raised her head and looked at him as if she intended to continue, but after a moment she looked away and said, "So what do we do?"

Jake leaned down and kissed her gently, then pulled away. "I'd say we should make the best of what time we have."

She smiled down at him. "Would that perhaps involve you fucking me?"

Jake chuckled. "Maybe. Or perhaps you fucking me."

Amanda giggled. "One way or another, it looks like one of us is going to get fucked."

"Or both of us."

Amanda raised herself on one elbow and used her free hand to caress his chest and abdomen. After a moment, she slid her hand down to his cock. It was semi-erect, but as she wrapped her hand around it, it quickly began to harden.

Jake closed his eyes. "Mmmm," he murmured. "That feels nice."

She gently squeezed the taut sack of his balls, then gripped his shaft in her palm and began to stroke it. "Thank you, Jake."

Jake opened his eyes and looked up at her.

"For everything. For teaching me about pleasure. I couldn't be lying here doing this if you hadn't swept me off my feet on your balcony."

Jake grinned up at her. "The pleasure was all mine."

She returned his grin. "No, it wasn't. But I won't argue."

"Since you've got me hard again, maybe you would like another pony ride."

She smiled. "I've got a better idea." She rolled to position herself on her hands and knees, her bottom turned toward him. She looked over her shoulder and gave him a big grin. "In Texas you told me I had the sweetest, tightest ass you'd ever fucked. Any interest in confirming that observation?"

"Oh yeah," Jake said as he turned toward her and rose to his knees.

"Well this is cute," he said as he nudged between her legs. "When did you get the tattoo?"

Amanda looked back over her shoulder, grinning at his surprised expression. "I got it a few days ago. Just as a reminder of my visit to Texas. My friend, Sarah, introduced me to a brilliant artist."

The tattoo, low in the small of her back, was a horse's head surrounded by bluebonnets and Indian paintbrush. It was about four inches in diameter and beautifully done, still bright with fresh ink.

"It's really pretty. The horse looks a lot like Ginger."

"Doesn't it." She grinned mischievously before leaning forward and resting her breasts on the bed, tilting her ass higher. "I'll bet you'll find some lotion in the bathroom." She wiggled her ass. "But don't take too long."

****

Jake retrieved a small bottle of lotion from the toiletries in the bathroom. He slipped on another condom and knelt behind Amanda's tempting ass. He had met women who could be coaxed into anal sex, and a couple who, if pressed, admitted they sort of enjoyed it. But he had never met a woman who so readily offered her ass up for fucking as Amanda. As far as he knew, she'd had anal sex twice, once with him in the cabin and again with him and Justin on the balcony of the lodge. But here she was, tilting her ass up and wiggling it eagerly in invitation.

He nudged forward and spread the perfect globes of her bottom with both hands, revealing the pink rosebud ring of her anus. He dribbled a generous amount of lotion on her ass hole, then used a finger to push it inside the tight ring. As his finger slid in up to the second knuckle, he heard her sharp intake of breath, then she exhaled with a soft sigh. He removed his finger and positioned the head of his cock at her back opening. He dribbled more lotion on her anus and his cockhead, then began to slowly push his cock into her ass.

Amanda let out a sharp cry but didn't pull away. Instead, she took a breath and arched back against his cock, pushing the head inside, followed by several inches of his shaft. "Oh God," she gasped. "It's...so fucking...tight!" She gave another sharp cry as Jake slid his full length into her, but this time the cry was from pleasure, not pain.

"Are you okay, baby?" Jake asked. "Does it feel all right?"

"Yesss! It feels incredible. Fuck me, Jake. Fuck my ass. Make me come."

Jake held her hipbones and began to fuck her

with deep steady strokes. With each stroke, she released a quick sharp breath, slamming her ass back against his driving cock. Reaching around her hip, he found her pussy, her slit wet with arousal.

"Yesss!" she moaned as his fingers slipped between the moist folds. "Fuck me with your fingers. Shove your fingers in me."

Sliding two fingers, then three, into her hungry core, he felt her tense up, felt her anal muscles clenching around his cock. She was lying with her head sideways on the bed, her mouth open, her eyes shut tight. In her outstretched hands, she was twisting the sheet up into tight knots, as her ass slammed back against his driving cock.

He sped up the pace of his thrusts and began to finger fuck her pussy more and more rapidly. Her moans were louder now, coming in breathless pants with each thrust of his cock in her ass. "Now, Amanda. Come for me. I'm going to come in your ass." She gave a loud cry, shuddering in pleasure, and he felt her climax, her hips jerking in involuntary spasms. It was all he could do to hold on to her thrusting, bucking hips as her orgasm forced his pleasure higher and higher. Finally, he couldn't hold back. A wave of ecstasy surged up and out from his groin in all directions, setting every nerve ending alight as he ejaculated deep into her ass in fiery pulses. He held her hips tight against his pelvis as he came, feeling her quivering in the last throes of her orgasm. Finally, they collapsed on the bed, sweaty and exhausted, trying to catch their breath. Jake held himself on stiffened arms to keep from crushing her and, after a couple of minutes, felt his shrinking cock slide out of her tight rear.

As he got up to discard the condom, Amanda sighed contentedly. "That was amazing." she said. "But if you want any more fucking from this filly, you're going to have to feed me."

Jake ordered room service and, while they were waiting on the food, they showered together, soaping each other clean while they shared wet kisses and caresses.

Room service rang just as they left the hot and humid bathroom. He wrapped the towel around his waist and quickly went to get their food.

They ate sitting at a small table overlooking Central Park, wearing fluffy cotton robes and making quick work of the thick pastrami sandwiches on fresh rye with slices of provolone and spears of kosher dills.

When they finished the meal, they moved back to the large bed, propping themselves up on pillows against the ornate headboard. Amanda snuggled against his side, her head on his chest.

"So how are Luke and Justin? And Julie and Rosita?" Amanda asked softly against his chest.

"Rosita's fine. And so is Julie. She has a new foal to take care of. By the way, we named the foal you saw Mandy."

She rose up quickly and looked at Jake. "Mandy? Really? After me?"

"Yes, after you. And she's a wild little thing, too. I'll show you a photo later." Jake saw her eyes begin to fill with tears.

"Thank you, Jake." She leaned forward to kiss him, then laid her head back down on his chest.

"Luke and Justin are both fine. Though I think Luke was a bit disappointed to be left out of your last evening on the ranch."

"Does Luke know about you and me and Justin, out on the balcony?"

Jake chuckled. "Sugar, every hand on the ranch knows about that."

Amanda blushed rosily. "I guess I need to learn to climax a bit more quietly."

"No. Letting go—completely—is what sexual

pleasure is all about."

"I know," she said. "I learned that from you. And from Justin and Luke. I certainly let go that night."

"You did," Jake said. "It was incredible to watch."

"I was excited. It was so damned erotic having two men at once. And having you watch made it twice as exciting."

"Would you want to do it again?" The words were out before Jake could stop them.

She rose up and sat cross-legged on the bed facing him. "Seriously, Jake? Like I told you in Texas, yes, I would. Under the right circumstances. With the right men." She paused. "And with you there."

"Watching?"

"Yes. Or participating. That night with Luke and Justin, I really wanted you."

Jake felt a surge of pleasure at her admission.

"But to answer your question, Yes, I'd enjoy another threesome"

"Or foursome?"

She gave him a sly grin. "Or foursome, if it included you. But I don't need to do it anytime soon. Right now, at this moment in time, the only man I need is you."

Jake smiled at her. "And right now, in this place, the only woman I need is you." He tried to keep the note of wistful sadness out of his voice but, from her expression, he hadn't succeeded. Here, and now...would be over by tomorrow.

Amanda soon left for her apartment. "Get some rest, Jake." She said as she left. "I think tomorrow is going to be a big day."

Chapter Twenty-Five

The private auction for the "Gunslinger" illustration was held in the large conference room at PP&C the next morning at ten o'clock. Eighteen Western art collectors who had attended recent auctions had been contacted concerning the somewhat unusual sale. Of the eighteen, six collectors of Randell's work accepted the invitation. Three bidders were at PP&C in person and three were attending via video conference. Sarah was there in one of her outrageous outfits, along with Jerome Dansforth from Dansforth Auctions and two Randell experts.

Of the bidders attending in person, one was a wealthy collector from the East Coast. Another was a California rancher who raised racing thoroughbreds. The third was woman in her fifties dressed in a business suit Amanda estimated cost at least two thousand dollars. The sophisticated woman was on one cell phone and had a spare phone on the conference table in front of her, ready to place bids for a collector who wanted to remain anonymous.

Some of the bidders knew each other personally and, while there was a general atmosphere of geniality, there was also an element of rivalry and tension among the collectors. To demonstrate their intent, each bidder had deposited five hundred thousand dollars in escrow should they place the winning bid and not be able to immediately cover the sale amount.

The most unusual part of Amanda's plan was to invite the two experts on Randell's work to offer an on-the-spot evaluation of the piece.

Amanda met Jake at the office and ushered him into the conference room, introducing him to Richard, Sarah, Dansforth and the six collectors. On meeting Jake, Sarah gave Amanda a knowing look that made her blush.

Richard brought the meeting to order and asked Amanda to explain how and where the illustration had been found. The canvas sat on an easel at the end of the conference table, and the bedroll it had been wrapped in was lying open on the table.

To add further to the validity of the work's provenance, Amanda had created a presentation using photos she had taken of the cabin's interior and exterior. She did not discuss the forged painting or the blankets and pots Winslow had destroyed. She did have photos of the first phase blanket and Onapi pot Chi Long had purchased, which added even more validity to the provenance of the painting.

After creating a compelling outline of the illustration's provenance, Amanda asked the experts to speak.

The curator from the Western Art Museum in Montana spoke first, giving his background and his evaluation of the painting. His presentation covered both artistic and technical considerations and took almost an hour. His conclusion was that the painting on the easel was a genuine Charles Marion Randell.

The publisher responsible for *Rawhide Outlaws* spoke next, telling the small audience he had compared the work to the still existing rotogravure copper plates for the *Fast As Lightning* illustration and to a printed version from the June 1889 issue of the periodical. According to his references, "They match perfectly."

Jake watched the events unfold with keen interest. He'd been to many cattle auctions, with fast talking auctioneers who seemed to have extra sets of eyes when it came to spotting bidders, but had never been to an auction quite like this one. Jerome Dansforth himself conducted the sale and, after twenty minutes of almost silent bidding, the collectors attending by video conference had dropped out. The East Coast collector soon followed, reducing the group of bidders to two: The horse rancher who had flown in from California, and the woman taking instructions by phone from the anonymous bidder.

When the bid reached thirteen million two hundred thousand, the woman bowed out. The California collector had just acquired his third Charles Randell painting. The final bid had come so quietly, Jake asked if he had heard correctly.

"Did I hear that right? The bid was thirteen million?"

Richard smiled. "You heard right. It was thirteen two. The collector will pay our fee, but you will have to pay Dansforth. And capital gains taxes of course. But you and your brother should both end up with four or five million each."

"Holy shit." Jake couldn't keep from grinning. "For a drawing of a cowboy."

"It's a very good drawing of a cowboy." Richard smiled at the Texan. "Why don't we go and meet your buyer?"

Jake shook hands with the collector, a happy man who had just arranged the wire transfer of thirteen point two million, plus the broker's commission, to PP&C's bank. Then they went to Richard's office to direct the wire transfer to Jake's bank in Austin. Sarah and Amanda chatted with the experts Amanda had cleverly arranged to bring in.

Once Amanda joined Richard to discuss final logistics, Jake returned to the conference room and called Justin, bringing him up to date on what had happened.

****

Amanda stood in front of Richard's elaborate desk, waiting for him to speak. He was smiling broadly.

"Good job, Mandy. Bringing in the experts for authentication was brilliant."

"Thanks, Richard. There were times down in Texas when I wasn't sure anything good would come of our efforts."

Richard turned serious. "I know, Mandy. Jake told me what happened with their cousin, Winslow, on the day you left. That must've been horribly frightening."

"Believe me, it was. He was a madman. And now he'll never walk again," Amanda responded sadly.

Richard's broad smile returned. He picked up a check and handed it to Amanda. "We don't offer hazard pay, but this is your bonus on the sale of the Randell illustration, the Onapi pot, and the first phase blanket."

Amanda took the check, smiling at Richard in return. "Thank you, Richard. I appreciate this very much." She glanced down. The check was for twenty five thousand dollars..

"And this," said Richard, handing her another check drawn from a different bank, "is from the Morgans. It's a finder's fee. They said you were the one who actually found the painting in the cabin."

Amanda took the check, surprised. For a moment, she thought it was another twenty five thousand dollars. Then she counted the zeros again. " Two hundred fifty thousand dollars! My God, Richard. I can't take this."

"They insist. You found the painting, knew what it was. Knew what the Indian artifacts were worth. And in Justin Morgan's somewhat colorful opinion, you 'saved their fucking bacon.' Their note at the bank is due day after tomorrow. Now, they can pay it."

"Richard, really...I can't..."

"Mandy, after they pay the auction fee, the Morgan brothers will have netted at least twelve million before taxes. That check is for less than two and a half percent. It's not an outrageous fee at all."

Amanda's eyes started to well up with tears, but she sniffed them back. "Then I guess I need to go say thank you, don't I?"

"I think that would be very appropriate, Amanda. Very appropriate."

Amanda walked slowly to the conference room. She pulled Jake aside, insisting she shouldn't be paid so much for simply spotting the bedroll in the cabin rafters. "Jake, this is a quarter of a million dollars."

"I know." Jake said. "And because of you, Justin and I have about five million apiece. We can pay off Daddy's note. You literally saved our ranch. So take it and enjoy it."

"All right," she finally acquiesced. "Just assure me of one thing." She lowered her voice. "This isn't because of...of our personal..."

Jake burst out laughing. "Because of our fantastic time in bed?" Jake asked. "No sugar, there's not enough money in Texas to pay for that."

She smiled at the last statement, pulling him into a big hug. If Richard and the rest of the group hadn't been there, she would've done much more than that.

Chapter Twenty-Six

"What shall we do now?" Jake was trying to keep a grin from smothering his face, but becoming a multimillionaire made it difficult. Amanda certainly wasn't trying to hide her glee.

"That should be up to you, cowboy. You're a guest in our city."

Jake thought for a moment. "I want to see your apartment."

"Really? Why? You're at one of the finest hotels in the city. With a big bed. My bed's not half that nice."

"That's a hotel room. I want to see where you live. Where you sleep. Wake up. Where you watch TV."

"I don't watch much TV. But if you want to see where I live, let's go. It's a quick cab ride away. I just hope I put my dirty underwear in the hamper."

"Oh, I'm particularly interested in seeing your dirty underwear. Or you being dirty in your underwear."

A fifteen minute cab ride had them at Amanda's apartment in a well-kept brownstone. She showed Jake around the small but elegantly decorated space, a tour that took about three minutes. They ended up in the bedroom.

"That looks familiar." Jake pointed to the plaid shirt she had stolen from him at the ranch. It was hanging on the doorknob of her closet.

"That's mine. And you can't have it back." She sat down on the edge of the bed. "So, now what?"

Jake sat in an upholstered side chair in the

corner of the bedroom. He thought for a moment, then said, "Take off your clothes. Slowly. I want to see you naked again."

Amanda tilted her chin and let her eyes slightly close. She gave Jake a sexy smile. He crossed his legs and relaxed. "Strip for me," he said.

"There isn't any music."

"Just take everything off. You don't need anything else to be sexy."

"What shall I take off first?" She asked naughtily.

"Those stiletto heels. What do they call them? 'Fuck me pumps?' Then take off your skirt." Jake had a plan and didn't want to be deterred by her impish behavior.

"Not my top first? Most men want to see a woman's breasts first, don't they?"

"I'm not most men."

"No. You're not." She slipped out of her sexy open-toe heels.

Once the shoes were off, she unwrapped the skirt and tossed it aside, leaving her only in her top and underwear. She was wearing sheer thigh-highs with exquisite lace tops. The effect was startlingly erotic and he had to adjust the front of his jeans to accommodate his growing erection. He tried be inconspicuous but caught the hint of a smile that crossed her lips. He cleared his throat. "Now your panties."

She stripped off her nude lace thong, tossing it to Jake.

He held up the tiny garment. "You have really sexy underwear."

Amanda giggled. "Underwear are granny panties. I wear lingerie." She smiled and stood facing him, naked from the waist down except for her stockings. Jake could see that her smoothly shaved pussy lips were already wet with her desire.

She put her hands on her hips and tilted her head, silently asking, "What's next?"

"Now your top." Jake watched her intently.

The silk top came off easily. He was pleasantly surprised to see that her bra was scalloped in front, leaving just the tip of her nipples and the top half of her areola exposed.

"That's a very sexy bra." He growled in appreciation.

"I like to feel my blouse rubbing against my nipples." She lifted her hands, palming the cups of her bra and thumbing her nipples. She was giving him a look of pure seduction.

The look was working, too. He felt the level of his arousal increasing exponentially, racing toward meltdown. His cock was growing larger and he shifted in his seat and adjusted his fly, not bothering to hide what he was doing from the little minx.

"Am I making you uncomfortable?" She continued to tease her nipples with one hand but let her other hand drift down to cup the smooth flesh between her legs.

Jake grinned at her. "Are you the same shy little mouse I caught on my balcony a couple of weeks ago? Just look at you now, teasing me into a raging hard-on. What's gotten into you?"

Amanda smiled, keeping her eyelids lowered. "Hmm. You got into me. My inhibitions have been shredded, thanks to you."

Jake leaned back in the chair. "That's something I'm very proud of. Now face me. Spread your legs apart." She followed his instructions exactly.

"A little wider." Damn she looked sexy in just her bra and stockings.

She spread her legs wider. "Are you trying to see if my pussy is wet?"

"I know your pussy is wet. Now take off your necklace." He'd been fantasizing about those pearls all day.

She gave him a curious look but reached back and unclasped the string of pearls.

"Now hold it by one end behind your back, between your ass cheeks." Again, she did as she was told.

"Reach between your legs and grab the loose end. I want you to pull the necklace up so it's snug between your pussy lips."

A look of understanding crossed her face. She smiled and lifted the string of pearls until the strand was hidden between her pussy lips. She grinned at him. "Jake Morgan, you are wicked naughty."

He smiled. "Now slide it back and forth. Slowly. Pull it higher in front so it touches your clit."

"Like this?" She pulled the string of pearls forward, then back, then forward again.

Jake smiled when he saw her catch her breath, her expression changing from light humor to surprise, then arousal. "Yes. Now, a little faster. Be sure it rubs across your clit."

She pulled the necklace faster and faster, bending her knees and tilting her pelvis forward. She was still looking at Jake, her gaze mirroring the unexpected pleasure he'd introduced her to.

Jake slowly unzipped his jeans to lift his raging erection out while he watched her pleasuring herself. He wrapped his hand around his cock and stroked upward, feeling the tight skin covering the rigid shaft. A luminous drop of pre-come appeared at the tip and he used his thumb to smear it over the velvet smooth corona. He could hear the quiet "thrrrup, thrrrup," as the silky pearls slid between Amanda's labia, could see them glistening wetly with her juices. She had closed her eyes and tilted her head to one side. Her mouth was half open, her breath coming in shallow pants. *Damn, there is nothing sexier than a woman deep in her pleasure.*

"Are you going to come, Amanda? Show me how much you like to orgasm. Make yourself come." Jake urged, needing to see her climax.

The pearls were a blur now as she pulled them rapidly back and forth. Then her head went back, and she moaned loudly. "Ohhh! Ohhh, my God! Yes! Yes! Oh God, yes!"

Jake saw that she wouldn't be able to keep standing through her orgasm. He leapt up from the chair, kneeling to catch her just as her knees buckled and she crumpled to the floor. He ended up on his back, holding her against his chest. He held her until the trembling stopped before lifting her onto the bed. He moved back to sit in the chair. In a few minutes, he heard her breathing steadily. He had never met a woman like her, knew he never would again. But the chances of her coming to Texas, or of him coming to New York, were zero and zero.

Finally, she stirred, slowly opening her eyes, and lifted her head to look at him. "Did you just talk me into having a sexual relationship with my jewelry?"

Jake laughed out loud. "You seemed to enjoy it."

"Oh, I did. Those pearls are my new favorite toy." She gave him a sexy look. "So what else have you got on your naughty mind, cowboy?"

"Where do you keep your vibrator?" Jake asked, stroking his cock slowly.

She started, surprised at the question. "What?"

"Your vibrator. The one you teased me with in Texas. Where do you keep it?"

Amanda's cheeks turned pink. She sat up on the bed, then leaned across and took a sock out of her nightstand drawer. She lifted it by the toe and the vibrator slid out into her hand. She turned the knob at the base and the vibrator hummed to life. "Is this the one you mean? What do you want to do with it?"

Jake stood and started taking off his clothes. "That's up to you," he said. "Leave your stockings and bra on. Show me how you pleasure yourself. I'd like to see you make yourself come again."

"I'm beginning to think you are a voyeur."

"Oh, I am. No question. I love to watch and you love to be watched. That's why we make such a perfect couple."

****

Amanda watched him take his boots off. Then he stood and took off his jeans. He had pulled his hard cock through the opening in his black briefs, which formed a sexy background for his erection. She propped some pillows up against the headboard and lay back, spreading her legs. She played with the vibrator, using the tip to tease her nipples and then stroke her clit. By the time he was completely undressed, she was breathing heavily, working her way toward a shimmering climax.

Jake stepped over to the bed and knelt next to her face. Her lips parted as she moaned softly in pleasure. She glanced up and saw the desire in his eyes as she worked the vibrator deeper and deeper into her pussy. She felt his cock touch her lips and she opened her mouth and sucked him in, working her tongue wetly along the underside of the hard shaft. She took him deep in her throat, her cheeks hollowing as his hands reached out to tangle in her hair. She heard him moan and saw his head tilt back as his hands tightened on her head. She turned the humming vibrator up to full speed and pressed it tight against her clit. In seconds, she was moaning, ready to orgasm. As her climax approached, she sucked him with increasing speed, desperately wanting to taste his cum in her mouth as she came.

Jake came when she did, squirting into the back of her throat while she kept the vibrator against her clit. "Ahhh God," he growled, his fingers tightening in her curls, his hips thrusting in quick strokes as he fucked her mouth.

She swallowed several spurts of his hot cum and then had to break away, the cresting waves of her own orgasm taking control of her body. With a loud wail, she lifted her legs and pressed her thighs tightly together, surrendering to the currents of pure pleasure that surged through her body.

As she came down from her climax, she turned the vibrator off.

Jake was grinning at her. "That's quite a toy you've got."

She sighed and closed her eyes. "I like your cock better. No question about it."

"Then you should definitely have it. I'll be hard again soon.

****

Jake took a condom from his jeans and lay down beside her, studying her face.

God she's beautiful, he thought, watching her as she lay on her back, eyes closed, her arms entwined above her head. It was as if she had surrendered to his will, offering her body for his pleasure and knowing her own pleasure would be her reward. Jake kissed her on the forehead then worked his way down over her eyelids and cheeks to her neck and shoulders, kissing and nibbling with gentle teeth, causing her to shudder slightly at his touch. When his lips reached her breasts, he took his time lathing each full globe with his tongue, wetting each areola before pressing her nipples tightly between his compressed lips. The stimulation apparently made it impossible for her to lay still and she began to writhe sexily beneath his caressing hands and kisses.

When his lips reached her tummy, he moved to position himself between her legs. His erection had returned with a vengeance and he was hard as a rock. He rolled the condom on, then pushed her knees apart to reveal the swollen pink slit of her pussy, shaved smooth and glistening with the creamy moisture of her arousal.

"What would you like, Amanda? Shall I eat your sweet pussy or fuck you? Do you want me to fuck you with my tongue and suck your clit or shove my cock into you?"

Amanda opened her eyes halfway, giving him a lazy, seductive look. He smiled down at her. "What would you like, sweetheart?"

She smiled up at him. She squeezed and caressed her breasts with one hand while letting the other drift down to stroke her clit. He watched her for a minute, then said, "You little exhibitionist. You do know how to give me a hard-on, don't you? Now what do you want, my tongue or my cock?"

"Eat me first," she whispered, "then fuck me."

Using his lips and tongue on the swollen wet flesh of her pussy, Jake brought her to the brink of orgasm again and again, each time backing off just before she slipped over the edge into ecstasy. By the time he lifted his head from between her upraised thighs, she was writhing in desperate, unrestrained passion. "Are you ready to be fucked, Amanda? Are you ready for my hard cock?"

"Yes," she whispered hoarsely. "Oh God, yes. Fuck me. I need you so bad."

Jake inched forward and angled his cock toward her wet, swollen slit. He had never seen a sexier woman in a more erotic pose. Watching Amanda caressing her breasts and playing with her pussy, her legs spread wide open, made his dick ache with desire. God he needed to fuck this woman.

When he was in position, he pushed her thighs back and lifted her legs to his shoulders, angling her pussy up for his dick. Then with one hard thrust, he buried himself in her core.

"Oh God, yes!" she cried. "Fuck me, Jake. I need you."

Jake fucked her with deep steady strokes, pulling his cock out until only the head was caught in her slit, then plunging the full length of his shaft deep into her pussy. Over and over, he thrust, his thick cock stroking her inner flesh, the friction of his flesh in her cunt igniting a flame in his groin that burned brighter and brighter.

****

Amanda clutched eagerly, desperately, at Jake's back and shoulders, riding a wave of pleasure that threatened to sweep her into oblivion. She couldn't believe his stamina, couldn't believe he could keep fucking her over and over and over. Finally it was too much, and the mini-climaxes she'd been having blended into one giant orgasm. "Oh God, Jake! I'm coming! Now! Now! Come with me!"

"Yes!" Jake, cried. "Yes, I'm coming."

Amanda felt him stiffen and hold still, then felt his cock jerking in sharp spasms in her pussy. She looked up to see him staring down at her as her own orgasm flooded up through the connection of his cock in her pussy, sending sparks up her spine, setting her nerves alight. At its apex, the orgasm lifted her out of her body, leaving her floating on currents of pure bliss. To her surprise, the physical pleasure that swept through her body was accompanied by an emotional feeling so intense she felt she would be consumed by sheer ecstasy. Unable to tell where her body stopped and Jake's began, she surrendered to the joy of blending into one being.

****

Jake's orgasm was intense and, as he surrendered to its ecstasy, he was certain he would never know such bliss with any woman but Amanda. Finally catching his breath, he lifted himself on stiffened arms and stared down at her, his feelings a mélange of physical pleasure and emotional bliss. Below him, Amanda slowly came back to full consciousness, her thick dark lashes blinking back tears. "I hope those are happy tears." Jake kissed her eyelids, sending the tears rolling down her cheeks.

"Oh, they are. They definitely are."

Jake got up and discarded his condom, then crawled back onto the bed. He lay on his side facing her, pulling her hips forward, pressing his shrinking cock against her tummy. He looked at her, studying her dark eyes, his gaze steady, penetrating. "I love you, Amanda."

She smiled. "You love fucking me."

"I do. That's true. But I love more about you. It's going to be hard not seeing you."

She giggled and reached for his cock. "It's usually hard when you do see me."

He smiled and then looked at her seriously. "I mean it, Amanda. I really care about you. It's more than the sex." He was saying things he had been feeling for days but had been afraid to express. He was sure she had similar feelings for him.

Amanda had tried to keep the conversation light hearted, but Jake was dead serious.

"Jake," she said, "we've only known each other a couple of weeks."

"I know. It sounds crazy. But I think there can be much more to our relationship than just sex. Or there could be, if we could spend more time together."

She stared up at him, then smiled. "I think I love you, too, cowboy. And there may be a way we can be together more."

He raised an eyebrow. "Really? How?"

"When I was in Austin last week, my friend offered me a job teaching art history. Nikki is the acting dean of the College of Fine Arts. She needs someone to replace a professor who had to leave suddenly. She wants me for the position."

Jake rolled to the side and rose to one elbow, staring at Amanda.

"It would be a two-year assignment. With an option to extend the term if things go well."

"And you would move to Austin?" Jake wondered.

Amanda smiled. "Well, New York City would be a long commute. So, I guess I would have to. Which means we could be together a lot more."

He was grinning now. "I like the sound of that. Would you like teaching?"

"I would. I've taught an undergrad class before and I liked it very much. I love art history. I think I'm good at it."

"I'm sure you are."

"The pay is lousy. Less than what I make now. But it costs a lot less to live in Austin than it does in New York. And Richard has offered to give me freelance appraisal projects whenever he can. And the generous check from you and Justin certainly helps make it easier to say yes to Nikki."

"So, you are seriously thinking about taking the job?"

"Yes. It would be a chance to see if there really could be more to our relationship than sex." Amanda studied Jake intently. "I haven't said anything because I wasn't sure how we felt about each other. But maybe it's something to consider. Maybe we do love each other. But we need to be together when we aren't fucking our brains out. Although, that certainly has been fun."

"It has," Jake said with a grin. "And I want a lot more of it."

"I do, too." She was quiet for a moment, seemingly lost in thought. Finally she took a deep breath and said, "Before we say anything about spending more time together, or me moving to Texas, I have to know something. Something important." She paused, her expression serious. "And you have to be honest with me."

"I will. Of course. What do you want to know?"

"At the hotel you asked me if I would ever want to have sex with other men. Have threesomes or foursomes like with you and Luke and Justin."

"And you said yes, under the right circumstances, with the right men."

"Yes. And I said I would if you were involved. But you need to know I'm serious about this. I really want it. I need to know if you would still love me if I had sex with other men."

Amanda cringed, waiting for an answer.

"So you definitely want more? More sex like you had with Luke and Justin?"

She lay still for a long moment, looking into his eyes. Finally she said, "Yes. I do. Not all the time. Or forever. But right now, I have to say I do want more." She hesitated, then took a deep breath and said, "If we want to have a serious relationship, a committed relationship, I have to know you are okay with another man in our bed." She paused, studying his expression. "Jake, I feel like, sexually, I'm just waking up. And that is thanks largely to you. I'm not ready to give that up. Not yet. I do want more sex like I had with Justin and Luke, and with you and Justin. But only if it includes you. I don't want to fuck another man just for the sake of having a different cock. I want you to be there, too, enjoying it with me. Watching or participating, whichever gives you the most pleasure." She looked at him, a hint of worry in her eyes. "Could you handle that Jake? Do you love me enough to let me discover my sexual boundaries? Enough to share me with other men. If you were always involved?"

Jake looked at her seriously for a long moment,

then he grinned. "Yes, I could handle that. Although it wouldn't be a case of me "letting" you do anything. But I would love to help you explore possibilities."

"You would do that?" Amanda was amazed. And grateful.

"Yes. I would. I hope I've already shown you that, by sharing you with Justin and Luke. And we may have more opportunities than you might expect."

She gave him a curious look, waiting for him to continue.

"Justin has been talking about using some of his money from the sale of the painting to start an adult dude ranch. He has been looking at a small spread just an hour north of Austin. He thinks it's perfect for city folks to come play ride 'em cowboy. Or cowgirl. It has a swimming pool and a large sauna. He says there are plenty of bedrooms for couples or threesomes—or moresomes—that want privacy. And a big main room for people who aren't worried about privacy."

"Oooh. Sounds naughty. And fun. Would you take me there to play?"

"I would. But how would you feel about me giving pony rides to other women?"

"How do I feel about you having sex with another woman?" Amanda wondered how best to answer. "Honestly, when I think of you with another woman, I get very...aroused. Especially if I am part of the scene, too. It makes me wet." Amanda flexed her hips against his rising dick.

Jake grinned. "And it makes me hard. I could get off watching you make love to another woman."

Amanda grinned and shook her head. "I'm not committing to that. But who knows what can happen in the throes of passion? Things could get very hot. And a move to Texas is sounding better and better all the time."

"I know you have to make the decision that's best for you," Jake said. "But I really hope you take the position at the university."

"Then you'll be glad to know I called Nikki this morning. I start with the summer semester next month." She bucked again against Jake's now straining cock, her hands clasping his firm ass. "Now slip on a condom, cowboy. I think we have time for one more hard ride."

About the Author

M.M. Bordeaux lives and works in middle America and has had over two dozen erotic short stories published in national publications. *One Hard Ride* is the author's first full length erotic romance.

Bordeaux enjoys writing about independent women in interesting settings who are exploring—and expanding—their sexual boundaries. Bordeaux likes masculine heroes who are sensitive to the heroine's sexual journey and strong enough to commit to romantic love that leads to a happy conclusion.

Visit M.M. Bordeaux at
www.mmbordeaux.com

To chat with M.M. Bordeaux and other Wild Rose Press authors of erotic romance, join us at www.groups.yahoo.com/group/thewilderroses.

Also Available

Candy's Kisses

by

Carys Weldon

City girl Candy Merrill can't see herself falling for a country bumpkin. But her best friend's cousin, Levi Bishop is hard to resist in his tight jeans and country charm. This has to be lust at first sight...because it couldn't possibly be love.

It's been a long time since Levi has kissed a woman as sweet as candy. And this Candy is looking for a guy who can kiss her socks off. Levi's never been afraid of a challenge. But after one kiss, he's hooked on sweets. Now he'll just need to get Candy to see past their differences and show her she needs him for more than kisses.

Chapter One

"This is dumb. Let's go."

"No," Erica stubbornly grouched. "He'll come. I swear he's not like most guys. There's got to be a good reason for him being late." She turned to the bartender. "Give us a second drink, please."

Candace winced. She was nobody's idea of a "drinker" and the bar meeting had been the first bad omen for the blind date with Erica's cousin. All the way there, her ears had been ringing with her mother's mantra. "Where you meet a guy sets the relationship. Meet a guy at a bar, you can't complain when he likes to drink."

That was something her parents had struggled with. Her father drank. Her mom always complained and went to church—alone—to pray for him. The bible was always between them. The fact that "even Jesus drank wine daily" did not help the situation.

Candy's mind rattled over their arguments as she sat there, feeling utterly stupid for having a blind date in the first place, and even more ridiculous for meeting a guy in a place that might give him the wrong impression of her. If anything, Candy was not the typical city girl, singles bar and nightlife type.

"You look pretty." Erica smiled. "He'll love you. I'm sure of it."

"Right. No one else does. Why should I expect this guy to walk in here, take one look, and go nuts?" Candy pushed at her dark auburn mass of unruly spiral curls. "Just so you know, there are no expectations here."

The bartender scooted a couple of frozen margaritas toward them. "Thanks," Candy whispered and took a sip. It was strong and gave her an instant brain freeze. "Wow! That hurts."

She didn't want any more. One drink was her usual limit—a completely social thing. Normally, she nursed that half the night. Glancing at her watch, she said, "Really. He's a no-show. It's forty-five minutes now."

"Levi isn't like that."

The bar Erica had chosen was a busy place on the far edge of town with an urban cowboy feel. The strains of Boot Scootin' Boogie by Brooks and Dunn began, and a flurry of Barbies, belt bunnies, and bimbos rushed the floor with a questionable crowd of boot wearers right behind them. Candy was temporarily distracted by the sudden urge to go and give the boot scoot a try. Squelching that temptation as fast as it came, she turned on Erica with her disappointment in life in general.

"And he is so thoughtful he called the minute he got held up." Candy sighed. "Really, let's take stock here. He wasn't asking for a date. You set him up with a girl he's never seen and never cared to meet."

"That's not true." Erica reached over and tucked Candy's bra strap in. It peeked repeatedly from under her boat-neck cotton T-shirt. Apparently, it was driving Erica crazy. She'd fixed it three times.

Candy pushed her hand away. "What's wrong with him, anyway? A guy who's thirty-one and single, lives on the family farm. What's that say to you?"

Erica frowned. "He's a farm boy?"

"And I'm a city girl. I'm seeing problems already. But no. There's more than that. If he's so good, why hasn't somebody snapped him up and given him four kids by now? Isn't that what farm boys do?"

"He's not really a boy anymore," Erica muttered.

"Even if he is a cousin, I'm telling ya, the guy looks good in his jeans, with or without a shirt. You gotta see him."

Erica averted her eyes, staring at the door, as if willing her cousin to appear. Her friend was a big believer in manifesting destiny, making things happen by wishing them to be. But this desire for them to be related by marriage just wasn't working out. Levi was the fourth cousin Erica had set her up with. Noah, Kyle, Danny, and now, Levi. Admittedly, the others had been hot but missing something she needed—like a total love at first sight thing. Now, Candy's heart had lost hope. After all, if Levi was all that great, why hadn't Erica hooked them up first?

"You gotta meet him."

Candy studied Erica's profile. It was a head turner. Erica had bleached blonde hair, perfect aquiline features, and looked a lot like Morgan Fairchild and Paris Hilton. Not quite as skinny but thin enough to spin men in circles. Candy hated that and loved it at the same time. She got a lot of fall-out attention when Erica passed guys off. But neither of them could find true love. It was so disheartening. What did it take?

She was a little too curvy to be happy with her body. Not that she was fat exactly, but no one would call her thin. She had full hips. Her waist wasn't bad, but her breasts weren't all that great. Nothing a farm boy could call melons. So, what most people noticed was her wide ass, and it was pretty flat. That's about all she could say for it. Erica swore she looked great in her jeans, though. And who was she to argue with the fashion queen?

"Why are you keeping it such a mystery?" Candy tried not to be annoyed, but with every ticking second, she felt more and more unwanted.

"I told you how old he is and that he has blue eyes and black hair, and that he isn't a bum. And he's not into sheep."

Sipping her margarita, Candy glanced around, nearly choking on it when Erica reminded her of the worst question she'd ever had to ask about a man. Worry had been replaced with snickering laughter when Erica assured her, "No. He's a cow boy." Candy had wondered about the guy ever since.

Erica reached over and gave her back a wallop. "I wish you'd get over that."

"Swear you won't tell him I asked about sheep. I mean it, swear."

"You want my blood oath?" Erica shook her head, happy, way too happy. "I don't think it would be prudent for me to give a promise on this. I'm sure I'll need the dirt sometime in the future."

That was how Erica was. And now that Candy thought about it, it was probably how Levi had been twisted into agreeing to the blind date. Suspicion filled her mind. What did Erica have on him?

"Please say you're serious that he doesn't have a weird thing going on with animals. Sheep or cows, or anything else."

"He does have a dog he's pretty partial to. Or two." Erica's lips slid sideways, and she rolled her eyes heavenward. "Please. He's great. And, believe it or not, I don't have any knowledge of anything being wrong with him...except one thing, and that's not too bad, really. But it's the kind of thing he'll have to tell you himself."

A fairly handsome guy headed toward them, but Erica caught his eye and shook her head with a frown and a wave, sending him in a veering direction away from them. Several men had come over, but Erica had staunchly sent them away, announcing they were meeting someone. Now, they were looking pathetic. Stood up.

And that last one, to Candy's mind, was the final straw. "I just want to go."

"That drink's putting color in your cheeks." Erica smiled at her. "You really look good, Candy Laine."

Ah, the stupid nickname. "Please don't call me that when he shows up, if he shows up."

Erica's pep talk made Candy want to cry. She was twenty-six and dying.

"I think he talked to your other cousins and found out stuff about me, then decided not to show. Why doesn't he have a cell phone? What guy in this day and age doesn't have a cell?"

"There's no service where he lives, I think. He has a land line in his house. Maybe his truck broke down on the way in. Who knows? Oh. There he is!"

Erica practically fell off her barstool, standing up, waving. Candy did not believe her eyes. The guy at the door was beyond sexy. A Marlboro man without the cig. A romance cover model with his shirt on. And oh, how tight was that black T-shirt? Tight enough to outline a serious set of abs and to stretch across arms that were obviously used to weight lifting or some other strenuous activity.

He was tall, too. Who couldn't like that lean but bulked up look? Candy reached up, checking the errant bra strap, pasting a hopeful smile on her face, reminding herself not to hope too hard. He'd probably stay for one beer and be gone.

Holy heavens. She couldn't help noticing his below-the-waist-action when he caught sight of Erica and strode toward them. Levi's jeans said cowboy, cowboy, cowboy. They were long and boot cut but appeared well-worn. Not commercially aged. No holes. Clean. That was the biggest thing Candy noticed about him. He had a fresh look, like he was his own man—straight from the farm. An old world sort of guy. Honest. Everything Erica had promised.

Her gaze dropped. His black, pointed toed boots screamed real, real, real cowboy. They were freshly

287

polished. Candy didn't know any men who polished their boots. Or any men who had those kind of, honest to God, shitkicker boots. Certainly none who had boots that might have walked through a corral or climbed on a horse. She was a city girl, born and bred. So, this guy appeared to be an enigma.

He wouldn't want anything to do with her. They would never get along. All her doubts and fears came to the fore, but rushing behind those were bold faced sexual attraction. With every step he made, Candy felt her insides coiling tighter, spiraling downward, a wetness pooling lightly in her panties.

The minute he got within two feet of them, Erica wrapped her arms around him. "Levi! I thought you stood us up!"

It was weird, how Candy's gaze focused low and her mind went straight to the gutter. She couldn't manage to take her eyes off the way he automatically slid his arms around Erica, squeezing gently then letting her go and setting her back on her feet in one smooth move. The need for a caressing hug caused a pang in Candy's heart.

"Hey. I wouldn't do that to you. I said I'd come. Thanks for waiting. I got hung up."

His voice, sexy, slid over her in a warm way, even though he was talking directly to Erica. But it was his hands stealing her attention—long fingers, big, strong looking—and his forearms...how did a man get forearms that muscular? Lifting hay? How much did hay weigh, anyway?

The tongue-twisting thought made her want to giggle. She tamped down the urge.

"Let me introduce you to my friend." Erica pulled Levi the last step or so toward her. "Candy...Candace Merrill. This is Levi Bishop, my cousin."

The fact that she tacked on their relationship made Candy grin. Erica was so silly. Of course he was her cousin. How many times had that been stated before?

"Nice to meet you." She held out a hand and finally forced her gaze upward to really take in the man's facial features. As he took hold of her fingers, his eyes lasered through hers. Feeling at a distinct disadvantage, and shorter than ever, she slipped from her stool and went weak in the knees.

He didn't hold onto her hand, but she couldn't remember him letting go or touching her more than that first second. But her whole system zipped with electricity from the contact. Her heart raced. She noted the feminine wetness again, and blood rushed to her cheeks.

Could a man be that pretty and that rugged at the same time? Besides the fact that his eyes were a true sky-blue, the long black lashes surrounding them accentuated the pupils. His hair was collar length and didn't look like it had seen a barber in a while. Most of the guys Candy dated were short trimmed. Levi had long sideburns that pointed in a bit toward his lips.

Which moved, pursing a second before he spoke. She keyed in.

"I've heard a lot about you." His voice had such a smoothness, quiet and low, the tenor of it sent another coil of need through her center.

"Really? I'm sure it was all lies." She had no idea why she said it. Nervous? Yes. A smart crack to cover it up, and maybe because she didn't trust Erica completely. Her friend wanted this to happen so bad, she probably had embellished the truth some. "She's made you out to be the mystery man of the century. Weird, huh?"

"Is that right?"

His gaze slid toward Erica and seemed suddenly unsure. Candy watched the emotion flit across his features. He'd looked so confident, waltzing in, striding across the bar with purpose. But now, she couldn't put a finger on it, but he was awkward.

That expanded as Erica looked between the two of them and said, "How 'bout we get a booth and just talk for a few minutes?"

"All right." He seemed agreeable, glad for the suggestion.

Candy grabbed her drink. She was going to need it, probably. She was grateful he'd given her time to get through one before showing up.

The guy was too handsome. Too perfect for a girl like her. She had so many flaws. He was a hard body and she was too soft. He was picture perfect and she...oh why had she done this stupid spiral thing with her hair? Her hand tangled in the ringlets hanging at her temple. Her newly manicured solar nails got caught and it took a second to get them out. She pretended to scratch her head.

Great. He'll probably think I have head lice or something.

She thought about the odd emotion that had slithered over his face. It had unsettled her. He had to have something wrong with him. Some secret or the mystery man comment wouldn't have made him uneasy.

Candy didn't know if she was out of her league or what, but she felt uncomfortable. Mostly because she desperately wanted to see something wrong in him. Self-sabotage climbed into high gear. Look for it. Look for it. There has to be something.

He probably has an ex psycho bitch girlfriend that Erica never heard about, a girl in his past like all his cousins had. How could a man that looked like that not have an ex or two hanging on?

"You want something to drink?" Erica picked up hers.

"Let me think about that." His lips turned up a bit at the corners, adding to his appeal. Again, she noted his voice had a deep but easy resonance that titillated Candy as if it had reached right inside her belly and squeezed her pussy. She felt a tingle down below. That was a new experience for her. Turned on just by a man's voice? That didn't happen to her every day.

Geez. She darn near went sky diving in his baby blues. Swimming in the crystal ponds. They didn't look like there was any guile behind them. Maybe she'd imagined that look of discomfiture. Candy sighed, glancing at his tight, body hugging T-shirt again. The moment stretched, it seemed, to breaking point in a slow-mo that had Candy thinking way too much about running her fingers over every inch of his upper body. She wondered if he had a "farmer's tan" or was just as tanned under his shirt.

What was on his mind? Did he like what he saw? Would he care to know her skin was milky white everywhere?

She wanted him to think about all sorts of things, all having to do with her—her eyes, amber; her hair, auburn; her build—as it was. God, she wanted him to like what he saw, just half as much as she liked what she saw in him. Once again, her gaze skipped to his. Could a guy get eyes any bluer? Or hair any darker? More silky? And she damn near wanted to drool over his biceps. Skittering nervous glances. One thing was for sure, she was afraid to make eye contact for more than a second.

Reality snapped. He wasn't ordering a drink right away. He wasn't sure if he wanted to stick around for a whole drink? No problem. She understood. One look and he wasn't interested. It happened.

Disappointment skewered through her. She couldn't help feeling a little sad as they went toward the first open booth Erica spotted. The guy towered over her, keeping close, bringing up the rear. Candy didn't look back. She didn't stop to think about who should sit where. She just slid past Erica and in, ending up in the middle, in the back. Erica scooted left, sat down and pointed.

"Why don't you sit there?"

Levi didn't have any choice. He dropped into the booth on the other side. And the minute he was in, his knee bumped Candy's.

"Sorry," he said, but he didn't move it away.

"It's okay." She sucked hard on her skinny straw. She needed another drink, maybe.

This close she could smell him. He had on some heavenly aftershave, and it wasn't some cheap pharmacy brand either. She didn't know what it was, but the richly blended scent of pine and musk made her senses swim.

"So, you work on a farm?" It was the only thing Candy could think to say.

"Yep."

Lazily, he leaned back and eyed her. She knew the minute her hair totally registered. It was too short now and the perm had gone a little tight, although it still hung past her shoulders. Candy hated the fact that she'd given in to fear that her "regular" hair was turning men off. The bouncy curls were a big difference from the long straight stuff's natural look. Erica swore it was a fun, cute style that suited her features really well.

Self-conscious, Candy pushed the springing curls out of her eyes. "I work in the call center for a phone company."

"Where Erica works. Right?"

"Yep."

Candy felt sure the whole thing was a bust. Two sentences out of the gate and they'd had a couple of yeps already. One word answers were never a good sign.

"Do you like it?"

She winced. "Kinda."

Did it sound lame to like a job where all she did was call strangers? Probably. But she liked chatting without physical appearances bogging things up.

"Do you like working on your farm?"

He gave her a full-toothed smile, and she melted. Sitting up straighter, then leaning closer, he asked, "What would you think if I said I loved it?"

He loved it? She couldn't swallow. She couldn't think. He was in her face, daring her to call him...something. Daring her to argue the point or to judge him.

She cleared her throat. "I'd say a man should love what he does...for a living." Then she stuttered. "I m-mean wh-what's the point if you don't?"

"Exactly. A man shouldn't be miserable all his life."

Did that mean he was miserable or not? Or had been at some point? She wasn't sure.

"You want a drink?" Erica, pusher of alcohol to ease the situation, got up. "Let me get you something."

There was a waitress, but she was on the other side of the room and apparently not in any hurry to leave the table full of men.

"What do you want?" Erica pushed the issue, flicking her blonde hair away from her face.

Levi smiled evenly. "How about a Coke?"

"A rum and Coke?"

"Nope. Just a soda." Levi stared Erica down.

Disappointed, Erica gave in. "Oh. Okay."

They watched her walk away. Candy wanted to know what made him late but felt it would be rude to ask.

"I've never been on a real farm." It sounded stupid even to her own ears, but she had a great need to fill the silence, to keep from thinking too hard. That always got her into trouble.

"Probably never wanted to be, then. Huh?"

So much for getting the home tour. Candy played with the straw in her drink.

"No. I mean, I never knew anybody from the country. It was never, you know, an option."

"Serious city girl, huh?"

She wondered if he liked brown eyes. Did hers remind him of cows? They were big. Her dad used to tease her about that. Her big cow eyes. Cows don't cry, he'd say just to stop her tears. To make her argue that she wasn't a cow. She felt like one, though.

"I don't know about serious." She gave him a little smile. "Are you a serious farm boy?"

He chuckled out loud. "Boy?"

His bulging biceps and forearms snagged her attention again. Oh, hell no. This was no boy.

She squeaked. "It went with the girl thing."

Was he counting every freckle or what? He stared through her skin or something. Could he see her insecurities? The heart of her? If he could, he'd know it was running ninety miles an hour and tripping all at the same time.

Candy felt she was failing the test, whatever it was. She hated that, but how to bail herself out? Normally, she had a pretty good sense of humor. Normally, she didn't care if a guy didn't like her. She expected them all to be jerks. She'd met so many of them.

"You're a pretty girl."

That was unexpected. Her eyebrows went up. She blurted, "Said the pretty man."

"Ah. Mutual admiration. That's a good start. Isn't it?"

A good start? "I guess."

He leaned toward her again. "I have to tell you that I don't usually go for being called pretty."

"You don't?"

"Nope. Those are fighting words."

"Oh. So you've been called that before?"

He grinned again. "Once or twice."

"You could make a living doing underwear ads, if you wanted to."

Holy crap. Had she just said that aloud?

"I'd have to come into the city more to do that. And," he seemed apologetic, "I don't think I wanna do that."

"You don't like the city?" All her hopes crushed in a second.

"I hate the city, but I was talking about posing in underwear for a billboard picture. I think my mother would roll over in her grave and come back to haunt me. She was pretty big on modesty."

She would have cried right then, over the I hate the city thing, if he'd looked away. This would never work. Not to mention, she was just joking about the underwear thing. Man, he was too serious.

"I might," he hesitated, "might be talked into taking private pictures, though."

Candy squeezed her eyelids tight. Don't picture it. Don't picture it. Too late. She had him in Calvin Klein's on black and white film in a poster on the ceiling above her bed. She would never sleep again for picturing that. Already, she saw a million nights staring at her ceiling, thinking about this moment.

She had to laugh inwardly at herself. "Too bad I don't have a camera. Now I'm wondering if you wear a thong, bun-huggers, or boxers."

"What do you think a farm boy would wear?"

Ooh. She winced. The farm boy/city girl thing resurfaced. "Probably not a thong."

"You got that right." He, too, wrinkled his nose in distaste. "You'd have to hogtie me to get me into one of those things."

Hog tie? What the heck was that? She couldn't ask. That would make her look all the more stupid.

Erica returned, carrying three drinks. Candy killed her margarita off. Two down. She had to quit after the third. It would be an all-nighter. She could nurse it until closing if they were there that long.

"What did I miss?" Erica's too-bright, assessing gaze split from one to the other. She plopped into the booth. "Oh. You did not go to the city girl/country boy thing already, did you? I only left you for two minutes."

Yes, and skipped straight to his underwear and posing for porn pictures. Oh, Erica would absolutely kill her for turning the conversation like that.

"You were right about one thing." Levi palmed his soda glass. "She's prettier than pumpkin pie with whipped cream on top."

Candy turned on Erica. "You did not describe me like that, did you?" So grateful to leave the underwear convo behind, Candy glared at her friend.

"Pa-shaw." Which meant Yes, of course. He's a country boy. Food metaphors are the way to go.

Outraged on principle, Candy asked, "What else did she say about me?"

"That you get grumpy pretty easy."

That was true. But it didn't make Candy happy. "And you still came to meet me?"

Levi shrugged. "What girl doesn't?"

"Not me. I'm the soul of pleasantry." Erica lied, but neither Candy nor Levi argued the point. He grinned, though, and Candy knew he was being prudent. Erica was known for things like dumping drinks in people's laps and smacking people upside the head.

"If she told you I was a city girl, and you hate the city, why did you come?"

"Curious, I guess."

"About what?"

"Pumpkin pie. And I had three visits this last month. Sort of intrigued me. Plus, Erica was relentless in demanding I take a break from the cows to do this."

Three? The other cousins? Candy looked toward the door. Curse Erica for pinning her in the booth. She needed to go home.

"So," Candy squeezed the words out, "why bother?"

The guy needed to get up and walk away and call it good, so she could cry in her drink and on her friend's shoulder. Why in hell hadn't she been born a country girl? That had been a problem for all Erica's cousins.

That's what was wrong with her? A girl couldn't help where she was born and raised. She didn't understand these men from Erica's family.

"What did they say? I'm sure they lied." Erica practically growled. "Throw it out. I'll discredit every one of them." But before he could say anything else, she said, "Better yet. Why don't you tell us why you were late?"

"I was pulling a calf."

"Pulling a calf?" What did that mean? A calf was more important than a date?

"Sometimes heifers have trouble. The calves get stuck. We have to reach in, wrap a chain around their front feet and winch them out."

"Ow." Candy envisioned the process. The thought of it hurt. Reach in? Wrap a chain? Holy friggin' Maloney.

"It wasn't expected. I didn't have time to call."

"Farm emergencies rule Levi's life," Erica explained. "This is why he never keeps a girl long enough to fall in love or get married. That and the fact that most girls don't wanna live on a farm forever. Cows stink."

Well, Candy didn't think she did, either. Not if cows were more important than anything else. So, what was the point?

To be nice, she said, "I hope the calf and its mother are okay."

"Actually…" He took a swig from his drink. "The heifer didn't make it."

"What?" Candy didn't want to grasp his meaning. At least, she hoped she was wrong in her interpretation. She looked to Erica for confirmation.

"Oh, God." Erica groaned, her disgust evident in her tone. "Do not go into it."

Candy gasped with horror but pulled herself together and reached out to put a hand on Levi's forearm. "I'm sorry. I hope she didn't suffer."

His gaze landed on her touch and followed her arm up, over her shoulder—keying in on the peeking bra strap and then to her face. She felt his perusal like a living, crawling thing, tickling her skin all the way down to her nipples, up her cleavage, snaking along her throat, and over her lips, which he keyed in on.

She fought the urge to lick her lips, ended up rubbing them together instead, and then realized his gaze had skipped a beat and was now looking her in the eye.

"I wish I could say she didn't. She hemorrhaged. It was a pretty bad deal. Vet didn't get there fast enough."

"That's awful." She squeezed his arm. "What did you do with her?"

"Well, that's part of what took so long."

"Do not explain anything else," Erica warned. "It's too hot in here. You want to step out the back door, Candy, and get some air?"

There was no waiting for a reply. Erica climbed out of the booth and headed out. Candy didn't have a choice.

"I-I'm sorry."

Scooting around and off the bench seat, Candy asked, "Will you be here when we get back?"

He stood up, too. There was quite a difference in height. She had to tip her head to look up at him.

It was odd, the way she felt. Too afraid to walk away. Too sure there was no hope. Desperately wanting to beg him to stick around.

The alcohol hit her. She felt woozy, too. Dizzy. Damn.

"Oh!"

He scooped in, slipping an arm around her waist, dragging her against his chest. "You okay?"

"No, uh, I-I don't drink much."

She grabbed hold of his upper arm with one hand, and her other snagged a grip at his shirt. Focusing on her mouth, his lips descended upon hers, and she didn't know what stirred her more. His hold was firm, possessive. His lips were demanding, taking.

She gasped, and his tongue swept in. And suddenly, his lips softened, coaxing her for reaction. She melted against him, and realized his lower body had firmed where hers met his below the belt. Pupils widening, his eyes darkened with something she could only name as desire. Need swamped her whole body with a damp sweat.

Oh hell. The farm boy could kiss.

How long did it last? She couldn't count the seconds. It ended all too soon, though, and he set her on her feet before she even realized he'd lifted her off them, but he kept his hands on her until he was sure she was steady.

"Yeah. I think I'll be here. Now, go on. See what little secret Erica needs to tell."

Candy blinked. What had just happened?

Thank you for purchasing
this Wild Rose Press, Inc. publication.
For other wonderful stories of erotic romance,
please visit our on-line bookstore at
www.thewilderroses.com.

For questions or more information
contact us at
info@thewildrosepress.com.

The Wild Rose Press, Inc.
www.thewilderroses.com